Lucia
Where You Are

By

Daniel S. Keenan

PublishAmerica
Baltimore

49

First printing

This is a work of fiction. Names, characters, places, and incidents either are the product of the author's imagination or are used fictitiously. Any resemblance to actual persons, living or dead, events, or locales is entirely coincidental.

Library of Congress Control Number: 2006908341

ISBN: 1-4241-5597-5
PUBLISHED BY PUBLISHAMERICA, LLLP
www.publishamerica.com
Baltimore

Printed in the United States of America

To

For information on book purchases, book signings and author updates: www.publishedauthors.net/danielkeenan.

Acknowledgments

No work of art is ever created without the influences of others inspiring each word which springs from an emotion that the heart feels from their touch. *Lucia: Where You Are* is the result of such sentiment, and to those individuals who have contributed to who I am I dedicate this novel.

Research was paramount to the nature of *Lucia* as it is historically accurate as it pertains to the timeline. The Web site for the 463rd Bomb Group was instrumental in keeping this story on track. Although my efforts to speak with the surviving members of the group failed, I am in awe of their bravery and sacrifice and want to thank each and every one for their patriotism.

Edward Jablonski's *Flying Fortress* was a great source of B-17 history, procedures and personal accounts which gave me the confidence to write any scenario and appreciate that anything could happen because it probably did. The book made a personal testament that fact is stranger and more captivating than fiction.

I must extend my heartfelt and most sincere thanks to the Yankee Air Museum and the beautiful *Yankee Lady* of Belleview, Michigan. Their love of WWII aviation history and their determination to keep history alive inspired me to make an accounting of my writing to make it as historically accurate as possible and bring credit to the warriors of our nation who were but America's finest children. Never in history has America had a better showing of courage, fortitude and duty than did the boys and girls who became men and women in World War II. My experience aboard the *Yankee Lady* at the Reading, Pennsylvania, Air Show in June '06 placed me back in time, into the spaces I could only imagine that America's greatest generation lived, fought and died.

It was a surreal moment in my life, a life's ambition, a realization of my life's dream to fly in the most beautiful airplane ever designed by man. I will never forget the smells, sounds, vibrations and smiles of everybody on board and the warm courtesy of the flight and ground crews to answer my questions and allow me to help turn the prop prior to their roaring start.

The visual setting for the home of Rick Hamilton was the White Doe Inn in Manteo. The home of Kelly Stewart was the Island House of Manchese. Having a visual reference for the actions of my characters helped in the development of their personalities and the romance that evolved. The pictures of these homes and the visit I made in the spring of '06 will remain with me always.

I would be remiss without rendering the appropriate praise and thanks to Michelle Runey Taylor, M. Ed., who edited my book with tenderness and care. The time she spent within these pages can be seen with every coma and period. Thank you for your silent praise and suggestions. The marks of your affectionate tears will always remain between these pages, and in the lives of Rick, and Lucia.

I doubt, sometimes, if writing *Lucia* would have been possible without the music of Rolf Lovland and Fionnala Sherry of Secret Garden and their White Stones CD. I played it constantly during my writing. Their soft, beautiful music helped me to feel what I imagined my characters were living and helped me to describe it in the story. Music expresses so much and affects everything to include color, climate, temperature and emotion. Secret Garden is an ingenious duo who is inspired by love and nature. I owe them my profound thanks.

The main focus of this story is Bodie Lighthouse and credit has to be given to the National Park Service who now maintains this remarkable and beautiful structure. The care and maintenance of such an old stone-and-mason structure is magnificent.

I extend my friendship and devout admiration to the surviving members of the Gaskill family. Although this is a book of fiction it is built upon historical events and people. I used names familiar to history to bring realism and a soul to the book that would otherwise be impossible to attain. I pray that I have brought credit to them through the scenarios that I have created in my mind and placed here in this book.

1

It was late winter, March 1942, or what some northerners might consider spring, at a temperature of fifty degrees, on the Outer Banks of North Carolina that Rick Hamilton began his ritual cleaning of the Fresnel lens at the top of the Bodie Lighthouse. He had been cleaning the lens and at times helping the principal keeper, Mr. Gaskill, make minor repairs to the lighthouse since he was old enough to make the journey himself. He would also paint, do some woodworking and gardening on the grounds while he was a student at Manteo High School on nearby Roanoke Island. Rick enjoyed the peace that the trip over afforded him as well as the company that Mr. Gaskill and his two boys, John and Vernon, gave. Rick loved the command of the lighthouse, a tall sentinel which stood 156 feet high guarding the Oregon Inlet and the Pamlico Sound. A strong black and white edifice, it represented a beacon of warmth and safety to mariners for the past seventy years. It is located on Bodie Island, which isn't an island at all but connected as the southern tip of a thin sandy peninsula beginning in Virginia. Along this peninsula Rick saw sand dunes guided by weathered wooden fences with gray metal wire entwined between the thin boards to make the fence one continuous array of uneven boards. Atop and along the slopes of the dunes he would find areas of sea grass that nature uses to control the erosion. Rick would find gaps in between the sandy mounds from time to time so he could walk through to the Atlantic Ocean. Occasionally, he would find lighthouses of various heights and colors along the highway driving south from Manteo. The most famous of these was the

Cape Hatteras Lighthouse halfway in between Bodie Lighthouse and Nags Head. It had a beautiful earth-tan brick base with spiral black and white stripes. At 180 feet tall it could send a beam of light over nineteen miles.

Thinking back in time as he stood on the gallery of Bodie, overlooking the familiar ground and water, he remembered that he was drawn to the romantic flash of bright white light from Bodie as it pierced the darkness of the sky, the clouds and the fog since he was about five years old. It brought him comfort at home as he peered out his bedroom window at night, lying comfortably in his bed. It was, for him, a great friend and he wanted to give back, even if just a little, of what she so generously gave. So as soon as he was able, at the age of fifteen he started the little boat ride or drive to the island and struck up a friendly relationship with the lighthouse keeper.

Mr. Gaskill was a friendly gentleman, forty years old, graying hair and wrinkles in his masculine face from years in the sun. He had a beard reminiscent of the old faring sailors and pirates of the eighteenth and nineteenth centuries who were known to frequent the water and the shores of the Outer Banks. Blackbeard, in fact, was caught and killed at Ocracoke Inlet in 1718, which is just south of Bodie Island.

Mr. Gaskill had a sincere love of life and family and informally adopted Rick as his own on the weekends to do the little chores that made Bodie Lighthouse a special place. Rick took pride in the polishing of the lens and the brass, painting the twenty-two-foot-wide bands of black and white stripes and the grooming of the grounds. Mr. Julian Austin was the assistant lighthouse keeper who helped to coach Rick through some of the complicated procedures of lighthouse maintenance. The lens itself was almost an all-day affair as it is ten feet high and twelve feet wide or a little smaller than two vans standing on end, side by side. With his unquenchable curiosity he asked Mr. Gaskill about the lens and how it worked.

"Mr. Gaskill, this glass is the soul of Bodie. What makes it so bright? It must weigh a ton," Rick inquired.

Mr. Gaskill said with a smile and with the care of a seasoned teacher, "The lens was designed by the Frenchman Augustin Fresnel in 1822 which would take the light from a little 1,000-watt light bulb through its maze of prisms," as he pointed and traced the fine curves and lines of the crystal with his finger, "and focuses it out to sea about nineteen miles. This lens, this glass soul you so accurately called it, weighs about 6,000 pounds and is five times stronger than the conventional reflective system that was common prior to 1850. Bodie can reach out and touch mariners and land lubbers on the foggiest of days and the stormiest of nights to keep them safe from the shores and guide them to where they want to go."

Rick was thinking about what he said and asked, "With all of the lighthouses along the shore how would a sailor know that he was near Bodie and not Hatteras or some other one?"

"That is a good question, Rick. During the day all of the lighthouses along North Carolina's shore have a distinctive paint pattern. In fact, Cape Lookout can guide a sailor on a specific course by the way the diamonds are painted along the vertical spire. But to answer your question, at night each lighthouse has a distinctive light pattern or signal that identifies who you are looking at. Bodie, for instance, will flash 2.5 seconds on, 2.5 seconds off, 2.5 seconds on then 22.5 seconds off.

"You know, Mr. Gaskill," Rick said amazed, "you are right. I never really thought about it before but the flashes on the other lighthouses *are* different. That is really something!"

After a moment of quiet thought and looking at the ocean, Rick took a deep breath and said, "I bet Bodie has saved many lives by being here and with you and Mr. Austin making sure she is working and painted so cleanly."

"The number of lives Bodie has saved cannot be determined, but I dare say that many sailors have thanked God that she is here," the proud caretaker said.

"Do you have any stories to tell about Bodie and how she changed a person's life?"

Mr. Gaskill took a moment and thought, dipped his head and said, "I have a couple of stories, on a personal level, that has affected the heart and which has, in turn, changed lives. I know of families that came into existence because of the light that Bodie produces. This light was designed and built to protect but it also draws people to love. Strange, I guess, that I never really thought of that, but it does. In my years here looking at the shore I guess I can honestly say that I have seen hundreds of couples kissing, hugging and walking hand in hand under Bodie's beam walking along that shore," nodding east towards the ocean.

Then quickly and with a sense of urgency he said, "I swear, Rick, the power of Bodie really does reach further than nineteen miles. It reaches deep into the human heart. It captivates, sometimes hypnotizes, the mind through the eyes. It lights the heart and every corner within. It has been said, by local people that would know and by my father, that if a man and a woman meet under the light of Bodie that love is destined to evolve between the two, a love that will transcend oceans and will endure the depths of time."

He was amazed by his answer. It was certainly not one that Rick expected but words that he will never forget, even though he did not fully understand what he meant. Rick knew there was more to the story and hoped to find out more about it later, but, as things usually occur, a rekindling of that discussion did not happen, at least not on that visit.

The visits to Bodie Island began to become routine, but every trip, either by boat or car, always involved a discovery of something new and fresh. It could have been the actual trip and the feelings within the body and heart that the movement to Bodie made or seeing something not noticed before like a little box turtle crossing the road or a new sand dune that formed because of the previous night's storm. Rarely would the same route over to Bodie look the same except when he was within sight of and approaching the goliath structure that he cared so much for.

The Gaskill family was always playing and the boys were as rambunctious as children of eight and ten years old would be. One spring morning as Rick was cleaning the glass panes of the lantern room he heard the boys down below on the lower level of the lighthouse. They were playing on the beautiful spiral metal staircase with intricate molded details of art and workmanship rarely seen today. They would navigate themselves from metal rung to metal rung, hanging by their hands, maneuvering as they went to get higher and higher into the lighthouse. Not thinking too much about the dangers that were inherently present with play of that sort, Rick continued to work knowing that the kids were completely familiar with the staircase and were experts at "step navigation."

Suddenly he heard a clang and a thud on the floor. Thankfully, he thought later, he heard a boy cry. He ran down the 214 steps clanking all the way down only to find Vernon, the youngest, with a bloody tongue and his dad already at his side. His dad was patting Vernon on the back telling him everything was OK and to be a man about it and stick out his tongue so he could have a look. Almost as quick as Vernon stuck out his tongue, his dad pulled out his old wick-trimming shears that were so essential in the days before electricity and trimmed off the flailing piece of flesh that a moment before was the tip of his tongue. That was all there was to that incident. Injuries did not occur very often, or if they did, no one complained after that.

The nights were always the most special time of the visit, as one would expect, because Bodie would come to life. When Bodie started to shine, the residents from Manteo and other neighboring towns, to include Nags Head, would come over to enjoy the lighthouse, the shore, the dunes and the grasses made famous by the occasional hurricanes and daily winds. North Carolina had some of the best beaches in the world. There on Bodie Island it was a treasured secret that only those who live near by knew about. Rick knew its value and enjoyed seeing his friends from high school visit, what he would like to consider *his* little piece of heaven.

This was what Rick did just about every weekend until he went to Richmond College at eighteen years old in 1938. The summer before he left for Virginia he spent the Fourth of July with his friends at Bodie. He was invited to the lighthouse, not that he needed one by the Gaskills, but so they could throw him a birthday party. All of his friends were there—Tom, who was his baseball buddy since he was old enough to throw a ball; and Bobby, who used to wrestle with him in the mud. Once, during the hurricane of September 1936, Bobby almost drowned Rick. Rick coughed up mud and had dirt between his teeth for a while after that but believed in the saying "What doesn't kill you only makes you stronger." Rick became a fine wrestler thanks to Bobby but never considered himself good enough to pursue it in college.

His best friend was Sean Ryan, who was a tall young man with blond hair and a strong chin. His physique was muscular but not threatening. He had a great charismatic way with the girls at school and was fun to watch when he was making a move. His Hollywood smile and fun laugh made him the prize capture of all the popular girls. They were always competing for his attention. Sean and Rick actually faked a fight once in which Rick would pretend to bloody Sean's nose with catsup so he could get noticed and capture the sympathy of a pretty new girl named Kelly Stewart.

During the fight Rick had Sean down on the ground. While he was there Rick squirted catsup up Sean's nose as part of the plan. Gagging, Sean said to Rick, "Get off me! Damn it, that's enough!"

Sean staggered away holding his nose with a dirty handkerchief in dramatic fashion and walked to where Kelly was standing with some of her girlfriends. Rick just stood in the middle of a circle where several boys were gathered to watch the fight. With Kelly taking a pitiful look at Sean she said, "Are you OK? You have blood coming from your nose."

"Yeah, I'm fine."

"Here," Kelly said retrieving a hanky from her skirt pocket, "let me wipe this for you," as she carefully wiped his face of the red dribble that she recognized as catsup.

"Does it hurt?" Kelly said playing along.

"Oww," Sean said. "Just a little."

"What was the fight all about?"

"Oh, nothing really. Something stupid," he said, looking back at Rick, winking secretly. "He said I owed him money, but I don't. He is such a bully."

Kelly looked at Rick, and noticed that he smiled then quickly turned the smile into a snarl as soon as Rick noticed that she was watching him. She then said to Sean, "Yeah, you poor boy. He looks so mean. What's your name?"

"Sean. Sean Ryan," he said looking her right in the eye.

After a moment of silence Kelly asked, "Aren't you going to ask me my name…Sean?"

"I already know your name," he said.

Kelly, being only partially surprised at his response said, "Is that so? Now tell me how you came to get my name?"

"I noticed it on your notebook," he said, glancing at her books on the ground, "and I heard your friends call you by your name in school."

"Well, you just figured out everything, haven't you," she said to him, smiling.

"No, not yet. I still have to figure out a way to get you to go out with me."

Kelly stood there putting her messy hanky back in her pocket and said, "Why don't you go back over there to your friend, Rick, you know, that big bully, and figure out a way." Kelly turned away smartly and walked back towards her friends. They were all giddy with excitement as they walked away as a group, looking back over their shoulders with curiosity in their eyes to catch one more glimpse of Sean and Rick. Some were laughing but all were smiling and knew that Sean was smitten and that Rick played a large part in the game.

A week after the charade they were all by a small fire that they made on the banks of the Roanoke Sound, not far from Rick's Queen Anne's house on County Road. There they told Kelly about the ruse.

"You know, Kelly, Rick didn't really give me a bloody nose a week ago. Fact is it's a joke to even imagine that he could ever lay a punch on me, small, large, doesn't matter. It wouldn't happen. It was all a plan to get your attention," said Sean.

"Really?" she said acting as if she was thinking, pretending to be dumb.

"Yeah, really?" said Rick, taking a quick jab at Sean's arm. "Don't even think that if I didn't want you to get up that you would have, bub," he said to Sean.

Kelly said, "Well, I am relieved to know that. Really I am. I thought I was going crazy."

"Why is that?" asked Rick, knowing that Kelly was about to unleash a whipping on Sean.

"Since that day I had this urge…and now I know why. It explains why, for the past week, I have had this urge to stick a French fry up your nose," and with a shove from her and a quick embrace by him the cat was out of the bag, at least as far as the boys knew. She never was fooled.

Kelly was a very bright young lady who had an upper-class upbringing. She carried herself in a style rarely seen by roughneck boys who liked to work with their hands in cars, the dirt, and in athletic competition. Most of the time, she wore dresses of light material and pretty subtle prints that flowed and swayed when she walked.

Rick knew all along she knew the catsup play was a fake. You could see it in her eyes and the way she smiled at Sean and Rick for being so boyish. Perhaps it was the unique smell that fresh catsup had that filled the air that gave it away. She was too smart and for all the right reasons. Sean and Kelly were meant to be together. With her short brown hair, green eyes, and simple features, she complemented him when she stood next to him. The top of her head came to under his chin and fit in a groove that was made just for her, and they both knew it. A perfect couple, they always smiled when together. It was amazing to see what a fight can start.

She moved up from Wilmington with her mother after her dad died in an auto accident while driving to work one morning to his insurance business. She lived with her mother at the old Midgett house on Mill Landing Road in Wanchese. A colonial home, painted in light colonial blue with white windows, it had a white front and back porch about two feet off the ground. The dining room jutted out onto the corner of the porch with a semicircular bay window. Hanging on a front porch post was an American flag. There were several hanging plants hanging underneath the eves, decorating the home with color that spelled welcome to all guests. On occasion the boys would ride their bikes the five miles to visit Kelly rather than drive so they could enjoy the breezy and sunny day. It was a straight road that was not traveled very often which made the trip fun and carefree.

Kelly had a great mom who loved the social calls from Rick and Sean because they broke her spells of loneliness at times. She did not dwell in the past but there were times that she wished her husband was there to watch Kelly grow up into the beautiful, playful, intelligent and loving young woman that she was. She was a strong survivor. It was from her that Kelly got her strength and keen eye. She would offer the boys tea and cookies in true southern style on the shady front porch of her house. She would stay and chat awhile but would leave politely. You could tell she left reluctantly because she enjoyed them so much, but she would give the excuse that she had to tend to her chores that were ever present in a good-size house in the country. Sean went to visit Kelly whenever he could and she would do likewise. They were inseparable.

Life was good for Rick. It was the Fourth of July, his birthday was in a couple of days and college would start next month. His best friends were with him as they sat in rocking chairs on the front yard that they got from the caretaker's house. The house stood in front of Bodie Lighthouse facing inland. With the Gaskills, Mr. Austin, Sean, Kelly and her mom, Rick rocked peering out west towards Manteo over the Croatan Sound. It was a beautiful night with a million stars dotting the sky and a waxing moon standing overhead. They were anticipating a fireworks display from Manteo funded by Dare County at 9:00. The celebration began with a beautiful burst of red, white and blue, followed in succession by various explosions of white sparkles at different altitudes. The sparkles of cascading lights made moving shadows against the slick and smooth walls of Bodie and on the pretty grass upon which they all stood and sat. Looking over and on the water in front of the peaceful spectators, Rick saw a fireworks display, all its own. The still water of the sound made a black stage lit by the light of the moon and the brightest stars. The show on the water was augmented by the show over Manteo as it added a mixing of bursting and falling primary colors of red, yellow and blue onto the black surface.

The reflection of celebration lit the faces of all of his friends from the top to the bottom and into the depths of their eyes. The smiles were bright, as bright colors against a black mat of warm air always were. The love that each one felt for the other emphasized family. It was genuine and unique. They all had a common tie, a belonging to this land that made this time and place special.

Rick's love for Bodie and its polite behavior to blink on for only 2.5 seconds was never stronger. The structure was beautiful in the day, but on this night, with all that was happening in town, on the water, in the sky, and in the hearts and souls of his friends, and in himself, he never saw Bodie more mysterious, stunning and impressive. He glanced back in his mind to the discussion that Mr. Gaskill and he had several years ago about the lives that Bodie affected and the love that Bodie influenced. He began to understand, just a little, of what that remarkable and intelligent man meant because he was vividly feeling it, and seeing her awesome power in his life.

On that summer night in 1938, on a little strip of marshy land, Rick realized that his life was never going to be the same again. He knew that his life was taking a turn to destiny. Sean was going to assist Kelly's mom in the construction business she had just started up. Kelly was going to attend her first year of college at Meredith College in Raleigh, and Rick was leaving in about six weeks for Richmond. Although they were all excited about the changes, they were also anxious about how it would affect their relationships. Change always brings a bit of uncertainty, but they were still confident that they would always be there for the other.

Rick knew that he could always come back home and to Bodie to work in the summers. He knew that the Gaskills would always be there to welcome him. He knew that his little corner of heaven would always be there. The fireworks continued for about ten minutes, and after it was over, they made a little fire in the fire pit that the Gaskills had dug between the house and Bodie. They had cake and listened to Bobby play his version of "Happy Birthday" on the guitar as they sang. What a remarkable night.

Kelly was walking back to the caretaker's house with Rick and the Gaskills while Sean was helping Vernon put the fire out. With a big smile on her face, Kelly sweetly kissed Rick on the cheek as they walked and said, "Thanks, Rick, for a great time tonight. Everything was perfect. The sights and smells," and with a big inhale and smile said, "I feel, will remain with me forever."

Rick thought a moment. "Me too. It was a perfect night. Even the insects cooperated," he said, jokingly. "Everybody here means so much to me. Thanks for being here with me and my friend. He loves you so."

Sean ran up to the two of them and said, "Hey, what's going on here, you two," then put his arm around them both and walked the rest of the way with them.

Inside the house, Mr. Gaskill, his wife Mary, and their two boys stood by the fireplace in the front room and asked Rick to come over. There, Mr. Gaskill had in his hand a small black box wrapped with a small red ribbon with little embroidered gold stars.

Mr. Gaskill said, "Rick, you have been a part of my family, even if it had been just on weekends and the summers, but a part just the same. My wife, the boys and I wanted you to have this," as he handed him the little box.

Rick opened it, first untying the bow that was noticeably tied with care. Then lifting off the cover he saw two keys lying on top of North Carolina cotton. Rick knew immediately what they were as he had seen them on Mr. Gaskill's key chain.

"The family wanted you to have the key to this house and to Bodie. Next to us and perhaps even more, no one loves this place more than you. You are always welcome here. This is your home."

Rick was touched, as were his friends. A tear fell quietly from Kelly's green eyes. Sean put his arm around her. Rick gave Mr. Gaskill a hug saying, "Only *you* could possibly know how much this means to me. I will always hold these close to me wherever I go. I will come back. No place on earth means more to me. You know that or you would not have given me these."

He then turned and gave Mrs. Gaskill and his boys a hug in turn. "Thank you all for a great birthday," Rick said. "I think a person can be measured by the friends he," and, looking at Mary Gaskill and Kelly, said, "or she has." He continued saying, "I know that I am a better person from having known each of you. I will never forget this night and the family that you are."

2

Rick was a good student at Richmond College but he was missing home, Sean, and Kelly, and the trips to visit Mr. Gaskill and Bodie. On his first trip back home after his first year in school in late May, 1939, he found out that the lighthouse was no longer occupied full-time since the reliability of electricity made the cost of having Mr. Gaskill live there "unsubstantiated." Rick did a quick search for the Gaskills but found that they had moved to Coinjock, where Mr. Gaskill was assigned duties at the lighthouse depot. Since Rick had the key to Bodie, he planned to use it to carry out his ritual of commitment and care. Although the familiar faces would be gone, he anticipated he would still feel their company.

He went to Sean's house to see if he was home. Mrs. Ryan was elated to see Rick and invited him in for some tea. Being thirsty, he took her up on the offer. Mrs. Ryan began to tell Rick all about Sean and his new job. She told him about Sean being promoted as the contracting foreman and going to school, courtesy of the Roanoke Island Construction Company, to learn about design and architecture. She said that Kelly was back from Meredith College and brought her roommate with her to spend the summer.

"Sean went down to Wilmington, Rick, to buy some special lumber he needed for a job. He took Kelly and her friend with him. They should be back in a couple of days," she said.

"OK, that's great. That will give me some time to get a good start on Bodie and get her ready for the summer," he said.

After some time discussing how their respective families were and about school, Rick asked, "Do you know when the Gaskills left the island?"

"You know, Rick, I'm not really sure," she said. "I know it was just a month or two after you left for school though. Mr. Austin still works there for a time but will not be there for long. No one knows for sure but he is probably there part-time at best."

Rick thought that was kind of odd and quick, especially after he was given that wonderful birthday party and keys. He suspected that Mr. Gaskill knew he was leaving but didn't want to cloud the moment with unpleasantness. It was beginning to make more sense now, and those circumstances even gave the occasion of last summer more meaning.

His visits to the island recharged his heart, mind, and body and rekindled enthusiasm and excitement. Trips to Bodie, throughout his life, helped to build his character into the man he was quickly becoming. This trip was just one more emotional recharge that he needed after a long arduous academic year. He stood before the tall testimonial of human courage and perseverance and wished he could touch the optics again. He knew, however, that the temperatures within the lantern room, which protected the optic section with large panes of glass, trapped all of the heat energy from the sun and was too hot to even consider entering.

So, with the pride of an owner, he took out Bodie's key and unlocked the door of Bodie. He entered, leaving the door open, and looked through the two rooms on either side of the main entrance. He climbed the steps that he had climbed many times before opening the door at the top. He was immediately hit with a rush of fresh summer air and light, then with a back draft of hot stale air from the internal regions of the lighthouse. He emerged from the lighthouse and took a walk on the lower gallery around the lantern room. The view of the Atlantic Ocean, the Sound, and of Roanoke Island was breathtaking and, after a big sigh, he inhaled breathing in the salty Carolina air under a cloudless Carolina blue sky atop one of the most important of Carolina's jewels. He knew he was home again.

His eyes scanned the horizon for ships. He did not see any but did see families on the southern end of the peninsula playing in the surf and the sand. Seagulls were abundant and were known, on occasion, to hit Bodie's window panes, breaking the glass, sometimes throwing debris from the impact deep into the lantern room. With that thought, Rick walked around along the gallery and did notice a crack and a hole in one of the lower corners of a window. After a quick survey of the damage, he took a mental note of the supplies he would need and began working on a plan to repair the glass. He knew that, in any case, any repairing of the panes or cleaning of the lens would have to be done either at first light or not at all, until fall. The mornings would average about sixty degrees but he knew that the temperature in the afternoon could get as high as ninety. That would put the temperatures inside the lantern room well over 125. Getting Sean to help would be a necessity and it would allow a way for him to reacquaint himself with his best friend. He was looking forward to the task.

He would spend as much time as he could at Bodie cleaning the caretaker's house, cutting the grass, scraping and painting whatever needed it, or doing whatever it took to preserve the past and allow a future. Everything was still in remarkable condition despite the neglect of loving care that Bodie was used to. Rick set up accommodations in the caretaker's house once occupied by Mr. Gaskill and his family. He stocked the cabinets with canned goods and essential items such as water, toiletries, Orange Crush Soda, Pepsi Cola and, of course, cookies. He was somewhat surprised to see that the Gaskills left the beds, the linens, towels, candles, radio, a couch, dining room table, two chairs, and what he thought was the family pendulum clock on the mantle. He opened the glass door of the pendulum section and took out the key to wind the clock. He set the time and tapped the pendulum to begin its swing. After some thought he realized that there was something very soothing about the tick-tock of a pendulum clock, the comfort of home, and the security of family it represents. With a smile he remembered the last time he stood before that fireplace and the things that were said. The Gaskills knew that he would come back and would need some things. Even in their absence they made him feel welcome. "I miss them," he said out loud looking at their family picture that was left on top of a photo album on the end table to hear.

He picked up the album and thumbed through its pages. The very first picture was a picture taken at his Fourth of July birthday party last summer. Everybody was gathered on the front porch of the house with the joy of the occasion readily seen on their faces. Working through the album he came across many pictures of the Gaskills as a family from the first time Mr. and Mrs. Gaskill arrived at Bodie, having each child and holding them as infants on the porch or in front of Bodie, through the time that Rick entered their lives. "I had no idea that they took so many pictures of me," Rick thought as he continued to stroll through the pages and remembered.

He was grateful for the warm nights so he did not have to build a fire, which would draw attention to his trespass. He became a master of eating cool foods from cans and performing, sometimes, miraculous feats of electrical and sheet metal maintenance. Fresh water was captured from the down spouts attached to the rain gutters on the edge of the roof that filled barrels underneath. The gutters were a leaking broken mess. They always were, but, now because of the neglect, they were even worse. He placed putty in some of the smaller holes and seams but had to replace a ten-foot section along with a down spout. After a couple of trips to Harpers Hardware, the spouts worked like a charm. "Now all it had to do was rain," he thought. In the meantime, Rick filled milk bottles with water from home and stored them on the kitchen counter.

As he was walking to the back door, he noticed an old picture of Alexander Hamilton over the mantle of the second fireplace in the house in the adjoining room. He took a moment and walked over to the picture to read the caption, "Alexander Hamilton, First Secretary of the Treasury of the United States. Appointed by Geo. Washington…swore after a horrifying trip around Cape Hatteras that if he was to survive the trip and ever made something in his life would build a lighthouse on those shores. On August 7, 1789, President George Washington through the ninth act of the United States Congress directed that the states turn over to the federal government all existing lighthouses, those under construction, and those that are proposed. This act created the U.S. Lighthouse Establishment and placed the lighthouses under the care of the Secretary of the Treasury." Rick took a moment to think about Hamilton and remembered how he was shot in a duel with Aaron Burr in 1804 and how vengeance paid Burr a terrible visit on December 31, 1812. Hamilton being a patriotic gentleman made amends with himself and forgave the argument that he and Burr had. Hamilton had planned to do the honorable thing and deliberately aimed to miss. Hamilton took the first shot and did as he had intended. Burr being a man of attitude took his turn and shot Hamilton in his lower right abdomen, just above his right hip, mortally wounding him.

Now as history tells the story within North Carolina lore, Theodosia Burr, daughter of Aaron Burr and the wife of Governor Joseph Alston of South Carolina, left South Carolina sailing north on the ship *Patriot* to visit her father in New York City. A British man-o'-war stopped the ship and searched it then let it continue on its voyage. Legend has it that pirates then boarded the *Patriot*, had the passengers walk the plank, cast Theodosia adrift in a small boat with a portrait of herself, which was going to be a present to her father, then sank the *Patriot*. Eventually Theodosia found herself on the Outer Banks, insane and living with a banker fisherman. When a doctor came by to aid an aging Theodosia in 1869, the painting of her, which was hanging on a wall, was offered as payment by the lady caring for Theodosia. Theodosia, heard the deal, grabbed the painting and ran into the ocean, drowning. Later the next day the painting floated back to shore. It is said that Theodosia haunts the fog and the mist of the shores of the Outer Banks to this day. "Strange and odd how one of America's founding fathers was able to remind Burr of his misdeed and let him know that he has not forgotten him," Rick thought. Alexander Hamilton lives through every lighthouse along the eastern seaboard of America. "What a small price to pay for immortality," Rick said to himself.

Later in the week after Rick had visited with Sean's mother, Rick was settling down for dinner with his parents when Sean knocked and walked into the dining room of their house. The usual courtesies of waiting at the door until answered were waived for Sean since he was like a son to Rick's mom and dad. Rick got up shook his hand which lead to a punch in the arm.

Sean said, "Damn, Rick! It is good to see you. When did you get to town? How long you here for? What are you doing tonight?"

"Hold on, Sean," Rick said smiling. "I have been here since Monday and will be here until mid August anyway, but never mind that, Foreman! Already?" he said proudly.

"Yeah, it appears that I have leadership qualities that I did not know about. Mrs. Stewart liked the way I handled my work crew and now wants to send me to get some formal training in house design and architecture. It will have to be during the slow months, of course, but hey, what the hell, right?"

"Sean, will you join us for supper?" Mr. Hamilton said.

"Ah, no thanks, Mr. Hamilton. The dinner looks really good and wish I could stay, but I am having dinner with Kelly and her mom," he explained.

"I can't compete with that," responded Rick's mom. "Don't be a stranger, Sean. You come back and see us any time. Our house is always open and the stove is always warm," said Mrs. Hamilton sincerely.

"Thank you, ma'am. I'll be back, promise."

Sean turned to Rick and said, "Can you come by the house later? Kelly is dying to see you, and she has a friend you have to meet."

"Sure," Rick said. "I can't wait to see her too." With that arrangement being made, Sean left and Rick sat down to finish eating.

"Sean looks fit, doesn't he, dear?" Rick's mom said to his dad.

"He sure does. That construction business is really keeping him busy and will make Mrs. Stewart a rich lady, again. If he plays his cards right, he could be right in the thick of things when the economy picks up around here. What do you plan on doing tonight, Rick?" redirecting the conversation to him.

"Well…I don't know exactly. I guess catch up on the news around here and ask him for his help to fix a broken window on Bodie," he said.

"How is Bodie these days?" his dad said.

"OK, actually," Rick said. "I expected worse, but I do want to get that window fixed before I leave for Richmond in the fall, which means I need to get it done now before it gets too hot."

With his mother listening, "It is a great thing you are doing to preserve Bodie, Rick. It takes someone like you to do it without pay or reward."

"I just don't want to see it deteriorate to nothing," Rick said, "and I'm afraid if I don't do the little things, one day when I come back it will be gone. Besides, I do get a reward. I enjoy her."

Smiling, his mom said, "I know you do. As a little boy, I remember I would enter your room to see how you were sleeping and I would notice your little eyes open with your head on the pillow just looking out the window at her. It is no surprise to me, at all, that you are doing what you are doing. You are a good boy. You have a good night tonight with your friends. I'll clean up."

"Thanks, Mom," Rick said, and with a little kiss on the cheek, he left for Kelly's house.

It was another gorgeous night on Roanoke Island, about seventy-five degrees, and a full moon. It was so bright in fact that a person could actually drive the short distance to Manchese without headlights. The light from Bodie seemed extra bright. Its ray was casting a shadow of its own against the sand dunes and topography of Roanoke Island. The light seemed to lead Rick to Kelly's house with its horizontal pulses. Her warm light sat in the car with him all the way there. Although Bodie was miles away, she seemed so close for some reason. Other than the moon that was high in the sky Bodie was the only living thing tracking his travel.

Rick walked to the front door, knocked and Mrs. Stewart answered. "Hi, Mrs. Stewart, are Sean and Kelly here?" Rick asked.

"They sure are, Rick. They're around back," she replied.

Rick walked around to the back of the house finding his way by the moonlight, which was casting beautiful blue-gray shadows of the trees on the ground. He heard laughing and later saw Sean pushing Kelly on the tire swing that he put up. Sean saw Rick first and said, "Hey, Rick!"

Kelly quickly stopped the swing, got off and stumbled in her run to Rick, and hugged him. "Wow, Rick, you look great! Doesn't he look great, Sean?"

"Yeah, he is absolutely beautiful," Sean replied smartly.

Keeping an arm around Rick's waist, Kelly turned to her friend who was standing by the trunk of the tree and said, "Lucia, come over here. I want you to meet Rick."

From the dark shadow of the tree, she moved into the blue-gray light of the moon. At the instant he saw her for the first time, Bodie shined upon her face. Time seemed to stand still for an eternity as he looked into her deep brown eyes framed by dark shoulder-length hair. Her angelic features were lightly tanned from head to toe. Her image filled his view completely as his heart skipped a beat, and the temperature within his skin rose. He could have been in a crowd of a million people and all he ever would have seen was her.

"Hey, stupid, say hi or something," Sean said.

Clearing his throat after a vain attempt to say a word, Rick uttered, "Hi. Lucia, is it?"

Lucia looked at Rick and expressed amusement with her smile saying, "Yes. Hi. I am very happy to meet you," she said shyly enjoying his obvious boyish charm.

Unknown to Rick she was glad that he said the first words because she was having difficulty composing words herself also. She noticed Rick when he turned the corner of the house. His six-foot silhouette, made by the moonlight and the occasional flash of Bodie, made an impression she had never thought possible. Straight, erect, and clean she noticed that he walked with purpose and confidence. A man, she could tell, who could do anything he chose to. A man of intelligence and determination, a man who has loved and been loved but is missing something. She felt within herself the brightness of the sun and a hope that she thought avoided her.

"Sean said that Kelly brought a friend home from college but didn't say anything about you being so..." Rick said, searching real hard for words expressing his initial feeling. Not wanting to be presumptuous or forward said the only word that came to mind to finish the thought, "pretty."

"*Grazie*, Rick. I think perhaps that the lack of light has made me seem prettier than I really am. For that blessing, I am thankful. You are kind," Lucia said a little embarrassed.

"I can tell that you are not from here...you are Italian aren't you?" Rick said with genuine excitement.

"I am from Italy in a small village named San Gimignano. I know my accent is strong and my English is not so good..."

"No, not at all. No, that's not what I mean. I mean your English is great and

I think your accent is…well, refreshing. After being around Sean all my life and the folks of the shore, your voice is, well…just lovely. Anyway, how do you like North Carolina? Have you been to the ocean yet or seen anything around here?" Rick asked, instantly liking Lucia and showing it.

"I love your country. It is so much different from where I come from. The people are friendly and curious about me and Italy. It's nice. I have not been to your ocean yet but…"

Rick interrupted, "Oh, that's good. Please allow me to take you tomorrow, OK?

Rick and Lucia both looked over at Sean and Kelly, who had their arms around each other in a comfortable way, to see if they had any plans for Lucia that would interfere with that invitation. Sean and Kelly heard every word spoken between Rick and Lucia and were amused at Rick's unusual and uncharacteristic love-struck babbling. Sean looked at Kelly, Kelly looked at Sean, then they both looked at Rick and smiled.

"We have nothing planned," said Sean.

"Yeah, you two go and have fun," Kelly said with a throw of the hand.

Lucia looked at Kelly saying, "Kelly, I was hoping you and Sean would go along with us," she said with a nod, feeling that going out alone with a guy without her…at least not yet, would be inappropriate. It was certainly not in keeping with the strict Italian traditions.

Rick sensing this and understanding completely said, "Yeah, you two. You have to come with us. Besides, Sean, I have to ask a favor of you. I need to fix a window pane on Bodie's lantern room and I need your help. I need your advice. You know, tap into all that construction knowledge you have now."

"Sure. I can do that. How about you, babe? You want to go?" Sean said to Kelly.

"It sounds like fun," Kelly said. "It's been a year since I have been over there, since your birthday party, Rick. Yeah, let's go and get an early start. Lucia and I will pack a lunch."

Rick was just elated at this. His summer just took on a new flavor. "Great friends and now a new acquaintance," he thought, but not like any he ever imagined. Lucia made him feel different and out of sorts. He never had been at a loss for words before. He hoped he didn't look too stupid trying to talk to Lucia. If he did he knew that Sean would tell him, happily! But after all, that was what friends were for and now he had a mystery woman in his life. Lucia made him tingle inside and, even though he was still standing next to her, he couldn't wait to see her again tomorrow.

Lucia was a foreigner in a strange land with different customs, foods, and climate. The people around her spoke a different language, which wasn't a problem for her, as English was taught in Italian schools and was always stressed by her father. "If you want to be successful in anything you do, you have to be able to speak in the language of the person you are speaking with. It shows that you are polite, intelligent, and respectful," she remembered him telling her. So she learned it.

She missed and worried about her family at home working the vineyards and was deeply concerned about the gloom of war that was present, threatening destruction and even death at any turn of coincidence or chance. The great distance that her family put between her and the troubles of Italy was meant to protect her and to give her the greatest gift parents can give a child. That gift was an education, an American education. In her father's opinion, an American education was the best for a number of reasons. First, America was safe and powerful, a land of laws, liberty, and freedom of expression and ideas. Second, America would be a greater consumer of wine soon and he wanted to be at the forefront of this opportunity with Lucia leading the way. Third, he wanted his young beautiful daughter to experience the world, to see new and wonderful things. Experience was the best teacher and experience was about to make an impression that would shape her soul and live forever in her heart.

Meredith College had a fine reputation as an all-girl school. A college set on top of gently sloping hills with trees of pine, magnolias, and oak and a beautiful little lake. The campus was somewhat secluded from the rustle of Raleigh and the distractions that a big city could cause. The school was strong in languages and business education. Meredith had rules of curfew and visitation by boys, which her father absolutely required. Through correspondence with Lucia's father, Kelly was able to establish a trust with the Bellamonte family which allowed Lucia to go home with Kelly to visit the eastern shore of North Carolina. Kelly understood this trust and relationship and would not put Lucia in jeopardy in any way.

Kelly knew that when Lucia was with Rick she could not be in safer hands or arms, whatever the case might have been. Kelly knew that, somehow, she had to introduce Lucia to Rick. She knew that the first day she saw her standing by the window unpacking her suitcase in the simple, plain room that they shared. She anxiously anticipated the moment they would meet and she was not disappointed. Kelly had hoped that Rick would find a gentle woman that would complement him in all that he was, a woman that would help him evolve into a great and loving man. She saw in Lucia's smile the companionship that had eluded Rick all of his life. She saw this need in her also and saw Rick as her great complement as well.

Rick took Lucia over to the swing and pushed her while Sean and Kelly stood close by.

"Rick, you have to take Lucia to the top of Bodie tomorrow and give her a bird's-eye view of North Carolina," Kelly said.

"I sure will, Kell," Rick said in reply.

"Have you ever been to see a lighthouse, Lucia?" asked Sean.

"I have never seen one," Lucia said as she stopped the swing and got off. She turned to Rick and said, "Kelly told me that you have one?"

Rick chuckled politely and said, "Well, I don't have one. I tend to one called Bodie just across the water, over there," as he pointed to Bodie's light. "That is where we will be going tomorrow."

"It looks really lonely from here," Lucia's said, leaning over to Rick in a friendly way and to get a little closer. In a wispy voice and in a tone a little louder than a breath, she said, "It looks small."

"Yeah, from here it looks small…but it is bigger than you might realize," he said in the same low tone and with a coy smile. "Tomorrow I will show you and tell you all I know. I hope you will tell me all about your home in Italy."

"My home is much different from here," she said, stepping back so she could look at him. "It is much hillier and the trees are cypress, like your evergreens but much taller and thinner. Everywhere you look you see olive trees and vineyards, each one guarded by rows of cypress trees brought to Italy 3,000 years ago by the Etruscans. Small winding roads, well traveled over the centuries, lead to towns so intimate you would think it was one big home. Each home rested peaceably under a seamless terra cotta roof supported by stucco, stone, and brick walls. You can see Roman aqueducts still standing with stone and brick arches among the hills and the painted fields of red orchids, white lilies and royal purple bell flowers. My country is old compared to your new America. Everything here is new. My country lives and breathes time. It is ageless and never really changes."

Standing in amazement, Rick paused to visualize all that she said. Even Kelly never heard Lucia describe her home like that. Lucia was missing home. That was obvious to Rick and Kelly. They knew that trouble was ravaging her country and the pain that she was feeling was strong. They knew that behind her smiles and enthusiasm of being in America, that home and the concern for her family was not far away. Her thoughts of home were always just behind the color of her eyes.

"Your country and home sounds just beautiful. It would be great to visit it someday," said Rick.

With encouragement in her voice, Kelly said, "What about, after we all graduate, we come to visit. I'm sure there will be a way to do it," Kelly said to Lucia glancing to the others.

"You are all very welcome at my home. Momma cooks the best pollo rustica, mushrooms, olives, onions and a hint of garlic. Nothing in this world is better. Momma would love you. Please come and stay as long as you can, promise?"

As a group they all responded, "Promise!"

"With that lovely picture in my mind and a burning appetite, I guess I should get going. Tomorrow will start early and I have to pack some things. You girls have sandwiches to make, huh?" Rick said with a smirk.

"I will meet you there?" he said looking and pointing his finger at Sean.

"Sure. About 9:00. I will bring the kittens and the food."

"I will walk with you to your car," Lucia said to Rick.

With a smile and a nod responding to Lucia's offer, he looked to Sean and Kelly, "See ya tomorrow."

Walking slowly around the corner of the house Rick said to Lucia, "Try not to worry about your mom and dad, OK? I know it is hard being so far from home and all. Try to enjoy your friends. Tomorrow, I promise, I will make a great day for you."

"I believe you will too," she said with her beautiful smile. "I do not worry too much about my family. They are away from most trouble. It is the occasional straggler and the stories about the war that scare me the most. It's not knowing, from day to day, week to week, that puts the worry in my eyes."

"Your eyes are so pretty too. Look into my eyes, Lucia," he said turning her by her shoulders then pointing to his eyes that were as blue as a Tahiti shore. "Concentrate on these. When you feel lonely think of my eyes. When you are worried or scared think of these," he said looking deep into her chocolate-brown eyes. He then gave her a very strong and sincere hug, a hug appropriate of friends with a genuine concern for the other. He could not help but feel her full figure press against his chest as he put his arms around her hourglass frame. He felt her breath on his throat. A sigh of comfort left her heart and entered into his soul. The smell of her hair impressed his brain so forgetting would never be possible. The feeling of her arms around his athletic waist made him realize that this trip home would be like no other time. "Something is happening," he thought again.

Lucia was shy and always had been, but on this night, she wanted more. She was hoping that somehow Rick would touch her, that he would place his arm around her shoulder or his hand on her back as he guided her to the car. It was all she could really hope for or even expect, but to get an embrace? It was like the surprise you feel after being lost and suddenly found. She felt his heart race and the warmth of his chest as her cheek gently rested for a moment on his neck. She never felt more protected or secure as she did when Rick put his arms around her. She felt the power that lived in his heart and body and knew, from that moment on, that Rick somehow was always going to be a part of her life. She knew that going to bed that night was going to be different from any other. She knew that her dreams would be of Rick and the light of Bodie that visited her room also, except that this time, on this night, it would be with a special meaning that was not there last night or any night before.

3

The morning seemed extra bright for Rick when he woke up. He was certain that it really wasn't any brighter than the rest but he felt different, a bit strange. He felt an excitement that he never felt before and it showed in his rush to shower and eat a quick breakfast. He selected the tools he would need for the job that day and put them in the back of his car along with some fresh water and a couple of clean towels to dry off with after they washed the sand, grit and grime off their faces. He was anxious to be with Sean and Kelly, but he also knew he had a special reason to be appetent. He was going to see Lucia again and that thought made his mouth dry and his skin hot. He thought it was strange, in a way, that one night made all this difference in his day, a day that twenty-four hours ago would have been saturated with work and toil with a few laughs to break the tension, but now would have a very special smile, cooling a hot afternoon, waiting for him.

Lucia woke up calmer than most days. She just lay in her bed listening to the sea gulls that frequented the house, wondering about home and hoping that everybody was healthy and happy. Letters from home were not very frequent because the mail service was poor and unreliable in the country. She knew that the normal problems that existed at home were compounded by the war in Europe. Italy's involvement was only making things worse. Since meeting Rick the night before, she felt more relaxed and more at peace with herself than she did since she came to the States. She was looking forward to the day, seeing the ocean, seeing Bodie Lighthouse and, of course, Rick.

"Lucia, are you going to get up or sleep in all day? Sean will be by in about an hour and besides, I am sure Rick will be standing tall and all ready to see you again," Kelly said with a simper.

Lucia threw her pillow at the door as Kelly was shutting it. Lucia hugged her little stuffed animal dog that her father gave her before she left for school and smiled.

She showered and got dressed in a yellow linen sundress that she brought from home that was supported by two-inch straps that rested nicely on her tanned shoulders. The front of the bodice was flat with needlepoint embroidery of white and beige flowers arranged around tiny round holes arranged in horizontal lines that went all around the bodice. Near the neck was a little bow that accented the little linen-covered buttons that went down the middle in a row and stopped at the waist. The waist was gathered which began the pleats and ended just above the knee. The dress was made for the Italian summers and would answer any man's dream of Tuscan perfection. By the time she came out to the kitchen to help with the sandwiches Sean was already there, car packed, and ready to go to work.

"Wow, look out, Rick!" Sean said with surprise and a little envy that, hopefully, Kelly didn't notice.

Kelly turned to see what that comment was all about. "Lucia," she said softly and with amazement. "You look nice," Kelly said knowing that was a serious understatement.

"Nice? Hell! She's stunning," Sean said surprised and to correct Kelly. "Lucia, we are going to a little island that is sandy, marshy, and windy. Not to a party. Heck, it's only going to be the four of us."

With that statement Lucia smiled and Sean and Kelly did also knowing all too well that the intent was to make an impression, not to do any heavy labor. Kelly knew also that Lucia was a woman who could outwork any man and would work as necessary regardless of the attire. Kelly was not worried one bit about Lucia…it was Rick who better be on guard.

The trip to the island was perfect. Dusty white clouds speckled the blue sky. The breeze was warm and just strong enough to make the warm sun tickle the skin. Rick had put water on the gas stove for some Earl Gray tea, which he knew was Lucia's favorite through conversation the night before. He put out a couple of rocking chairs on the back porch facing the lighthouse and turned on the radio to prepare the place for his friends. He was just unlocking Bodie when Lucia arrived.

"Hey there, Rick!" cried Sean. "Come on over here. There is something I want to show you."

"Knock it off, Sean. Behave yourself," Kelly said in a tone to get Sean's attention but not loud enough to alarm Lucia.

Rick turned to his friends and began walking towards them. Kelly began a little skip jog to Rick and gave him a big hug. During their embrace and over her shoulder he noticed Lucia walking over next to Sean. Kelly, sensing that Rick just noticed her, whispered into his ear, "Your life is about to make a big turn. I feel it in your chest and saw it in your eyes last night."

"But is she…?" stammered Rick.

"She is closer to you than your little naive heart could possibly know."

Rick walked over to Lucia and, trying to find the right thing to say, just looked at her, again.

Sean beginning to laugh, said, "Come on, my poor, poor buddy Rick. Show us the cottage." Sean turned Rick's body, but Rick's eyes stayed on Lucia as they walked to the caretaker's house.

Before going inside Rick stopped with Lucia as she paused in her step to look at Bodie standing tall by the water just about a thirty yards from the house.

"This is beautiful. This has to be the most beautiful part of America I have seen yet. You and your family built this?" Lucia asked.

"No," Rick said half laughing, "I did not build this nor is it mine. I just do what I can to keep it, well…standing and…beautiful."

"This is really something. It is peaceful here," she said as her eyes gleamed over the marshes, the sand, and the dunes surrounding this repose of peaceful solitude. "This Bodie is so big. I can understand how she is comforting to people because you always know where you are. Being lost is scary. You are never lost as long as you can see her."

Rick, took his eyes off Lucia for a moment, looked at Bodie, and smiled again. "You know, I never looked at her that way before," he said. Then looking back at Lucia continued, "But you are so right. There is a certain love that is born here, a certain comfort that exists in her shadows…where you are. I'm glad you are here."

Rick took Lucia into the caretaker's house and showed her around. Kelly had already poured the tea for everybody and Sean helped himself to an Orange Crush Rick had stored in his cooler.

Rick took his friends out to Bodie and let Sean lead the way up the stairs followed by Kelly. Rick held out his hand for Lucia to take before she entered Bodie saying, "Watch your head in here once you get on the stairs and don't be frightened. It is kind of cramped and the gallery is thin, but it is strong. So don't worry. I am right behind you."

"I'm not frightened. I've never felt safer," she said.

The walk to the top took about five minutes. The temperature was getting warm as the effort to climb the stairs began to make the body perspire. The concrete-and-mortar walls helped to keep the inside cool but there was no movement of the air unless the bottom and top doors to the lighthouse were open making a natural chimney draft. The thin and long vertical windows that line up in a tall row along Bodie's length helped to alleviate any claustrophobic tendencies by allowing ambient light to enter the otherwise dark chasm of space. The clang of the metal steps as you walked gave a song which was unique and gave a joyous accompaniment to the journey to the top.

After the long climb, emerging from the inside of the top of Bodie was as close to being born again as was humanly possible. From the dark interior, lit only by the occasional narrow window, the occupants emerged into a blue, cool and breezy environment overlooking a vast blue-green ocean. It was capped by sea foam and waves of a thousand shapes. They stood and listened to the piercing voices of the seagulls, waves crashing on the shore a quarter mile away and the wind as it kissed their ears and whistled by the steel gallery and glass of the lantern room. The sensation could be compared to suddenly being given sight for the first time after having been denied the sense for fifty years. The emotion that was felt from the emergence from Bodie's interior was very personal and different than any other experience. Other people have described it in a similar way, with one or two variances, but all could agree that it was a moment that ranked among the grandest in a person's memory.

Rick looked at Lucia and knew that she was feeling what he felt when he climbed to the top for the first time about four years earlier. Seeing the joy and astonishment in her eyes and the expression of her smile allowed him to relive his initial experience and have another one born. Bodie had changed his life in so many ways and now had touched the prettiest of hearts in Tuscany. Bodie really did reach beyond nineteen miles. It had touched Rick's heart again through Lucia's, and Lucia's heart, missing home, was beginning to feel a new comfort of home 167 feet above ground, overlooking a Carolina shore with two American friends and one extraordinary man who had seemed to captivate her heart, mind, and spirit.

Sean, looking around on the gallery, said, "Rick, is this the hole you want to fix?"

"Oh yeah," Rick said almost forgetting one reason why they came up there. "We will have to take the whole pane out and replace it. We can get the piece up here using a pulley and I can put it in place by removing these metal strips and putting them back again. What do you think?"

"Sounds like a big job, but manageable. I can get a couple of guys to go to National Glass in Washington tomorrow and we can install it, say, Wednesday?"

"That sounds fine to me. Let me know the cost and..."

"We will settle all accounts later. Don't sweat it."

"It is really beautiful up here, Rick. I forgot just how pretty it is," said Kelly.

"It is where I come to get away."

Turning to Lucia and whispering in her ear, he said, "You can actually get dizzy looking at the moon from here on a clear night, not something I recommend at all by yourself. Looking over the water at night you cannot tell where the water ends and the sky begins. Each star reflects a hundred times on the surface of the water. It's the motion of the waves that makes the poetry and the stillness of the sky that makes the music for the song that echoes in your mind. I can imagine you standing here at night conducting the great symphony."

"That is a beautiful thing to say, Rick. Of course you know I would not ever come up here without you. I could never imagine wanting to. I look forward to coming back up here with you one night."

Rick smiled and put his arm around Lucia and Lucia, with a quick head touch to his shoulder, righted herself and just looked at the magnificent ocean scene. Rick, looking over at Sean and Kelly, saw that, they too, were in an embrace doing much the same thing that he was. This was a special place that few are able to experience. This was one way Rick could reward his friends for their friendship, a thought that, if his friends knew, would upset them because their friendship was freely given because they loved him, unconditionally, and not for reward. Rick knew that but still wanted to share something extraordinary and special. Bodie did that and she fit so well in describing who he was.

Looking at Lucia after several minutes, Rick asked, "Are you getting hungry?" Lucia responded with a nod of grace and a smile to match. The look upon her face made Rick's heart stop as he could tell that she had changed from the time he saw her by the car and now. He could tell that she had been touched by this moment and Rick. Her face had a peace only seen on angels and in dreams. He knew, somehow, that he had just become someone very special in her life. He realized at that moment that Kelly was right. "It is amazing," Rick thought, "what women know between themselves." Rick's life did turn a corner and along the walk of life he knew that Lucia was going to be there. "How did Kelly know?" Rick thought, but, just as quick as those words came to his mind he discounted them because he knew that Kelly always had an insight to him. Women have a lover's instinct, and it was undeniable and true in this instance.

Rick looked over to Kelly and said, "Are the sandwiches any good?"

Knowing that the boys were probably getting hungry said, "Yeah, come on, you guys. I'll feed ya," said Kelly as she entered the metal portal to begin the trip down. Sean followed.

Lucia looked at Rick saying, "Rick, it really is beautiful up here. Thanks for sharing this with me."

"Are you kidding, Lucia? I was meant to bring you up here. Within your brief little encounter with me and Bodie, you have done more to impress my memory than the biggest hurricane ever could. Thanks for being with me today."

The friends all had a lunch of turkey, tomatoes, and mayonnaise. The frolicking on the island continued with walks along the marsh and the grounds. They even took a walk to the ocean and walked along the beach collecting beautiful seashells. Sean found several sharks' teeth and added them to a collection that he had been working on since he was a kid. Rick and Kelly were beginning to get a bit red but, because Sean worked in the sun all day long, he just got a deeper tan. Lucia just got more beautiful; her skin was made for the sun. The radiant energy was just absorbed by her olive color which just deepened her spicy complexion. The sunlight that was absorbed was expelled harmlessly through her bright smile and the stars enmeshed within the delicate nebulous glow of her dark eyes.

Lucia said, with a smile and a distant daze facing the long shoreline of the beach, "I love the beaches here, Rick. The sand has a clean firm feel. The water is warm and the seagulls are so curious which makes them seem friendly. There is no fear here. A person could actually relax, if a person wanted to. I could just sit here all day and not do a thing and that would be enough for me."

Rick said, "I know exactly want you mean. I have spent many hours on this very spot up against that dune over there," pointing to the dunes where Bodie stood in the background, "just reading."

Lucia just closed her eyes, facing the sky, and took a deep breath while raising her arms to a stretch then resting them behind her head. She didn't say a word for a while after that and Rick did not bother her with conversation. Sometimes conversation just got in the way of communication and in this case silence said volumes. She was enjoying herself, and Rick was enjoying just being close to her. That was good enough for him.

Afternoon evolved into dusk and dusk into night. Rick packed some burgers earlier that morning and he cooked them over the fire pit with a makeshift grill that he had scrounged from a rusted BBQ that he found in the corner of the lot. After he cleaned and polished it, it looked as good as new. Along with some cool tea and a leaf of mint that was still growing in the old herb garden from the Gaskills, potato salad that Rick's mom made and the sequenced sky that God created just for them, the night was perfect.

Rick walked Lucia back to the car along with Sean and Kelly, holding her hand while they walked. Stopping at the car, they turned towards each other. Rick said, "Lucia, thank you for coming out here and spending the day with me. I really had a great time. You are so interesting and, I don't know…new, I guess. I enjoy you so much."

"I too enjoyed today, Rick. It is I who should be thanking you for such a great day. I know it would not have been possible nor would it have been so special without you."

"Will I see you again? I mean soon…this week?" Rick said with urgency in his voice.

"Yes, you will see me again."

"OK then," he said with a smile, "I will take that as a promise," and kissed her lightly once on the cheek. Knowing she was a woman of class and decorum, he did not want to come across as being fresh. He felt he had to be careful in his approaches with her because he still was not sure what she would consider inappropriate or out of line. He knew to do anything more might be considered not gentlemanly and did not want to risk anything sour with Lucia. He still had time. Caution and care, he felt, would take the high road. That little kiss however, sent chills through his body and made him shake to the point that it took minutes after she left to settle down and steady his legs.

Lucia sat in the back seat of the car alone which was fine to her as she really did not want Kelly to see the little smile she had on her face as she was already thinking about the day, tomorrow, and feelings of missing Rick. She loved the day so much and felt, in one way, she did not have the right to because her family in Italy was having troubles. On the other hand, she knew that feelings for Rick were developing and were about to get more complicated and deep. She knew that she would be going back to college in a couple of weeks and now…had another interest, a big distraction called Rick. Being by herself, right now, was exactly what she needed to do and was glad to be given the time to just think the events of the of that lovely day through.

The feeling that Lucia was experiencing was new and foreign to her. She felt she knew what was happening but she was not sure what could be done about it or if she should do anything at all but perhaps, just maybe, just let things happen.

She remembered what her mom always told her, "Think of your heart as a little firefly. Don't ever be afraid of showing your light. Fly lightly in the sky and with the wind, blow from tree to tree resting only when you are tired and love only the hand that captures you gently then opens slowly to let you fly again." Lucia missed home and will now miss America. It took years but like a storm approaching home, she realized the warm meaning of what her mother meant.

On Wednesday, as promised, Sean and a couple of guys from his construction company came by to assist in the lifting and placing of the glass pane into the space that Rick neatly cleaned out before they arrived. The job was not especially difficult with all of the help that was available, but it did have the challenges associated with height. Sean suggested that they place some kind of wire mesh around the lantern room to help absorb the impact of a misdirected seagull. Rick thought the idea a good one so he said he would research as to what kind of wire fence would be best and would let him know.

Rick was a very gracious host to the work crew and offered each one a can of Krueger's Beer he brought from Richmond after the job. As they passed the can opener, opening their brew with two triangle punctures along the top, they stood around telling stories of the new girls seen in town. Sean said, "You know, Rick, Lucia will be going back to Meredith next week. Kelly will be taking her back and will be attending summer school with her."

"Back? Already? I have another month before I have to go back. Why is...?"

"Relax, Rick. They had this planned before they even left college for the summer. Lucia feels she has to get back home to Italy and one way to do that, and get her degree, is to take summer classes. She can graduate a year early by doing this."

"She never let on that she was leaving. Kell didn't even say anything."

"Don't worry, bub. She isn't gone yet. We have several more days. Plenty of time to see her and, you know."

"OK. Stop it. You know better than that. You know Lucia is, well, special and different. I wouldn't...and you better not even try anything stupid. Damn, that girl is real class. Can't you see that? She comes from a different world," and pausing a moment continued, "... a different world. What she sees in me, I'll never guess."

"Me neither," said Sean with a friendly leer. Putting his arm around him and walking him back to the cottage Sean said, "Rick, relax. You are strung too tight. Kelly and I both know what is going on between you two. It is obvious to everyone in town. Take your time with her. I have a suspicion she feels the same and is dreading going back too. Why don't you guys hook up later in the week when you get time and, I don't know, visit? Check things out. See how she feels about school, home, the friends she has here. Then when she is relaxed, find out, in some way, how she feels about... you."

Seeing that Rick was really emotionally drawn into her leaving and having heard all that Sean had said, Sean continued, "You are a special guy and you have met a very special gal. What has happened to you happened fast. The differences between you two and the distances that you both will have to deal with will be difficult but I think it will be the hardships that will bond you two together. Next summer you will be closer than ever to her and her to you; but, enough of that, big guy. I have to get this crew back before it gets dark; big day tomorrow. You have a lot of thinking to do. Call me tomorrow night and let me know what you want to do. We'll all do something."

Rick saw them drive off with some dust drifting from behind the truck. As he watched the truck disappear behind a dune he turned around and looked back at Bodie, the fire pit, and the cottage that they all enjoyed several days ago. Bodie's glass was fixed and clean and the grounds pruned. An empty feeling of loneliness filled the center part of his chest as he imagined her not being near. "Somehow," he thought, "I am going to have to work through this. I'm going to have to get to know her better and spend as much time as I can with her...but be careful, don't scare her with words that are too fond. Be careful, bud. Be careful."

Rick did call Lucia and arranged to pick her up on Saturday afternoon. He had planned that Sean and Kelly would join them for a drive or something, but Sean wanted to spend the last weekend with Kelly alone. Kelly thought it was a good idea too, aside from the fact she thought it was important that Lucia and Rick have some private time knowing that they had things to discuss.

Rick walked up to the Stewarts' front door to pick up Lucia. At the sight of her walking to the door and even through the dark screen, spanning the empty spaces of the entrance that protected the interior of the house from the insects of outside, Lucia was stunning. Dressed so simply but undeniably beautiful she walked towards him with a natural dainty swing. Rick, as he always was when he first saw her after an intermission of being without her, was speechless. This time it was Mrs. Stewart who had to break the silence saying, "Hello, Rick. You ready for your day with Lucia?"

"Oh, hi, Mrs. Stewart. I am ready. I guess Kelly and Sean have already gone?"

"Oh, yes. They left early this morning."

"OK then, I guess we better get going then. I will have Lucia back later tonight."

"I'm not worried, Rick. You kids have a fun day."

Once in the car after and after a quiet walk from the front porch, Rick looked over at her and could tell that something was on her mind through the little disquieted lips that she had. He had become strangely so familiar with her. He was able to read her expressions and knew this look meant that something was coming.

"OK, Lucia. What is on your mind?"

"Just drive, OK? Take me somewhere so we can talk."

"OK. Sure, how about the northern part of the Outer Banks. We can visit Kitty Hawk, where the Wright Brothers flew their first heaver than air machine, that's not far, and then we can visit Currituck Lighthouse?"

Rick looked at her, and seeing her face and eyes, knew she didn't care. He reached over and touched her hand and by doing so she opened her hand and held it. He knew that something was troubling her; that it wasn't anything that he did but something from within or perhaps from abroad or both. He knew, instinctively, not to pursue the questioning now but after they got to Kitty Hawk and only then, if the opportunity afforded itself.

There was not much at Kitty Hawk, just some sand dunes, a sixty-one-foot granite Art-Deco monument in the shape of a wing on a sandy hill commemorating the December 1903 flight and little markers showing the length of the first, second and third flights, depicting how each attempt to fly was getting progressively longer. Atop the monument was a bright light, resembling the airport beacons made of surplus Fresnel lenses. Rick explained the historical significance of this place and how aviation had progressed since then. She listened, he thought, intensely but, in fact, was just listening to him speak, not really paying attention to what he was saying but rather to just his voice and gestures.

After about an hour there they packed up and continued to Currituck, which Rick had only seen once before. Currituck Lighthouse was strikingly different because it was all brick and red in color. The height was just a few feet shorter than Bodie and the lantern room was of similar shape and size. The grounds surrounding Currituck were markedly different as they did have some trees, landscaping, and greener grass than Bodie.

Rick thought this might be as good a place as any to see what was on Lucia's mind so he took her by the hand and walked with her towards a row of trees. They sat down under one and on top of a blanket that he brought along. Sitting across from her and holding both of her hands he asked, "Lucia, I know you hardly know me. I just want you to know I care about you and whatever it is that is troubling you. I'm your friend and want to help you. Do you feel comfortable with me?"

"Yes, I do and that is the best part of my life. Maybe too comfortable...I don't know. I do know that my feelings scare me a bit but only because they are new to me. I do trust you, more than you know. I am going back to school in a couple of days. You know that. Wednesday begins summer orientation and check-in," Lucia said with concern tainting her voice.

"I know about that. Sean told me last week after he helped me repair Bodie. Is that all that is bothering you? That you are leaving?"

"No, it is not. Understand, you comfort me but I still have family in Italy. They, by simply being citizens, are involved in a war that they did not want. It affects the entire country and my family is a part of it. The war affects the national economy and my family is forced to take on a financial burden. I feel guilty going to school over here for a number of reasons. First, is because it is expensive. I know my parents sent me here to get me away from the danger but I feel I should help them too. Second, my father is against the Mussolini Fascist government because they are dangerous to the Italian people. They have killed, no, murdered thousands who protest against him. The Italian communists are gaining strength which threatens my father's business. The government's alliance with Germany spells death to Italy and endangers everybody. One reason being, that it is well known that the Germans hate Communists. How can the Italians think that if the Italians were successful in their aggression in the north that the Germans would not turn and invade Italy and annex us to their plan? I know you do not understand everything I am telling you. I just wanted you to know that it is on my mind."

Pausing for just a minute she continued, "It is a war we cannot win, or as my father says, we should not win. My father resists. He actively resists and that scares me. Mussolini is ruthless and if my papa is caught..." she said exhaling deeply as she held her head in her hands.

Rick touched her head with his hand to let her know he was there, listening.

Lucia continued after she looked up at Rick, "He is a proud man. He resists in ways that, if found, would be executed and I fear my mother and friends who work the vineyards will be indiscriminately murdered too."

"Hearing all this makes the problems we have over here seem small," Rick said.

"Rick, this war is coming over here too. Another reason I fear is because I know that you personally will be involved in it somehow; Sean, too. I see how you guys are and you will not stand by while other men of America fight and I do not want to see you or Sean hurt."

"Aw…come on. There is no evidence to lead me to think we are going to war with Italy or Germany. The war is far away."

"You are smarter than that, Rick. Add it up. Germany invades Czechoslovakia then Italy invades Albania. And now, just recently, Italy signs the 'Pact of Steel' with Germany. England is nervous over Germany's aggression and the Russians are certainly sharpening their spears. Do you think, for one minute, that America will sit idly by while England is engaged with a dictator who threatens security in the Atlantic?"

"I had no idea that you knew so much. How did you find all this out?"

"I can read, Rick. I think most Americans are naive to the events in Europe. I wish…I don't know…I just wish it would just end and my family can be OK."

Putting his arm around her he thought of what he could say to comfort her. He knew that anything he could say would not be enough as her trouble was global and deeply personal at the same time. Rick's world was very small compared to Lucia and he knew it.

"Lucia, look, I am not going to claim to know everything but I do know this. The best thing you can do for your family is to do the best you can here in the States, and honor your father with a degree just like he asked. That is all you can do aside from writing when you can and keeping up on current events like you have. You have to stay safe. If he had to worry about you, don't you think that will just put him more at risk? Get your degree and let's see where the world is then. Let's not worry too much about things that we cannot control. OK?"

Raising her head she looked into his eyes through the tears of her own that have yet to fall. She knew what he said was right and she knew that getting her degree, just like her father wanted, was her ticket back home, thus her urgency to get it.

"OK. Now do you understand why I feel I have to go back to Meredith early? Please say you understand. Your understanding means so much to me."

"Sure I understand. It does not make the pain of missing you any less though. I am with you and you can count on me for anything you might need, just ask. I'm hoping in the years to come that I will get to know you well enough that I can determine on my own if you need something and then have the means to provide it to you before you have to ask. You have to know that I will do whatever it takes to help you."

"I do. You are a great comfort to me and I will rely on your strength to get me through the next couple of years."

"We have to communicate often. Write me and call, OK? Let's meet back at Bodie next summer," Rick said.

"I will write you, I promise. You are a very dear man and I will miss you. Now," she said looking at Rick right square in the eye, "I have one more person to miss and pray for. You are the most sincere man I have ever met and the best friend my lonely heart could ask for." Then she leaned over reaching for Rick's lips and lightly kissed him.

Rick and Lucia finished up the day touring the Currituck Lighthouse and the small community nearby. The drive back to Manchese was short, as Rick knew that this would be the last time he would see Lucia until next summer. His heart was pounding as his chest was developing a huge chasm of empty space that not having her would naturally make. Having said all that was to be said throughout the day, silence filled the car. A feeling of dread and woeful anticipation preceded a certain painful event that Rick knew would last until he saw Lucia again. Just a hold of each other's hand was all the communication that the two of them had. Fingertip to fingertip, a very sensitive touch full of tenderness for the other, communicated the respect and adoration that only a touch could make. Both of them knew what the other was feeling and both knew that the good-bye would be the hardest thing they ever did.

Rick pulled up to the house and just sat in the car looking at Lucia and she did the same, looking right back into his eyes framed with a face that only the union between sorrow, hope, and love could make. Rick walked her to the front porch of her house. When she reached the door she quickly turned and gave Rick an embrace that she knew would have to last until she saw him again. He knew it also and responded with a hug of equal strength. With one last passionate breath, he whispered in her ear, "I love you."

With tears in her eyes she turned and opened the screen door then, as if on cue, took one last look at Rick and said, "I know. *Ti Amo*," and went inside.

4

Rick's return to Richmond College had a lonely feel to it. Although he enjoyed the school, his friends and the city, he was wishing he could be nearer to Lucia. He immersed himself in his studies of history and Latin and enjoyed an occasional casting in a play. This year Richmond was doing a series of Shakespeare plays and sonnets. Rick was hoping for a bit part, knowing that competition would be tough for a lead character with the likes of Woody Harris, Dan Alexander, and Sloan Burns auditioning for every show. They were the best in their field and their talents were always sought by the directors Jack Welsh, Francis Daniel, and Bill "Coach" Lockey.

Night life was full of activities which usually involved going to fraternity row and mixing at parties. There he met and made friends with Richard "Dick" Humbert, who was a football, basketball, and track star. Dick influenced Rick and helped to develop him professionally and guide him physically by introducing him to extracurricular activities which Dick knew would help him pass the time.

Dick introduced Rick to the track coach, and after a brief tryout, he was able to become a member of the 440 relay. Track was a good distraction for Rick as it helped to fill his free time and did not interfere with his studies. Rick's entire life involved exercise of one kind or another and track was a great stress reliever for him.

The weekends in the fall were full of football and the pageantry that accompanied the competition. Dick was a tremendous offensive end.

Knowing a person on the team gave Rick just that much more to cheer for. Watching the team win was great fun but watching his friend play well was even more rewarding and exciting.

Rick took long walks along the Westhampton Lake on the cool days of October through December and on occasion would stop by the water and write Lucia a letter. With the Christmas holidays approaching and staying with friends in the Richmond area during the break he wrote Lucia a note hoping to express his concern for her happiness, health of her family, and his commitment to help her achieve her goals. She was never far from his thoughts, but the times being what they were and free time being at a premium, writing was difficult and mail delivery was slow and uncertain. The effort was made however, as affection would require.

December 18, 1939
Dear Lucia, my little Tuscan flower,

My days and nights are full of thoughts of you and hope this letter finds you well and happy. I have made several new friends here this year and everybody is so excited about the success our football team is having. I tried out and made the track team as I needed a sport to help me shorten the days and keep my mind sharp. The monotony of classes and study requires me to seek physical exertion so I can stay focused and ready for the monotone lectures. I am sure yours are much the same and know exactly what I am talking about.

The days are cool with the nights being even colder. The leaves have fallen off the trees which makes the sidewalks slippery but that is OK. I have learned to fall on my books, which softens the fall (only kidding). I don't know if the leaves fall off the trees in San Gimignano but here, it makes me feel lonely. Seeing the barren trees makes me realize how I must look deep inside my heart, with all the empty space that only you can fill. The nights get longer and I begin to wonder how you are and what you are doing and praying so fervently that you are OK.

I often find myself, when studying in Boatwright Library, looking out of the window looking at the lake that is nearby, thinking of home, and you and how pretty you looked when you were on Bodie's gallery last summer. Last night at a bonfire I saw a woman who resembled you in size and imagined she was you for just a moment…I felt very warm inside and smiled.

It is amazing, what just a few minutes can do to change a person's life, mood, or attitude. Those short weeks with you last summer put color within the empty spaces on the pages of my life and I find myself again so thankful that you emerged from the shadows of the oak tree and walked to me. I miss you, Lucia. I hope you don't think me forward or taking liberties that I have no right to take but I just wanted you to know that I am thinking of you and am looking forward to seeing you again.

I have not heard from you in a while, not that that really worries me as I am sure you are super busy, but I do get concerned and hope the news you get from your home is only good news. Knowing that Kelly is there with you gives me great comfort. I hope you trust me enough to tell me anything that is on your mind or in your heart. I hope you can sense, through my words, my heartfelt devotion to your safety, health, and happiness.

Please tell Kelly I said hi. I have not heard from Sean, but, that is nothing new. He never has been good at writing but I miss him just the same.

With a warm and affectionate heart,

Rick

Rick always felt better after writing his letters. At least within the time span of composing his thoughts and words he was with her and he felt that she was with him. He knew that the miles between them were tangible and not a real barrier. He *would* see her again.

Lucia was enjoying Kelly more and more each day. Kelly was a great friend and companion in all that she did. Lucia was majoring in English and was speaking and writing it better than most Americans. She was carrying a full load of twenty credit hours per semester and was maintaining a B average, which was remarkable for many reasons.

Lucia received all of Rick's letters and answered each one in turn and was disconcerted about the "I have not heard from you in a while…" line and thought she should write more often so he would not worry.

Kelly was quick to say, "Let him worry a little. It's healthy. Don't let him know too much about how you feel. Mystery is good and keeps guys on their toes. If they feel they've got you they will stop trying. Just write after he writes you. That's enough…for now"

Lucia, as fate would have it, also joined in athletic competition by making the tennis team. She would practice with Kelly her freshman year and became quite good real fast. She had a natural talent for tennis and had great hand and eye coordination. Her sense of speed and timing was superior. That, along with her natural athletic skill, mental toughness, and endurance, made her a true competitor. The tennis coach saw her serve one afternoon and asked Lucia if she would not mind trying out. Lucia explained that she had only been playing for a year and then only with Kelly. The coach was amazed at how good she was after just a year and with no formal training.

The coach said, "Lucia, you are a natural born athlete. I think after a few lessons with me, by the time you are a senior, you could be the best player on the team. What do you say you give me and the team a chance? No pressure. Just try it. If it is not what you want to do you can do something else. What do you say?"

"I don't know," she said. Then looking at Kelly said, "What do you think?"

Kelly did not want to influence Lucia but smiled because she knew this might be an opportunity for her to experience more of American college life. Lucia saw Kelly's expression and acknowledged it with a smile of her own.

"OK, Coach," Lucia said nodding.

"Great. I don't want to give you any false hopes but the tennis team gets one scholarship per year and Kathy graduates this year."

"Kathy? Who is Kathy?"

"Kathy Langford is the team captain and has been playing for us since she was a sophomore. I will introduce you to her and the team tomorrow. Can you meet us on the courts tomorrow at 2:30?"

"My classes don't end tomorrow until 3:00. But I will be there as soon as I change."

"There it is then. Please bring your schedule with you so I can see what adjustment I have to make with the scheduling of team practice. See you tomorrow. It was nice meeting you, Kelly."

Kelly just looked at Lucia and Kelly's eyes just grew.

"Lucia, did you hear what she said? You might be able to get your school paid for!"

"Would a scholarship pay for everything?"

"It depends on what kind of scholarship it is."

"It would be so nice to be able to help Papa with the tuition. Maybe I can help my family after all. Oh Kelly, this could be an answer to a prayer."

"The coach thought enough of you to invite you to play and to even mention it," Kelly said taking a breath. "I think she saw something in you that gave her the confidence that you could get it. I think you *can* get it and will."

Lucia made the team as a doubles partner and played as good as anybody on the team, although at 0-2 after a month of practice and play she would disagree that she was any good at all. Lucia was not a quitter. It was not in her blood to quit anything that she had started and was not about to start now. Her team depended on her and she practiced with a vengeance. Lucia had always been a team player. From working the vineyards picking Sangiovese grapes to crushing them with her bare feet, she was part of the Italian wine culture, the team, the Bellamonte family and a proud woman of unquestionable character, strength and integrity. This was a surprising chance for her to contribute to her family, and she was going to give her all.

Kelly wrote and told Sean about Lucia making the tennis team, and came to Raleigh to watch a match. Duke was a great school with a big student body population and was going to try to crush little Meredith. Lucia was aware of the rivalry and was determined to do her best to guard her lane and get as many first serves in. She had not won a match yet and knew that this game was important to everybody on the team.

Her team was tied in points and she was halfway through her doubles match with the game in the balance. Tie game and match to win, all on the serves of her opponent, Stacy Lorne, who was known to have the best serve on their team. Lucia looked up and saw Sean and Kelly in the stands and the excitement on their faces. Lucia knew then just how important this match had become.

Lucia had never played a better match. Her partner had a sore elbow but was holding her own; in fact, Lucia thought she never played better or hit the ball harder. Kathy and the coach were sitting in the team box anxiously waiting for Stacy's serve to Lucia. The ball was hit, landed just inside the serve box and Lucia moved quickly to return the serve with a hard forehand, which went right past the left side of the forward Duke player right into her lane and hit in bounds, Love–15.

Now it was time for Lucia's partner to receive Stacy's serve. The serve was hit hard and far, but just inside the inboard foul line. It was so fast that it caught Karen standing and just catching the ball with her eye as it whizzed by, Ace, 15–15.

Lucia was back to the end line, swaying side to side getting ready to receive Stacy's lively serve. Stacy bounced the ball several times. Marked her target with her eyes that Lucia noticed and hit the ball far and again next to the outside foul line but just inside. Lucia had begun her move to that spot before the racquet met the ball and because of that was able to be in position for the return. Another forceful forehand that went right back at Stacy and landed right at her feet. It was a difficult return for Stacy to make. She was just lucky to hit the ball at all and with a flop her return hit the net, 15–30.

Frustration was apparent in the posturing that Stacy was making. Lucia whispered to her doubles partner, Karen, to just relax and watch her eyes. "Her eyes tell you where the ball is going," she said.

Karen noticed her aim and went to the outside as the ball was hit. Stacy, suspecting a smash down the line, went to cover behind her teammate but Karen hit the ball right back to her serving position and caught her flat footed, 15–40.

So this is it. Game-Set-Match was on the line and Meredith's first victory over Duke in years. Lucia, the rookie tennis player, who just started with the team two months ago, now stood ready to receive the serve of the best player on Duke's team. The spectators were quiet again after a loud outburst from the last point. Lucia, swaying side to side and with a little sweat forming on her tanned forehead, bent her athletic legs to get ready to pounce on the fastest serve she had ever seen. Stacy, with intensity forced by determination, bounced and threw the ball up and served the ball so hard that Lucia barely saw it. Luckily the ball went way right and out. Lucia knew that the second serve should not be so fast because most players would let up a bit so that accuracy would not suffer. Lucia also knew that Stacy was not going to just give up but try to make a competitive point against her, stating, with authority, that she was the better player. She knew that Stacy was not that kind of "normal" player and was going to hit the ball just as hard and probably in the same place that she was most comfortable and that was the place where she had been hitting to all day.

Stacy took deliberate aim, bounced the ball, threw it up in the air, and hit it as hard as she could. Lucia, again anticipating the shot, was already moving when the ball was hit and was in position to return the serve. With a grunt she hit the ball right to Stacy's partner, who did well to just block the shot with her racket before the ball made a permanent dent in the middle of her face. The block was successful however, as the ball landed on Lucia's side of the court with a little bounce. Karen was there to tap it over but Stacy was charging the net to return it. Lucia saw the charge and dropped back to the end line to return it from the only place Stacy could hit it. Stacy barely reached the ball in time and lobbed it deep in Lucia's court, where Lucia was waiting, and hit the ball with such force as to make Stacy stumble and fall backwards reaching for the ball. Match point! The stadium erupted and the fans flooded the court. The coach and Kathy were the first to run to Lucia.

The rest of the team was close behind with Kelly and Sean amongst them.

Meredith's season was mediocre that year but that win made all the effort and sacrifice worthwhile and secured Lucia's position as the front runner for the scholarship.

At the athletic awards banquet, later that spring, Lucia received her letter for tennis. As the coach handed her the sweater she kept her on the stage a bit longer to make an announcement.

"I just wanted to tell everybody here, the athletes and alumni, that it was just pure luck that I was walking by the tennis courts one weekend last February. Lucky again that it was a warm day enticing this amazing person, Lucia, to play a round of tennis with her friend Kelly. Lucia is a guest to America from Italy. Sent here by her parents to escape the ravages of war, the threats and insecurity that saddens the human race. Lucia, born of righteous hard working parents, was raised to be the person you see before you. She is an academic scholar who should be getting her degree in English at the end of next year."

An applause erupted as everybody knew that getting a degree in three years was an accomplishment rarely seen; especially in a foreign country majoring in the local language, English.

"It is because of her academic accomplishment, athletic abilities and leadership potential that on behalf of the Alumni of Meredith College and the Athletic Department that I am pleased and honored to award Lucia Bellamonte of San Gimignano, Italy, the Morton Athletic Scholarship." Everybody stood and applauded again. Kelly had tears of joy in her eyes and Sean was as proud as a brother. Embracing each other and cheering, they both looked at Lucia knowing that this moment in her life would always be remembered.

Lucia was having trouble focusing through the tears that had accumulated in her precious eyes but was able to scan the audience for Kelly and Sean. She looked to the rear of the auditorium and saw, standing near the curtains, a familiar and distinctive shape that made her heart leap for joy and her feet run toward the steps leaving the short stage.

Kelly and Sean seeing her reaction were surprised and looked to where she was heading, Kelly smiled and kissed Sean after she recognized what he had done.

"I love you, Sean!" she said. "Why didn't you tell me? Oh never mind. That was the kindest thing you ever did...for Lucia and me," she said wiping the tears from her eyes.

Lucia was running as fast as she could through the crowd that was still clapping. She stopped only after she reached the silhouette formed by the light from the back window. Neatly standing with the biggest smile, and his arms outreaching for her, Rick quickly grabbed her. She embraced him again as if they never were apart. He held her just tight enough that she could just breathe. He waited an entire school year for this moment and didn't want it to end. Knowing that he would want something a little more to make his memory of her and this time everlasting, he recalled that smell was the sense that was most closely tied to memory, so he inhaled her scent, as he kissed the side of her neck so softly.

"I am so proud of you, Lucia. I missed you so much," Rick said in a private whisper.

She opened the embrace so she could look at him face to face and kissed him. Kissing was not something she did thoughtlessly, but she kissed Rick like she had known him all her life. There was something natural and transcendental about Rick. Familiar, yet something much more and it was germinating fast. Rick, too, was familiar with her. The simple touch of her warm, soft hands and the feeling within his body can be compared to being suddenly immersed under a warm cascading waterfall. The melodious look of her ancient mahogany eyes stole his heart the first time he saw her. The time apart, the letters, dreams and wishes for her had acted as fertilizer which had matured caring friendship into a devoted, faithful love. He responded to her by holding her waist and placing his hand in the small curve of her back. Suddenly realizing that they were in public, they slowly separated, turned, and walked back to the table where Kelly and Sean were still standing.

Approaching the table, Kelly ran to Rick, hugged, and kissed him. Sean was all smiles. He always enjoyed watching Kelly make of mess of herself over his best buddy.

"When did you get here, Rick?" Kelly said.

"I got in town just a little bit ago. The drive from Richmond was long."

"How did you know to come here?"

"Well," he said half chuckling and now turning and looking at Lucia having his arm around her, "Sean is not much of a writer but he did write me one letter telling me of Lucia's athletic successes and this banquet. I knew she would be getting a letter and wanted to surprise her," then looking at Kelly, "…and you. But I had no idea she would be getting a full-ride scholarship. I came to do the surprising, but instead, got surprised!"

Looking right into Lucia's eyes he said, "You are completely amazing," then kissed her quickly again.

Sean, with the smile of success well planted on his face said, "Well, Rick, it is good to see you again and I dare say the kittens are just tickled. What do you say we go out for a soda or malt or something, you know to celebrate, after this is over? I'm buying."

"Sounds great but I am kind of hungry for real food too."

"No problem. There is a soda shop down the road that has burgers and things."

They all sat down for the remainder of the banquet and Rick picked at Sean's plate eating what was left of his steak that was too well done for him. The baked potato was a bit cool but that was fine. Hunger tends to overpower manners at times.

Rick wiped his mouth with a napkin and said to Lucia, "I didn't know you knew how to play tennis."

"Kelly taught me," Lucia said.

Rick turned to Kelly saying, "I didn't know you played either."

"Well, I don't, really. I just like hitting the ball. Lucia is the one who grabbed me and made me play."

"I did not. I was just curious about the game. Besides you *do* know how to play and you play good too."

Sean saw an opportunity developing said, "What do you all say that one of these days, this summer, we all just go at it? Me and Kelly and you two. Loser buys dinner."

Rick saw a sure victory and a free meal, and said, "You're on, pal. With Lucia, I can't lose...at anything," and looking back at Lucia said, "ever."

5

Rick could hardly wait to do the usual visit to Bodie, but he felt strange, as if he had outgrown Manteo and the people there. Everything seemed different somehow. College was changing him. He knew that it would happen because his dad told him that the college experience not only educated the mind but gave you experiences you can't get at home.

"Casual and routine things at home will look different and smaller when you come back," his dad said before he left for Richmond. "College gives a person the full package. It teaches a person how to be socially responsible. It trains a person to schedule classes and free time and how to balance the schedule so you can do both and succeed. It introduces a person to different cultures and ideas. It teaches tolerance and cooperation. It will even teach you how to fail and deal with disappointment. You will learn that things don't always work out the way you expect them to, that there are always alternatives and that there is more than one way to skin a cat. Keep trying. Don't quit. Quitters never win and winners never quit."

Inside, he felt different. Home, and Manteo as a town, looked familiar but seemed different somehow. Everything looked simple, plain, smaller, and not as colorful as he once remembered them. The friends he had when he was in high school either got married, had kids, moved into a house in town, were working with their parents or friends, or not working at all but still living at home. Life went on at Manteo. It had been moving on without Rick for two years now. When he came across an old buddy, few words would be shared aside from the pleasantries of "Hi," or "It's good to see you again. What have you been up to?" Little quality information was ever passed on either side. Rick would begin to enter a conversation of what Richmond College was like and being on the track team, but after a brief time Rick would feel like he was showboating and would down play the experience. He felt his friends did not understand what living away from home was like and decided to just talk about things that they had in common, and that was this little pearl along the North Carolina barrier islands, his home.

Hurricane season in 1939 was quiet and Rick was thankful about that. Bodie was in good shape. No major repairs were needed on either the caretaker's house or the lighthouse. He spent his first day back just cutting some grass, removing some debris from the grounds and touching up the paint on the structures. Fortunately, black and white paint was abundant everywhere and easy to acquire.

He took a trip to the top of Bodie and took a look around. He saw that things looked much the same. He noticed that the gallery was beginning to rust and would need some chipping and paint before he went back to school. He also noticed brown splotches along the metal roof on the lantern room indicating rust and a need for paint also; a task he had never seen or done before because of the difficulty and dangers of the job. This was another job that he would need Sean's advice and help on.

After leaving Bodie, Rick went right to Kelly's house to see Lucia. When he arrived he saw Lucia standing with Kelly and Sean by his car packing the trunk.

"Hey there, beautiful," Rick said to Lucia.

"Hi, Rick. I haven't been told I'm beautiful in a long time," Kelly replied directly.

"You know, your brain isn't right. I told you that you were beautiful just last Christmas," Sean said with a smile. Kelly picked up a stick and chased Sean around the car until he let her catch him. He then lovingly disarmed her and hugged her.

As this was going on Rick approached Lucia and said, "Packing? Going home so soon?" he asked jokingly.

"No, Sean is going to Wilmington for the day. He will be back tomorrow night."

"Is Kelly going with him?"

"No. Although she will not admit it, she will feel guilty leaving me behind."

"Really?" Rick said. "We'll see about that."

Walking to the playful duo Rick said to Kelly, "Why aren't you going with Sean to Wilmington?"

"I can't go, Rick. I have things to do here."

"That's nuts and you know it. You pack your kicks and threads and go with Sean. I will take care of things here. You know I will. I promise she will not leave my sight."

"See, I told you. Why don't you ever listen to me?" Sean said to Kelly.

"When have you ever been right?" she smartly replied with a shove.

After some coaxing, Kelly went to her mom and told her of the opportunity and her mom just told her to be careful. Her mom knew that Kelly was a young woman and very responsible. After all, she was a college girl now.

After Kelly ran inside to pack her things, Rick said, "Sean, I need to paint the top of the lantern room on Bodie and the gallery is rusting. I would sure appreciate your help. It will be a tricky job and will have to be done in the cool of the day."

"Sure, bub. I will pick up some black metal paint. We will start in the morning the day after tomorrow. I will bring a harness and a couple of workers."

"OK, I will be there early, ready to go."

After they had left, Rick looked at Lucia and said, "How about you and I going to Bodie tonight and I will show you the ocean by moonlight?"

"I think that would be wonderful. I have never seen the ocean at night."

"Get ready, my sweet, for an experience you will never forget. Without light your senses of hearing and touch are forced to work harder. You can hear everything, the sea foam popping, the tiny hermit crabs walking about, and if you try real hard, you can hear the starlight breaking on the water like tiny pieces of glass. The warm sea breeze, when it brushes the hair on your arms, will give you goose bumps. Then when you look up at the moon and breathe the air, you thank God for life and the perfect view."

Lucia gave Rick a smile that would steal a sailor's heart from the sea. Rick, seeing that look, warmed all over and got weak at the knees. Clearing his throat and noticing that it would be dark soon said, "Look, I need to run home and shower. You get ready. I will be back in an hour and we will go out to dinner, then I will take you to Bodie, OK?"

"Sure, Rick. I will be ready," and kissed him sweetly.

Rick, noticing that Mrs. Stewart was on the porch, yelled, "See ya in an hour, Mrs. Stewart." She responded with a little wave and Rick got in his car and drove off.

Rick showed up at the Stewart home a little after an hour, as he forgot the lantern he would need to climb Bodie at night, and had to return home. Approaching the house he noticed how the lights on the porch cast a pale yellow light on the walls and rails of the whitewashed house. Mrs. Stewart greeted Rick at the door and told him that Lucia would be right down and offered him a glass of tea. Lucia came down from the stairs wearing a pretty light blue sleeveless dress that flowed naturally around her body and dropped into gathered folds designed into the fabric. She placed over her left ear a pink hibiscus flower that Kelly had growing in her backyard. Rick choked on the cold tea as he saw her stroll down the short staircase.

Mrs. Stewart, noticing and hearing Rick's surprise of Lucia's simple yet beautiful appearance, said half laughing, "Rick, my God, are you OK?"

"Ahem, yes, ma'am," he said clearing his throat. "I'm good. Wow, this is good tea," he said, looking at Mrs. Stewart then looking quickly back at Lucia having a difficult time taking his eyes off of her.

Mrs. Stewart, enjoying this playful drama, said under her breath, "You are such a boy."

Rick had arranged for a table on the outside balcony overlooking the Shallowbag Bay at his family's favorite restaurant, called the Rusty Nail. The restaurant was famous for its seafood fare, especially their New England clam "chowda," as it was spelled on the menu. With warm breezes and candles protected by hurricane glasses on round tables, the dinner at sea level was perfect. In the sky, white, calm puffy clouds preceded the rain approaching far from the west. Lit by the rising moon, their outer fringes looked like cotton candy drifting slowly by with nowhere in particular to go. The night sky was turning a dark charcoal gray which would soon turn to black as black could be. The sky would distinguish itself as heavenly only by the blinking eyes of the angelic stars peeking between the clouds.

Dinner conversation was very casual. Rick was very curious about her home in Italy but was careful not to ask questions that would lead to her missing home too much. He learned that her family had lived on the same land for over 300 years and that they were always growing grapes. Grapes have been grown and harvested in the area surrounding San Gimignano since the Etruscans settled in the area around 600 B.C. Chianti wine was the main product of their harvest which was the most common in the Classico zone between Sienna and Florence. The Bellamonte family had been known to grow the fattest and juiciest grapes in the region, a reputation that her father was very proud of and would die to protect.

Lucia mentioned that she was the first Bellamonte, of memory, to ever leave Italy and doubted that if it were not for the war that she would be there today. She explained that her family had always regarded education as important and critical to the success of their business and life in general. Since she was an only child, her father, she thought, felt he had to be protective, especially since his only child was a daughter. He felt she needed to attend the best school possible, especially since she would inherit the business.

"I am glad you feel comfortable enough with me to tell me these things, Lucia. Since I have met you I have paid more attention to the articles in the *Richmond-Times Dispatch* about the problems in Europe. Things are not well over there. I feel your dad did the right thing. He loves you. He did the only thing he could do. Any parent who loves his children would have done the same thing," Rick said.

"Please understand, Rick, you have become very close to my heart in a very short time. I did not come here looking for love or even to meet boys," Lucia said.

Then, after a pause of a minute which seemed like hours, and after a feudal effort to fight back the emotions that tears were sure to follow, she said, "There is something else you have to know. I wanted to wait for a better time or perhaps, no time at all, hoping that, I don't know, somehow, something would change so I can stay with you. I thought of not telling you anything and just leaving after I graduate, but I know that would hurt you. I would never want to do anything unkind but, rather, I want to be the gentlest and dearest friend in your life. Being with you and thoughts of you occupy my days and nights." Then after a quiet moment of obvious reflection she shook her head and said, "Why couldn't you be an Italian man living at home!"

Rick, taking everything she said in, was very confused. He was not sure what the problem was but knew he had to break the tension and bring some relief to the situation that was developing.

"Hey, hun," Rick said pausing. "I'm not sure what this is all about, but let's get out of here. Let me pay the bill and I will take you to my special place. I want to show you something."

With that, Rick paid the bill, drove Lucia to Bodie, and walked to the lighthouse. Rick lit his lantern and unlocked the door. He put the keys back in his pocket and held the lantern inside with one arm so Lucia could enter into the lobby.

"I will lead the way up the stairs. Watch your step and head. I will shine the light so you can see. Once we get to the top and before we go outside I am going to have you close your eyes. Don't worry or be scared, OK?" Rick said with loving care and confidence.

The climb to the top took a little longer than usual and it was a bit warmer than her first trip up but the day was a warm one and the heat had not yet had the time to dissipate from within the lighthouse.

When they reached the top Rick took Lucia's hand and opened the door to the gallery, 150 feet above the ground.

"Now close your eyes and don't open them until I say, OK?"

"OK," Lucia said with a smile and a tight grip on Rick's hand.

Rick very carefully guided Lucia onto the gallery and faced her to the ocean where the moon was thirty degrees above the horizon and only partially covered by one lonely bright silver cloud in the sky.

"OK, Lucia, open them."

Lucia did not have to say a word. Her breathless sigh and the covering of her mouth with her unstressed hand was worth all the words, in any combination, that Webster or Shakespeare could possibly put together. The reflection of the moonlight in her eyes was like star dust interfused within limpid pools. One single tear fell from her eye and rested so comfortably on the cheek of her face. Her skin glistened as the subtle twinkles of dancing starlight from the ocean in front, and the moon and the stars above, took up residence in her unnatural beauty and made her skin their home. At an instant, and as quick as light traveled from her figure through his eyes to his brain, he knew that whatever or however man defined beauty in the past it now had a new meaning. It began in Tuscany and now resided atop Bodie. One bright light meets another at the most perfect place in the world.

Rick did not want to spoil this moment for her so said nothing but just looked at her and the God-given celestial and earthly beauty before him. He thought of how fortunate he was to be alive with Lucia and prayed that he could be with her to help her through whatever trouble saddens her eyes.

"Rick, this is the most remarkable view I have ever seen. If I had not seen this with my own eyes, I would not have thought this view possible. Thank you…for everything, Rick," she said reaching for him.

Looking up at him she continued, "You are an amazing man and I love you for everything you are and will ever be. Thank you for being so nice to me and taking care of me. You give me more comfort and security than you will ever know."

"You warm my heart. You are the most beautiful woman I have ever seen. Whenever I am with you and you touch me and when I kiss you…I shake. I lose all track of time when I think of you. I search you out in my memory whenever I am lonely. You…fill every part of my day…my life. I adore you and want to help you in whatever is bothering you."

"There *is* something I have to tell you. I'm not sure where to begin or how."

"Sit down here," said Rick as he pointed to the side of the gallery. "Just sit there and rest your back against the lantern room wall and stretch your feet out over the walk."

They both sat down. Rick was very anxious to hear what she had to say and held her hand when she began to speak.

"Italy is different from America in so many ways, Rick. People and families act differently and have different customs. My parents are very traditional, as I have said before, and arranged a relationship for me to secure the family business. This arrangement was made when I was five. I have never seen him but know he waits for me when I return."

"Who waits for you, Lucia? What are you talking about?"

"My parents promised me to marry, Rick," Lucia said. "The man is Barone Pallanti. I don't know too much about him except that he is six years older than I am and is the son of Paolo Pallanti, who owns one of the largest vineyards and producers of Chianti in Sienna. My marriage to Barone would merge the two families, which would make Bellamonte-Pallanti wine the biggest name in Tuscany."

"That just doesn't seem fair; you marrying a guy you don't even know? What are you going to do?"

"Before I met you I was going to graduate, go home, get married and have a dozen kids just like I am supposed to. Just like my mother intended except she did not expect to have a difficult time in my delivery and now cannot have any more children. My mother was promised to my father the same as I was. My mother explained it to me when I was sixteen, saying that I will learn to love him. It will take time but just bear him many sons and he will love you too."

"That sounds shallow and unreal to me," said Rick in disbelief.

"It would sound unreal to you because it just isn't done here. In my country it is common. My family evolved and prospered through this tradition."

"OK, now things have changed. We met, you love me and I love you. I don't want you to go back."

"I have to go back. I have no choice. It would disgrace my family if I don't return and face my responsibility. I'm not going to run, Rick. I…" Lucia said and stopped suddenly. She looked at the open dark ocean for words that could explain her dilemma.

"What can I do, Lucia," Rick said softly, interrupting. "I want to help."

"Just love me and no matter what always know that I love you. You have given me so much more than I ever wanted or expected...ever. Be my best friend."

"That's easy."

"You say that now but it won't be easy. I will be thousands of miles away in a year and in a place you have never seen or even understand. Italy is no longer the place I knew as a child growing up. Danger will be in every shadow and I will be wishing you were walking with me to protect me as you do here."

"Knowing that you are there in that environment will eat me alive. I'm not sure what to do. I know I have to do something though."

"You cannot do anything but be yourself. You are so unique this world. Just live and with any luck at all, perhaps someday..."

"I will find you. My happiness, my hope, my faith in love is where you are. You take it with you," Rick said interrupting.

With a limp hand he stroked her face and wiped the tears from her eyes with his thumb. He kissed her soft lips with the moistness of the ocean below, and felt her breath as it exited her nose on his cheek. Kissing her was a union of the soul, a harmonious joining of two hearts tormented by a certain departure, but tempered by a prayer that their futures would intersect again.

Rick and Lucia sat on the gallery. They just looked and loved each other until close to midnight. After he drove her home he walked her to the front door, lit by a single light on the porch that Mrs. Stewart kindly kept lit for them. Her sweet little light blue dress caressed the top of her calf as she turned to him. Without a word he took her in his arms, with the affirmation of a mature gentleman, and kissed her. The simple power of the kiss served as the crowning testimonial of their love for the other. Their lips gently, softly touched and barely moved. His arms wrapped around her waist barely touching but with his hands feeling every curve of her back. Her hands held his hips through which she felt his strength and eternal love for her. Close and without moving, their communication was powerful. A bond was developed that would endure, that would remember, that would be the nurse to help them both to get through the tough times ahead, times that would test their love and patience and above all would try their dedication and commitment to each other.

Rick was getting Bodie ready for Sean and his crew a couple of days later in the early morning hours while it was still dark and cool. At dawn Sean pulled up in his pickup with one guy in the cab and one in the back. They were a professional crew who knew how to work difficult jobs with height as the major challenge. They were masters of rigging a harness. The morning brought a thick fog which Rick appreciated because it kept the steel cool but was concerned about the dampness which made it slippery. As the crew began the rigging Rick was surprised to see Sean put the harness on.

"Sean, what are you doing? You should let one of those guys climb to the top," Rick said, with deep apprehension.

"Nonsense, I know how to do this. I shingled the steeple on Mount Olivet United Methodist Church last winter."

"I should have known that. That explains the crooked rows. You have to lean when looking at it to get them straight," Rick said while mimicking the lean.

"You're a riot, you know that?" Sean said while he struggled with a clamp around his leg.

Sean climbed the stairs with Rick and Kenny to the gallery of Bodie. Donny, the other crew member, was on the ground serving as the anchor watch and supply man. The sunrise was beautiful as it always was from the Outer Banks but this time it had a special look. The thin fog bank was falling and the top of Bodie was just appearing through the top. Looking at the sunrise from that vantage point made the cloud floor appear like the spill of light whipped cream. All three of them just paused a minute and peered across the fog to see a crescent of the sun as she began, again, her timeless ark across the sky. Bodie had never disappointed Rick and his friends in the beauty that she provided. She gave a different perspective of things not seen by most people. "How unfortunate they are," he thought. "This view was just one more."

"Wow," said Sean.

"Wow is right," said Rick right back, valuing this moment.

Getting back to the task at hand, Sean started to get ready to mount the lantern room. Throwing the rope over the top of Bodie, he had Kenny tie it to the railing of the gallery on the other side with about twenty-five feet of slack. He threw another rope as the pull line to help lift him to the top, which was about an eight-foot lift to the steel roof. He threw one more over to the ground where Donny could serve as a safety and an anchor to his harness. There, he would be supported by the tension on the pull line since there was nothing for Sean to grasp on to on the smooth surface of the roof.

On his command, they all pulled slowly with obvious, practiced skill. They lifted him to the top where he immediately slipped testing the slickness of the black and dusty surface.

"Wow! It is slippery up here. This is going to be trickier than I thought." With strength and pure determination he reached the peak wanting to work himself down and around as he painted.

He cleaned and dried an area with his rag, painted and moved around to another adjacent area where he repeated the procedure. He did this until he reached the first ridge of several along the top. He hopped his body over it and without any warning at all and in a flash he was off the roof, over the gallery and falling fast. No one was really in position yet to stop his fall because they did not anticipate the suddenness of his move even though they did expect that a move was going to occur. The anchor on the ground tightened the rope that was attached to the trucks hitch and, after a fall of about twenty feet, the fall suddenly stopped with a POP!

"Holy shit, Sean!" screamed Rick. "You OK?"

Sean just hung there with a grimace on his face while his harness swung and rotated.

"Sean, God damn it, say something!"

Sean looked up at Rick, saying half laughing and half in pain, "Man, that will straighten your spine. Owwww."

"You hurt?" Rick yelled once more.

"Stop screaming! I'm fine, but I will be sore tomorrow. Pull me back up."

"Bullshit," he said to Sean.

Directing his next sentence to Kenny on the gallery said. "Lower him down."

Donny screamed up, "Is he OK?"

Rick said yelling back, "Yeah, he is fine but he is coming down. Nice job on the rope. You saved his life."

"It's not the first time. I'm used to it," Donny said quite casually.

Rick looked at the face of Kenny on the gallery. He just smiled and shrugged his shoulders.

"Not the first time? What did he mean by that?" Rick said to Kenny.

"Just that, we are always ready, nothing new. Well, we better get back on it before it gets too hot, huh?"

And with that surprising casual exchange Donny came up and finished the painting while Sean served as the ground anchor. Donny was more skillful and a lot quicker. When it was all done they had paint left over to do the gallery's catwalk. It was a good day's work. "Hopefully," Rick thought, "it would last several years." Rick was not anxious to do this again.

After they completed the job, cleaned up, and had a couple of beers to celebrate their cheating death escapade, apparently again, Sean looked at Rick and had a look in his eye that Rick knew spelled mischief.

"What are you thinking, Sean," Rick said slowly, accented with caution.

"I got an idea."

"I figured that much."

"Let's trick the girls to thinking I was hurt in the fall. That would be a hoot. Wouldn't it?"

"I don't think that is a good idea at all. You shouldn't tease like that."

"Come on. We could have Donny and Kenny carry me on a makeshift stretcher I have in the back of the truck. I can moan and make sounds like I'm in pain. Hey, after all the tricks Kelly pulled on me over the years, she's due."

Looking at Donny and Kenny, Rick saw that this is just one of many pranks that these jokesters have probably been doing for some time.

"If you get clobbered, and I hope you do, I am just going to stand back and watch and, if Kelly needs help, I will hold you down."

"You're on, buddy pal. It will be like old times."

"That's why I know you are going to get clobbered," Rick said shaking his head, smiling. Under his breath and walking to his car Rick whispered to Kenny and Donny, "Stupid Sean, cheating death once in one day is lucky. Trying to cheat it twice is…well…my money is on Kelly."

Kenny said, "We always enjoy watching Sean get beat up."

Sean's pickup truck was the first to pull into Kelly's driveway. Kenny pulled in at such speed that a big white cloud of dust rose above the trees. Kelly and Lucia walked out to see what the noise was all about when they saw Kenny and Donny go to the back of the truck and drag Sean out on a hokey stretcher formed by two long pipes and a piece of green canvas. Immediately Sean started the charade with moans and motions of pain. Kenny and Donny were placating and supporting the action with ambulatory measures such as looking for tourniquets and bandages.

Kelly ran over almost in hysterics. Above the commotion and the chatter Rick looked over at Lucia, who was still standing on the porch not far away with a look of concern. He smiled at her and secretly shook his head. Lucia took a deep breath in relief and smiled back. Through it all Rick heard Kelly yell.

"What! You jerk! You're not hurt! I'll kill ya!" as she began to hit him. Sean fell from the stretcher laughing. Kenny and Donny took the stretcher back to the truck and got ready for a fast get away.

63

Rick walked to Lucia.

"Don't worry. It will end in a couple of minutes with them kissing and all of us going out to dinner." No sooner than he said that Sean was hugging her on top of him laughing as she continued to weakly punch him. Donny and Kenny were laughing as Kelly stood up slowly then darted towards them. They both bolted out from the truck and ran down the street. Sean went to Kelly and hugged her again and kissed her and she kissed him back.

Witnessing this scene Rick said while still looking at Sean and Kelly, "Love has never been more fun," then pausing, "or dangerous."

The summer went fast as fun times always do when the mind is at rest and relaxed. The four of them traveled down the Outer Banks visiting Ocracoke Lighthouse and Cape Hatteras Lighthouse, which was the tallest lighthouse in the United States.

They spent several days touring New Bern, which was the capital of colonial North Carolina. They all enjoyed visiting the place where Pepsi-Cola was created by Caleb Burnham in 1898 and drinking the ice-cold pop from the soda fountain.

They visited Tryon Palace, the former residence of the British Royal Governor, William Tryon, of North Carolina in the eighteenth century. Lucia loved the architecture and the gardens of the estate the most because they reminded her of her home in Tuscany. The color of the brick and the arches on the house were remarkably similar, she said. Rick had a camera and took a breathtaking picture of Lucia sitting down by beautiful roses and pots of flowers of various assortments. Rick thought back on this day later and realized that it was the only picture he ever took of her. Her beautiful tan skin shined in the summer sun. The shade of a nearby tree blessed her face with a touch of shadowed grace that kissed Rick's heart with a vivid memory that would last him forever.

The summer also included fun on the sandy white beaches, looking for fancy seashells and sharks' teeth. Lucia loved to body surf. She was better than anyone in the group. She loved to swim and play with the children and bury Rick and Sean in the sand. Lucia was naturally happy and enjoyed life with all of its variety. She never forgot to say thank you, even at times when it was not required, and was always the first to offer assistance when there was a sense that some might be needed. Lucia was a lady of class, born for greatness, and Rick was beginning to miss her. Rick felt the eventual pain grow more each day in his chest and was preparing himself for the farewell that he knew would rip his heart from his body.

The night before Lucia and Kelly went back to school, Rick took Lucia for a walk along the beach that Bodie guarded. The night was warm and the water cool as they strolled half in and half out of the surf with their bare feet. Rick noticed a clear stone, polished by a hundred years of sand in the shape of a heart. It would have gone unnoticed except the wet, polished surface reflected the moonlight right into Rick's eye. He stooped down and picked it up and handed it to Lucia.

"I think this being the only stone I noticed on this walk and being in the shape of a heart should mean something, don't you?" said Rick.

"It expresses everything that I have experienced here perfectly," Lucia said then kissed the stone.

"I'm going to miss you, Lucia. My life has never felt stronger or more purposeful since I met you. It is hard to talk about, I mean, to put my feelings into words. Seeing you like you are now makes me crazy. I never imagined anyone could look…I don't know…like you and make me feel so strange. Every time I see you it is like seeing you for the first time. Remarkable," Rick said taking a breath, "I fall in love with you all over again every time I see you, and I mean every time."

"I know. I will miss you too but much more. Miss is not the right word. I'm not sure if one word can express how I feel or how I will feel. I have grown to be so fond of you over the past couple of years. Those years will always be the most special because they were with you. Being without you physically close or even having the chance to be with you is how I guess death would feel."

"I don't want you to think that next year and the years after will be any different. I will always be with you. I know about Barone and the promise. I try to forget it…"

"You cannot forget it."

"I know. I can't help to think that two people who both feel were meant to be together can't be. I feel, deep inside, that we will meet again, either on purpose or by chance…but I will see you again."

"Rick, I hope so. I want that so much. I try not to think of what could have been if…"

"Sometimes it is nice to think or dream about if."

"It is. I'm bad to think of such things, but I do," Lucia said gasping for breath.

Rick stopped their walk and turned to Lucia. He looked into the face of the only mortal joy and love he had ever known. He reached into his pocket and pulled out a small box wrapped in gold paper with silver metal aluminum stars that he cut out of foil and glued on. Around the little box he tied a light blue ribbon of gold tangled stars of various sizes.

"I want to give you something that I hope you will wear every day until I see you again."

"Rick," she said with a low whisper. "I love the wrap! I have never seen a prettier package in my life." She kissed him softly and said, "I will have to unwrap this carefully because I do not want to hurt the stars."

"I knew you liked stars so I took extra care to make them as perfect as I could. It took me most of an afternoon to do it."

"It's beautiful, Rick. Really, everything you do and touch is just perfect."

She unwrapped the little box carefully, not tearing the paper that she knew he took so much time to fold so perfectly. After she opened the box she gasped and pulled out half of a lighthouse pendant attached to a silver necklace.

"Oh, Rick, this is so beautiful, Half a lighthouse? This must mean something, right?"

Rick put his hand in his other pocket and pulled out the other half of the lighthouse on a silver chain made for him.

"I have the other half of our lighthouse and will wear it always until I see you again. Lucia, look into my eyes and hear me. I love you. I fell in love with you the moment I saw you in the shadows of Kelly's oak tree. There is absolutely no denying it and I sense you feel the same about me."

"Yes, I do," she said with tears beginning to swell in her eyes.

"My love, my heart, my life, is…Lucia, where you are. I know I will find you. Believe, just believe."

Lucia raised her head and looked at Rick with eyes full of expression and passion.

"I believe by all that is holy and through all the prayers I have ever prayed that I was born for you. You are my destiny. I know that I came to America to meet you and to be with you now. I believe in my soul that I will see you again. I know in my heart that I will love you always and want to make love to you tonight."

"I love you, Lucia. I honestly do. You mean so much to me. Its crazy but I don't want to make love to you though unless you are really ready for me. I honor and respect you too much for you to regret tomorrow being with me tonight. I would rather wait than risk anything we have now or ever hope to have, if that was at all possible."

"How can I regret loving you? How can I regret giving myself to a man I know I will love me forever? Isn't that what a man and a woman who are in love are supposed to do? I cannot imagine nor do I wish to imagine being with any other man. You are remarkable. I never wanted to be with anyone more than I do with you now. There is no regret in my heart, no doubts but just a promise that I am yours."

"This has been a great day and tonight is just about as perfect as any could be, Lucia. I *will* love you forever. Not doing so would be untrue to you and me and the us that we have become."

Rick kissed her with passion and adoration as it began to rain.

"Come on. We need to get inside. Bodie is just across the street," Rick said.

They both ran to Bodie as the rain got heavier. Rick and Lucia arrived on the front porch of the caretaker's house drenched. Rick went inside and grabbed a couple of candles and brought them outside to the front porch. He lit them and placed them on the table by the two white rocking chairs he had placed outside earlier in the summer. After they were lit he looked at Lucia as she was wringing out her dress, lifting one side to well above her knee. The white dress became transparent, being as wet as it was, and clung to her hourglass shape like a second skin. He never saw Lucia wet before, at least not in this way. He never imagined that her breasts were so full or her stomach so muscular and flat. When she turned to the side to remove her shoes he noticed the subtle curve of her hips as they joined the upper part of her buttocks which curved downward meeting with divine perfection to the back part of her muscular leg and thigh. Her hair was straight and reached mid back. Wet, her hair was as black as midnight. The water on her bare arms allowed the contours of her muscles to be seen the same way her wet dress outlined the white undergarments she was wearing. Rick's body was responding and was ready to love her.

"Lucia, you…are…beautiful," Rick said emphasizing every word.

"Oh, sure. I'm soaking wet."

"I swear, I have never seen you or anything more beautiful than you are right now."

Lucia looked up for the first time since getting on the porch and noticed Rick with the top two buttons on his light blue short-sleeve shirt unbuttoned exposing and outlining his muscular chest. Rick was an athlete and the years of strenuous workouts defined his body as being purely masculine. Lucia noticed how the upper part of his shirt sleeve stuck to his upper shoulder exposing the entire length of his wet arm. He was pure muscle. He had the body that every woman would dream they could lie next to on a stormy night but on this night Lucia knew he was all hers.

Lucia finished taking off her shoes and walked to Rick with a sultry sway that spelled trouble. Rick, never having been with a woman before, was a bit anxious but knew, by how his heart was pounding, what to do.

No words were spoken as she walked to him; none were needed. Both knew what was going to happen next. For both of them it was their first time. Both knew where the other was and knew they were going to be with each other, at least this time and in this way, forever.

Rick led Lucia into the house lighting candles on the way until they reached his upstairs bedroom. On the nightstand he lit one candle which cast a hint of white and yellow light throughout the room. With the light casting dancing shadows upon the wall and illuminating Lucia's gracious loveliness that Cupid brushed with his wing, he began to unbutton the front of her dress, never taking his eyes off of her face. She was doing the same, feeling his chest, slowly moving her hands down the middle row unbuttoning each button in turn then opening his shirt and pushing it over his back where it fell to the floor. Examining his damp chest briefly she looked back into Rick's eyes. Rick pushed back the top of her dress having only unbuttoned the long row as far as her waist. Her dress fell to the floor easily exposing her voluptuous body. She reached behind herself and unsnapped her bra and dropped it onto the floor. Rick unbuckled his belt and pants and stepped out of them. Effortlessly, he picked her up and laid her on the bed, which she sank several inches into. With clean white linen, a soft mattress to lie on, and two new pillows to rest her head he lay next to her. He explored her body with loving curiosity as his hands touched the pearled surface of her skin. They kissed each other like no two people ever have, with so much care and compassion for the other. Delicate touching and adoration prompted the joining of their bodies.

Rick and Lucia were one in heart and spirit and would always be together, this way or another for as long as they lived. Destiny had put them together and now would have to play a bigger part to see them through an uncertain future which would begin tomorrow.

6

Rick's junior and Lucia's senior year were academically and athletically successful. The year was accompanied by challenges that a lonely heart would bring but they both endured them. Writing was the only avenue of approaching each other's tangible needs. Rick would take a letter that Lucia wrote and smell it and imagine her touching the paper. He would study the writing and look for prints or marks of any kind that she might have left. On occasion she would press a small flower in one of her textbooks and mail the dried remnant to him. He would place it in a little corner in his dresser with the others she had sent over time and looked at them every day. Lucia sent Rick a small picture of herself sitting by the bank of the lake on Meredith College's campus. That quickly became Rick's most prized possession and placed it by the picture he took of her at Tryon Palace the previous summer.

Rick sent Lucia an article from the *Collegian*, the school newspaper, about him and his track team. Lucia taped that to her wall. It was extra special not because of what it said but because it had the team photo and an enlarged picture of Rick in the lower right hand corner.

In the last letter he wrote to Lucia before she went home, he included a poem of a prayer he said most nights before he went to sleep. He wanted her to have it, to hold the words, so she would never forget him or what she meant to him:

Prayer

The moon casts a blue hue on the sand.
Funny, how I did not see that until now.
I must have seen it a thousand times upon Bodie's shores
but never noticed it until I fell in love with you.

Blue moon, dream catcher of the sky,
Bless Lucia.
Hold her close and bless her with the smiles of the Saints.
Comfort her sorrows and bring peace to her fears.
Show her your poetic passion of a million stars
And bring her joy.
Her comfort is everything to me.
Her happiness is mine.
Shine brightly on her path.
Never let her stumble.
Bring her strength and wisdom.
Bring her the fruits of a bountiful life.
Bring her hopes and dreams, a reality of unmeasurable joy.

Show her days without rain.
Show her storms without thunder.
Show her pain without tears
But never let her love without feeling.

Show her songs with a melody.
Show her the colors of the rainbow.
Show her the power of a whisper
But never show her love without a dream

Sing her passion lullabies when she lies to slumber.
Waken her gently with your kiss.
And always lead her through the day with your promise of lunar shadows
on the beach that she loves so much..

The year went by quickly and before it had hardly begun she was gone.
Rick had accumulated over twenty letters the last year and read each one over

and over again routinely. After final exams at the end of his junior year he rushed home to see Kelly to see if she had any additional information about her, her feelings, or her intentions. His entire focus was just seeing Kelly, hoping for a word that would spawn hope and generate an idea that would help him recover her.

Upon seeing Kelly he asked the expected question. She simply said words and phrases that he already knew, that she loved him, missed him, and prayed for him every night and every morning.

Kelly said, "She said that she wished that things were different, that she is and will always remain your best friend. She said that half her heart lives within your chest and that she will always wear the best half of her life around her neck." After saying that, Kelly noticed the half lighthouse pendant around Rick's neck.

"Rick, this is what Lucia has. It is exactly the same thing."

"No, it is not quite the same thing. I have the other half of what she has."

After she studied it a little longer she acknowledged her misperception.

"What an amazing present! I have never seen anything so romantic before. You are a darling, Rick. Where did you get it?"

"I had it made by Diamonds 'N Dunes in Manteo last summer. I drew a picture and they had it made. It cost a little bit but cost isn't what's important where Lucia is concerned."

"Well, it is remarkable. She never took it off. She even wore it playing tennis."

"I miss her, Kelly. Being here in Manteo is tough. It's killing me. I don't know if I can stay here this summer. There are too many memories here. I just wanted to see you."

"Poor Rick. You're lovesick," Kelly said putting her arms around Rick's head and putting his head on her chest.

"I plan to go to Bodie for a quick visit tomorrow and if things are all right I am going back to Richmond to go to summer school, graduate a semester early, and find some way to see her again."

"Sean will be disappointed he missed you. Both of us will miss you. We were hoping…well…I know this is difficult. Lucia was having a terrible time her last week in Raleigh, too. She wouldn't eat and hardly slept. My gut feeling is that somehow you two will hook up again. Don't rush it."

Rick kissed Kelly and said good-bye. Home *felt* different the previous summer but now it *was* different. He could hardly wait to leave because Lucia's spirit still walked the ground all over Roanoke Island. He was not looking forward to his trip to Bodie. For the first time the sight of Bodie and the security that it would normally provide was not present. A pain jerked in his stomach as he looked at the gallery in which he and Lucia spent one of their nights together and the house that they shared their most private and intimate feelings and expression of love. It was enough to make Rick's heart begin to murmur a whimper crying tears of its own color.

Rick managed to walk the grounds of Bodie Island and surveyed every building and every corner of the property on pure muscle memory as his conscience thoughts were thousands of miles away. As if Bodie anticipated Rick's feelings, all was well. Rick was relieved as he really did not want to spend too much time there, at least not this summer. He was too sore and needed time to heal.

Summer school was hot. Richmond summers were unbearable with humidity reaching 90 percent and temperatures sometimes hitting the 100-degree mark. If it was not for the occasional dip in Westhampton Lake and the private times to think on the little island in the middle, Richmond might not have been the getaway that he hoped it would. As it was, however, Richmond was just the place he needed to compile his thoughts and relive his memories. He found strength in the quiet times and set into motion a resolve that he would see her again.

Rick took a full course load during the summer and hoped to graduate in December '41 rather than the spring of '42. With any luck at all he could apply to the Department of State in Washington, D.C., and perhaps get attached to an embassy in Italy. He even decided to take a second language, Italian, to help his chances. It would still be a long shot, but it was the only thing he could think of doing.

For the next six months Rick did nothing but study and run track. The intensity of his efforts was noteworthy but made him a social recluse. The letters from Lucia during the previous semesters helped to give the day something special to look forward to. After she graduated from Meredith College, a dark loneliness fell over his heart. It was really hard to think of history, literature, and Latin when his mind was so preoccupied wondering what was going on in her life, whether she was happy, sad, married, single, alive, or dead. It was almost more than he could bear. His only exit from his mental anguish was what he was doing. School work and exercise in the weight room and track were excellent distractions and helped to relieve the stresses, anger and tension that often results from agony of this kind. The university campus and surrounding areas were absolutely beautiful with trees of every shape and size giving countless unbroken and hilly roads upon which Rick could jog or walk, if he chose to.

He made the usual contacts with Kelly and Sean through brief letters asking if they heard from Lucia and how their business was doing. Their letters to him expressed concern for him and wishing he would come back to visit for a while but they understood why he wouldn't.

Rick's parents understood their son and knew that he was simply doing what he needed to do and that he was alright. They supported his decision to work right through to graduation and visited him during the summer of '41 for a week. Rick took them to see Maymont Park, which he loved to visit, and walk on the weekends. The gardens were some of the prettiest his parents had seen. Hollywood Cemetery, just outside downtown Richmond, was a favorite spot they visited. It was there where Confederate heroes such as President Jefferson Davis, Generals Jeb Stewart and George Pickett were buried along with Presidents Tyler and Monroe. In one corner of the graveyard was a large granite pyramid where 18,000 Confederate veterans, mostly from Gettysburg, were buried underneath in a mass grave. Rick's parents were amazed at the size and beauty of Richmond and were proud of their son's accomplishments far from home.

Their visit did a lot to relieve the strain that had been building up in Rick's mind. It helped him to focus his attention on priorities that he had to resolve to get ready for a career after graduation. Rick's father knew U. S. Senator Josiah W. Bailey of Wake County who had an office in Raleigh. Senator Bailey gave them a contact in the State Department to send a resume and application to and recommended that Rick do it as soon as possible. Senator Bailey gave Rick a letter of recommendation and told him to make sure it was on top.

By October he had accumulated all the necessary documents, minus his final transcripts, and mailed them to the State Department. Now all he had to do was graduate and wait.

On December 7, the focus and course of his future changed forever as it did for millions of people in America. America was now fully committed to the war in the Pacific. Within a week America was at war in Europe with Germany's declaration of war on the United States on December 11. "We are in for the fight of our lives," he thought, and knew that he had to participate. He knew that Sean would probably join the Army or Marines and had to get home as soon as he graduated to figure out what he was going to do now since, obviously, every able-bodied man would have to fight for America's right to exist. Recruiters were everywhere. It was exciting and scary at the same time.

He took a moment to reflect on what Lucia said about the war coming to America and her prediction that Rick and Sean would participate. "She was right, again," he thought. Looking out into space he just thought, one more time but this time with a mature sense of urgency, "Please live, Lucia, and be careful. It just might take a little longer before I can get over there. Dear God, bless her and protect her; My love and my life, *Il mio amore e la mia vita.*"

After his last class in December he began his trip south, and as soon as he arrived in Manteo, he drove to the Ryan's house searching for Sean. As luck would have it, he was home. After a short conversation with Sean's parents, Sean walked into the living room after being called in by his mother, drying his hair after his shower.

"Hey there, buddy pal! If I had known it was you I would have put on a better towel," he said grinning from ear to ear.

"Man, am I glad to see you," Rick said excitedly.

"Yeah, me too, Rick. What has you in a buzz?"

"The war, man. The war! What are you going to do?"

Sean looked over at his parents then back to Rick and said, "Remember Pat Dixon? He was the president for the class of '36 in high school. He joined the Army Air Corp last year and is now flying. I thought I would volunteer, before I got drafted, to fly or do something with airplanes."

"Airplanes?" Rick said under his breath, a new thought dawning in his head.

"Yeah, I know you have to be an officer to be a pilot but I thought I could be a mechanic or something if I'm not allowed to fly."

"Have you talked to a recruiter yet?"

"I was going to in January. I will be in Greenville to pick up some tile and thought I would ask some questions then."

"I'll have to tell my mom and dad but I am going with you."

"I could use the help. I already lost two guys from my crews and will lose many more before long. Mrs. Stewart will have to start hiring older guys to do the work and soon too. I don't want to leave her and Kelly without having trained replacements."

"I'm yours, Sean. Use me as a part of your crew. I want to help."

"Done," Sean said with a handshake. "Look, let me get some clothes on and we can talk awhile. Help yourself to some Nehi or something in the fridge."

Mrs. Ryan was in the kitchen baking a cake when Rick came into the room. "So Rick, how was Richmond? Now that you are a college graduate you have any plans?"

"Yes, ma'am, I do actually, but I'm not sure which road to take. That is why I need to talk with Sean."

Mr. Ryan called for Rick from the living room, "Rick, call your folks and ask them to come over for dessert and drinks. It would be great to see them again."

"OK, Mr. Ryan," Rick replied from the kitchen. "They don't even know that I'm in town yet. This will be a great surprise," Rick said to Mrs. Ryan.

Rick called his mom and both parents arrived about twenty minutes later. Mrs. Ryan offered cake and drinks of their choice to all of their guests. Everybody had a piece of chocolate cake and a glass of cold ice tea. Mr. Ryan told Mr. Hamilton of Sean's intentions to join the Army Air Corps, which noticeably disturbed Mrs. Hamilton.

"Mom, you know that this war involves everybody. We all have to contribute. I'm considering joining with Sean," Rick said gently to his mom.

"I know," replied Mrs. Hamilton. "It will just take some getting used to the idea of seeing you two boys, in what seemed like yesterday, playing in your underwear, with the hose in my front yard, now being all grown up and getting ready to join the military to fight a war." She looked over at Mrs. Ryan for reassurances and saw in her eyes that she was feeling the same way.

"Mom, it *was* yesterday, or just about. It was last summer!" Rick said trying to break the seriousness of the situation. His mom and Mrs. Ryan snickered remembering that warm afternoon.

Rick's parents knew that Rick was planning something and knew that it involved the war. This was a good way to discuss the difficult topic. Rick's parents were relieved that they were with the Ryans, in this forum, to discuss it. There was comfort when you were with others sharing the same feelings.

This conflict would recondition their lives and would require the support from family and friends from every corner of Roanoke Island. Everybody would have to support the other now. One family—One nation. Everybody would share in the victories and everybody would share in the losses. No one wanted to talk about it but some of the losses would be very personal. Everybody knew it. Everybody knew that their little corner of heaven on earth would be touched by the ravages of war and death. Everybody knew that business would have to change and that the daily common lives that peace brings would be uncommon. Fear and an uncertain future would fill their hearts and minds, accompanied quickly by a prayer that everything and everybody would be alright. Change is always difficult and change just hit Roanoke Island hard. One thing can be said, however, that behind every tear was a lion's heart and a passionate resolve that American victory was certain and that the citizens of this community would proudly serve and survive, one way or another.

Sean and Rick visited the Army recruiter in Greenville and enlisted in the Enlisted Reserve Corps of the Army Air Corps. It was a smart way to avoid being drafted, which was certain, and to get their choice of a branch of service. Both young men chose the Army Air Corps to be aviation cadets. Although acceptance into the program was not certain the recruiter told them their chances would have been worse if they had waited. They had to enter a waiting pool for an indefinite period of time but since Rick had a college degree his chances were better than Sean's. The recruiter told Sean to take some math classes and to get ready to take some job specialty qualification tests that involved aptitude and motor skills. Rick was told that he would have to take the qualifying tests also.

During their waiting period Rick worked hard with Sean in the construction business. Many of Sean's crews were taking Sean's lead by enlisting in the service, which left a lot of work to do without the usual manpower to do it. Many young men chose the Marines Corps and Navy being recruited out of Elizabeth City. Those recruits did not have much of a wait and were gone within a couple of weeks of signing up. It was only because of Sean's and Rick's desire to fly and a possible commission that they had a longer wait than the others.

Sean and Rick did not mind the wait, though, as it gave Sean time to train the replacements who were usually older men or sometimes women. Sean's major challenge was getting them familiar with the routine, tools of the trade, and working as a crew. There were some challenges in getting their trust and Sean trusting them, especially when they had to do a job without supervision. As time went on, Sean realized that times were tough and were going to get tougher. Everybody needed a job and nobody wanted to jeopardize it by being less than what Sean expected. They all put in an honest day's work for the decent wages they were earning. Soon, trust was flowing in both directions.

The number of jobs fell quickly as new home construction and renovations reflected the uncertainty of the times. Building materials, rubber, and metals were being directed to the war effort and there was talk of rationing fuel.

Everybody had to play a part. This was definitely a national effort. The only new jobs were proposed government contracts. Sean was actively trying to secure some of those bids once they came out. Most of those contracts, when they were announced, were predicted to be in the Wilmington area building housing and quarters for ship builders. Other locations were at Bluethenthal Field as well as in Elizabeth City and near Camp Davis, Topsail Island for the Navy/Marine Corps, and at Montford Point in Jacksonville.

On April 1 Sean got a notice that the Roanoke Construction Company was given a partial award to start building barracks and support facilities at Montford Point in Jacksonville, North Carolina. This was the bolt that the business needed to keep it going. He also knew that success at this job was absolutely imperative if he was to be considered for any future contracts. He assembled the best crew he had to take the five-hour journey south and set up a base site. He also had to make sure that he had competent personnel back on the island to handle the business there. Now Sean would see first hand how successful the training of his crews were and if they could work on location away from Roanoke Island by solving construction problems such as design, contracting, purchasing, health and welfare, and morale issues. He would have to test each man's loyalty and work ethic. At home, he would have to get Mrs. Stewart and Kelly acquainted with the operations side of the business and familiar with the foremen of each crew. Everybody worked together well and was determined to make this transition as smooth as possible.

In May Rick made a trip to visit Bodie, in what would be his last trip before he got called to duty for training. Sean offered to go out there with him but Rick just wanted to be alone for a while. Time softened the emotional and lonely heart that the missing of a loved one impresses. Rick was happy that he could go back to Bodie without that pain. The pain evolved into a new matured confidence. He knew that the choices he made were going to put him on course with history and perhaps, just perhaps, a chance to be a little closer to Lucia someday. Rick always had a thought or a belief that with every step he took he was getting a little closer to where destiny had him going. The journey's length and hazards were uncertain but he knew that Lucia was somewhere out there.

He put some of the special items in the Gaskills' house away such as the pictures, and locked them in a closet downstairs. He disposed of some perishables, dumped the water after he finished a general cleaning, and locked all of the windows. He walked over to the mantel clock, opened the glass door that accessed the pendulum and just stood there a moment and listened to the sound, concentrating on the echo that it made throughout the house. He remembered, to the point he could actually hear, the sounds of laughing, the casual conversations that were made with the Gaskills, Sean, Kelly and Lucia, and the front and back door leading to Bodie opening and closing. "I'll be back," he said, then reached into the clock and stopped the pendulum swing. He wrapped the clock in a pillow case and carried it upstairs to put it in the closet he reserved for the most precious of things. He went into his bedroom and paused for a moment. He looked at the candle that he lit when he was with Lucia their last time together and noticed that it was burned down to the stump. He looked at the open shades, dusty floor, and furniture and noticed, with deep surprise, the heart-shaped stone that he found and gave to Lucia when they had their last walk on the beach together over a year ago. He kissed the stone and placed it with the candle remnant within the clock. He immediately got a dust cloth and mop and cleaned the room from top to bottom. He stripped the bed of the clean sheets, folded them, placed them in the linen closet along with the clock and locked the door. He draped a plain white sheet over the bed, dresser and end table to keep the dust from accumulating on them. It was a special place; he wanted it preserved and kept that way.

He went to the top of Bodie to give her a good cleaning, and to take a moment to look around the area since he was not sure when he would be back. His schedule with Sean was starting to take all of his time. Contracts were being awarded and it was certain that Sean was going to be awarded some of them.

After cleaning the lens and remembering his first days there and all the events of his life in between, he took the time to feel them again. He saw the people standing on that back porch that have taken him to where he was at that point in time. He took another look over the familiar beaches and marshes surrounding the lighthouse. He knew that it would be this moment now that he would have to reflect upon to get him past the trials that wait for him tomorrow and the promise that he made to Lucia, on that very spot, that he would find her. Looking over the water and facing east he said aloud to intimidate fear and doubt, "I promised you that I would find you and I will. Just stay alive."

7

In late June Rick got his letter inquiring if he was still interested in the Army Air Corps. Rick said he was but wanted to wait for his friend Sean because they were told that they would be able to enter together. On July 16 they both got their orders to report to the San Antonio Aviation Cadet Center in San Antonio, Texas, which was located at Randolph Field for Pre-Flight Training by 0800 (8:00 AM), August 17, 1942. Now it was official. Rick and Sean were to be cadets for aviation training. Becoming pilots was not a guarantee but they were going to be given a shot at it.

Sean's last scenes with Kelly were tearful and brief. Mrs. Stewart told Sean that she would take care of Kelly and would make sure Kelly behaved herself. Mrs. Stewart loved Sean as the son she never had. That love and concern was never more evident as it was that morning on her front porch.

With swollen eyes and a touch of lipstick she hugged Sean and said, straightening his shirt and collar, "You run along and don't worry about us here. We will be waiting for you when you get back. Thanks for everything…for taking care of us Sean. You…take care of yourself…" she began to say, and then with a kiss on his forehead she turned and went inside before the situation became unbearable.

It was decided by Sean and Rick that it was best that Rick did not see Kelly and Mrs. Stewart the day they left since the dual parting might be more than anybody could bear. Sean felt confident that he was leaving Kelly and her mom in good hands. The business was headed in the right direction as the

Roanoke Construction Company was recently awarded two more government contracts in Wilmington that should see them through the next couple of years. Sean's parents said that they would check in on the Stewarts from time to time which gave Sean more security in his heart.

Rick's good-bye to his family was hard. Rick's mom cried, of course, and his dad shook his hand as if he did not want to let go. His grip was strong, steady, and full of pride.

"You take care of yourself, son. I am so proud of you. Write as often as you can."

"I will, Dad," he said, then, walking to his mom one last time, he gave her a hug and a kiss on her cheek.

"Come on, Mom. You can't worry about me. I am your son. You have raised me up to be the man I am. How could I do anything less than what I am doing right now? You know that I am doing the right thing and I know you are proud of me. Everybody has to do their part. No more tears, OK? I will send you pictures of me in my uniform. I will keep you with me every step of the way. I love you, Mom." Reaching into his bag he pulled out his Teddy bear, "Goggie," that he got when he was a baby. He always had it close by for sentimental reasons but never told anybody in fear of ridicule. "Here, Mom, when you are missing me use him as your pillow."

"Where did you find him?" she asked in amazement.

"In order to find something it had to be lost, right? I always had him. I guess I kept him all this time because I knew that one day I would give him back to you, to give you the comfort that you so often gave to me."

"I love you too, Rick, my little baby boy," she said wiping the tears off her cheek. Taking a proud look at Rick she said, "My, have you grown," she said trying to gain composure and straightening his hair with her hand. "Where has all the time gone?"

Clearing her throat she said, "Now, you get or you will be late for your train. Just go now."

"OK, Mom. I love you guys. I will make you proud."

About that time Sean pulled up in his pickup to give Rick a ride to his house where his parents would drive them to the train station. With a wave from their windows, the latest contribution to the war effort from Manteo left and was headed to Texas.

Randolph Field, and Texas as a whole, was a flat, desolate place which was perfectly suited for training pilots because there was plenty of space to crash and not get anyone but yourself and your instructor hurt. The Administration Building was a beautiful spire that looked like it was built to impress young cadets. It was the largest landmark for miles which, no doubt, served as a VFR (Visual Flight Rules) navigational beacon for rookie pilots to recognize and get a bearing as to where they were.

Sean and Rick reported in to the Aviation Cadet Center and were quickly indoctrinated to the military way of life by being given uniforms, health care items, supplies, duffle bag, linens, a haircut, and a physical exam. Both cadets were run to the barracks that they would inhabit for the next twelve weeks while the Army Air Force Classification Center would administratively process their pay and allowances, orders, and classifications.

The twelve weeks primarily consisted of physical training, calisthenics and class work which included lessons in basic flight essentials, navigation, and Morse code. Sean and Rick did well in their indoctrination classes. Sean was a natural with the mechanics of navigation, whereas Rick mastered aerodynamics and theory of flight. After eight days of their arrival they were notified that they were classified as "Pilot." Rick thought that was strange since he had yet to touch an airplane but was glad to see that at least the paperwork was progressing.

After twelve weeks of intensive training and graduating on November 13, Sean and Rick were transferred to Jones Field in Bonham, Texas. Jones Field was a civil contract flying school that based the 302nd Flying Training Detachment. It had one 1,200-foot runway which was plenty for the PT-19A training aircraft. Jones Field had four auxiliary airfields in the area, three of which was within eight miles of Bonham and one, Cravens Auxiliary Field # 3, which was twenty miles. These airfields allowed aircraft to practice touch and go's, EP's (Emergency Procedures) and approaches, without interfering with the traffic pattern of the primary control zone of Jones.

After checking in, Rick and Sean walked around the base and airfield. For the first time the reality and consequences of their choice to fly were felt. The sounds of the single-engine, tandem-seat open-cockpit monoplane, along with the smells of the fuel combined with the dry, dusty Texas air, stirred excitement in their blood from which started a fever they never felt before. It was a great first day but their fever would get hotter three days later when they sat at the controls, wearing the B-3 leather flight jacket, hearing the commands of "Clear...Contact" being yelled to the ground crew, and the engine beginning its first turns of roaring life.

Rick was very nervous about his first flight. He heard horror stories about attrition rates and the demands and stress that the instructors put on the students. He studied procedures and checklist items sometimes with Sean but mostly by himself. He thought he was prepared for his first ride but once the plane was strapped on and the instructor was in the back seat everything took on a different feel and personality. Fortunately the first ride was just that, a ride. The instructor pilot did most of the flying, giving Rick a quick feel of the controls for a minute or two. The first flight was thirty-seven minutes and it was the thrill of Rick's life. Sean did not enjoy it as much however, as he lost his lunch in the cockpit and had to clean it up when he got back.

The first flight made Rick realize that he had to get organized in the cockpit. He had to arrange his checklist and learn where to place things such as his checklist and paper to write on. Sean had to do the same thing but also had to learn where to put his barf bag so he could get to it quickly when necessary. All of these preparations were necessary and not yet second nature. Their flight instructors told them "not to stress yet", that "it will get worse before it gets better" and that "flying really is fun." Rick was certainly ready; Sean wasn't too certain of anything yet.

When the cadets were not preparing for their flights they formed up to do calisthenics, formation runs, military drill, jump rope, and recreational swim. Some cadets had to learn how to swim. The swim instructors were very professional and patient taking their time with each group or individual as necessary. Sean and Rick considered the swim fun and used the time to relax, enjoy the guys and the training experience because they both knew that tomorrow they were going for a real "graded" flight.

At 0500 Rick woke up, not that he slept well anyway, showered, dressed and walked to the mess hall. There, he met up with Sean and two other students, Tab "Beaver" Beverly and Tom "Bunky" Pruitt. Both were southern boys from Florida just as green as they were but with carefree attitudes. They had a serious business demeanor, however, when it came to study and flying. Both wanted to fly since they were kids. Both had parents who flew with National Airlines out of Miami and both knew the inherent dangers associated with the job. Tab and Tom's fathers volunteered, soon after the war started, to serve as instructor pilots with the Army Air Corps. National Airlines operated a portion of its fleet for the Air Transport Command and operated Army Air Corps contract schools for pilots, mechanics, radio operators, and navigators. Nonetheless, both parents were needed to operate the airline from Miami, Florida with G. T. Baker, founder and president of the airline.

Rick walked to the briefing shed with the other three cadets firing procedures back and forth at each other. Aircraft and engine limitations were fair questions that could be asked at any time. Everybody knew them cold. Everybody was confident that their first flight was going to be "a piece of cake." Sean had his barf bag in his right breast pocket, which Rick wanted to joke with him about but knew that now was not the time. "This afternoon, if all goes well," Rick thought, "perhaps we can share a few laughs."

Rick met his instructor pilot, Mr. Bill McMillan, retired Pan American Airways captain who flew Boeing 314s in the Pacific. Fortunately for Rick, Bill was asked to come out of retirement to serve as an instructor pilot. Bill had a tremendous reputation on the base as being one of the best instructor pilots because of his line flying and check airman experience with Pan Am. He loved the flying business and it showed. He knew all the tricks and knew how to teach them.

After a twenty-minute briefing, Rick gathered his things and walked to the plane with Bill.

"Start with the engine on the preflight and I will follow you along the way," Bill instructed as they approached the blue and yellow bird.

Rick stowed his gear in the cockpit, unlocking the controls and doing a thorough cockpit check as Bill did the same for the rear seat.

Rick's preflight with Bill was smooth. Bill asked him questions along the way and pointed out some things about the aircraft that were just not written down in manuals that Rick found more interesting.

Bill allowed Rick to start the engine after the proper "Clear...Contact" signal and followed him closely on all of the controls, which meant the instructor had his hands close to the controls but not on them in the event the instructor had to make a real fast adjustment or correction.

Bill did the takeoff having Rick ride the controls and power. Bill never stopped talking, explaining everything he was doing from power and mixture settings, to saying procedures out loud. Bill would demonstrate a procedure or maneuver once or twice having Rick ride the controls then would have Rick fly the aircraft with Bill having a close hand near by. Maneuvers included takeoff, level off, climb and decent, level turns and landing pattern procedures at Brown Field. Total time was one hour and ten minutes with Rick logging forty-five minutes as first pilot which was very unusual.

Bill was an extraordinary instructor because he wanted to give his students as much time as possible "on the stick". His feelings, when it was explained to Rick at the post-flight briefing, were, "I don't need the time. You do and you need to start accumulating it fast. You are a natural at this, Rick. I'm impressed but don't let that go to your head. Never get too relaxed because if you do you will die and if you are piloting a plane with a crew or passengers they will all die with you. They are all depending on you to be a professional at all times," Bill said pointing to the flight line.

Continuing in his debriefing, he said, "This is dangerous enough work just flying around here doing pattern work. The real danger is flying where people don't want you to be and the enemy is trying to shoot you down. You have to be a solid pilot, competent in your abilities and knowledge of normal and emergency procedures. You have to have an instinct to fly when the manual no longer applies. That will come with time in the airplane and experience flying it. Be afraid. That is good as it will keep you alive, but be fearless in your duty; straight and level, greasy side down. Make the plane do what YOU want it to do is the best advice I can give you."

Rick thought a moment of what he said, and said, "Mr. McMillan, I can see how you have such a great reputation and I appreciate you and your experience more than you know. I promise I will pick your brain for as much information as I can get and will also promise I will be as prepared as I can be for every flight I have with you. I just have one regret."

"Really, what might that be?" Bill said with a curious look.

"That my friend Cadet Sean Ryan doesn't have you as his instructor."

"I heard of Ryan. He is the boy who barfed all over 440-1 a week or so ago."

"That's right," Rick said holding back his laugh.

"Sean is going to be OK. Throwing up your first flight is not that uncommon. Mr. Holden is a fine instructor but just like with every other cadet Sean has to be ready. We can't let anybody move on to the next level or get winged who we don't feel can take the pressures of piloting a plane in combat. Our job as instructors is to test every one of you. Sean will be tested. You will be tested, and if for any reason we think you or any cadet could be a risk, we will recommend reassignment."

"Yes, sir. That is understood and appreciated."

"Look, good flight today. I think you and I are scheduled again in two days. Go study."

Rick left and went back to his quarters, showered, ate and tried to find Sean. Sean came back later that morning. Rick saw him walking to the barracks from the airfield when he was walking from the mess hall after lunch.

"Hey, Sean, wait up!" Rick yelled across the compound picking up speed from his walk turning it into a jog towards him. "How did it go today?"

With a smile on his face, Sean said, "I never had so much fun in my life, and look," as he pulled his barf bag from his flight suit pocket, "it's empty!"

With a big slap on the back both of them walked to the barracks together, telling each other of their flight. On the way they hooked up with Tab and Tom, who were just walking out. Of the bunch, Rick accumulated the most first pilot time, which made him the envy of the guys, but each were proud of the other and felt a bit more secure and confident of their positions in the program and their decisions to fly.

Rick did his first solo after having flown seven hours in two weeks. Sean soloed after nine hours a couple of days later. After each had soloed the pace of the training picked up so that by the time they graduated from primary at Jones Field, nine weeks from reporting in, they had accumulated over fifty hours of flight time, of which seven hours were solo. At graduation the class was officially known as the Cadets of 43-F.

The next day, December 19, the four cadets left for Perrin Field near Sherman, Texas, to begin the basic training phase by flying the Consolidated Vultee, BT-13B, otherwise known as the "Vibrator" because of the rattling noise made by the sliding canopy. The Vultee was powered by a 450 HP Pratt & Whitney engine turning a two-bladed variable-pitch stainless-steel propeller (prop). The airplane was almost two times heavier than the PT-19A. Because of the variable-speed prop, the procedures were more complicated and would serve to be the downfall of many students. Rick and Sean were aware of the challenges and were eager to tackle them. Tab, who had some experience with the variable-speed prop, explained how it was more efficient as it provided more speed to the airplane with less engine RPM. After a brief informal class over a beer at the Cadet Club, they all understood how it was more efficient than a fixed prop (solid wood or metal).

Training began with a cockpit familiarization in Link trainers. The Link simulators moved, side to side, up and down to simulate the pitch and roll of the actual aircraft. Every student began radio navigation training in the Link by flying point to point, tracking in and out on a radio signal on a specific radial (beam) on a 360-degree electric compass. Needles on the compass would identify the actual radial you were on which allowed you to calculate your relative position to other points on the compass.

Movement of the trainer was accomplished by vacuum-controlled bellows connected to valves then connected to "the stick" and rudder pedals. The instructor sat at a desk near the trainer tracking the student's progress and giving the student simulated radio messages and Air Traffic Control instructions through the headphones both of them were wearing. The feel of air passing over the control surfaces of the airplane was accomplished by the use of Slip Stream Simulators. Rough air generators added turbulence during the static flight.

Rick and Sean took every opportunity to fly the Link. The instructors were very eager to assist in extra training when the schedule allowed. It was a friendly challenge to see who could navigate closer to a specific point identified by the instructors. The instructors were caught up in the competition as well. The best part of extra Link training was that it was not graded and always ended up with a debrief and a paying off of the bets at the Cadet Club.

As Mr. Rogers said, who was Sean's Link instructor, "All training is good training but it is always learned best when you are having fun doing it." It was something that Rick and Sean would never forget and realized just how true what Mr. Rogers said was.

Perrin Field was a bigger base than the previous two as it had nearly 3,000 personnel attached in either training billets or as students. Normal daily routine was similar to that of Jones Field as they still continued to do calisthenics, run, drill, and play some sports. Classroom studies intensified with a refresher of Morse code and a deeper study of engines, hydraulics, pneumatics, radio, and map navigation.

Flight training concentrated on applying what was learned in the classroom and the Link trainers to the actual performance of the task in the air. Navigation to and from a radio beacon and tracking on a course for a certain time or distance, making a coordinated time turn to intercept another radio signal and do the same procedure again and again was tough enough but to do the task while executing simulated emergency procedures and making the required radio calls was even harder. The real challenge and one that your life and the life of your crew depended on was an instrument approach, in which a student was under a hood and had to fly an approach to a runway just on instruments without any outside visual reference. Mastery of this piloting process was crucial because of its obvious importance; flying in bad weather was imminent. A landing you can walk away from was always considered a good one but a landing on an intended, friendly runway where a hot meal and a warm bunk waits was even better.

Rick particularly enjoyed the formation flying phase of training. Flying up close, within thirty feet and watching another plane was exhilarating. Being part of a multi-plane formation exemplified teamwork and pride. Before you could enter this phase you had to be competent in your procedures, have the trust of your instructor pilot, and fellow aviators. There was nothing more dangerous in aviation than having a careless pilot on your wing.

Rick and Sean planned a cross-country formation flight together with their instructors, as observers, to the Boeing Plant in Wichita, Kansas. Rick's instructor pilot for the formation phase was a pilot, on loan from Boeing. Mr. Denny "Always" Wright was often talking about a big bomber that Boeing was building that first flew in September, 1942. It was supposed to be bigger, faster and fly farther than the famed B-17. Rick was taken by the stories of the B-17 that Mr. Wright told and wanted to see the next generation bomber.

Rick remembered the meeting that he and Sean made to see Mr. Wright to ask him if he would fly with them to Wichita on their cross country and show them the B-29 that he talked about whenever he could.

"The B-29 is still being tested and developed, guys. I'm not completely sure if we could even get in the hangar. Security will be tough," Mr. Wright said.

Standing with Mr. Wright was another instructor pilot, Mr. Brad Powell also from Wichita.

Looking at Mr. Wright he said, "That is probably true but there is a chance it might be on the apron. I mean, if the cadets want to see it…that might be their chance. Besides, there are always a few B-17s there."

With the word "B-17" Rick's eyes lit up.

"If it is all the same to you I would be satisfied to see the B-17," he said.

Looking at Sean he said, "What do you say, Sean. You game?"

Sean looking at the two instructors, "Can you guys fly in two days? That is when we are scheduled for our hop. Out and back. One day."

Mr. Wright, looking at Mr. Powell and with a nod from him, said, "Sure thing. I'll tell Squadron Ops. Check the flight schedule tomorrow for times. Plan a VFR route with an instrument approach into Wichita Municipal Airport."

Rick and Sean immediately went to work on the route after checking the weather forecast at Base Ops. "Weather looks good so far," the weather briefer said. Now they just hoped that their planes worked and that "Murphy" stayed home rather than tried to upset their plans.

Briefing was scheduled for 0700 with a 0830 takeoff. All went as scheduled and they flew at 5,000 feet. Time in route was 2.5 hours and that went by fast. It was the best trip that Rick and Sean have had because it was the first time the two flew together, doing what they wanted to do, and going somewhere they wanted to go. Trips like that were rewards for hard work. Sean and Rick deserved it, and the instructors knew it. En route they changed the lead several times and the instructors showed the students just how close you could get an airplane to another in flight.

Mr. Wright took the wingtip of Sean's plane to within five or six feet of their own.

"You don't want to try this if your comfort level is not there and never exceed the comfort level of anyone else in the plane or the plane you are flying form on. You're OK, right?" he said with a chuckle.

"Yeah, sure. You can back off whenever you are ready. I'm more comfortable back there."

Approaching Wichita, Rick called Wichita Tower for landing instructions. Within range of the airfield Mr. Wright called out over the intercom to Rick, "Look down below by the large hanger. The silver airplane is the XB-29. Right next to it is the B-17—what a beautiful sight, huh?"

Transmitting to Mr. Powell in the other plane, Mr. Wright said, "Brad, see that?"

"Yeah, it looks like the boys' lucky day."

After performing a mid-field break in tight formation, which is when the lead plane would turn the plane quickly to a 45-degree angle of bank with the second plane (dash two) doing the same turn three seconds later, the two aircraft landed. Rick called for taxi instructions to the Boeing apron. Lady Luck again was on their side as they parked the two planes next to the B-17 with the welcomed aid of Boeing ground crews taxiing them in with hand and arm signals.

Rick's eyes were fixed on the dark green Flying Fortress as he hopped out of the cockpit and onto the concrete parking ramp. Mr. Wright and Mr. Powell met some of their friends as they came from within the hangar.

Sean walked to Rick after his aircraft was secured and tied down.

"Have you ever seen anything bigger in your life, Rick?" looking at the Fortress.

"I have never seen a prettier machine. It's huge. Amazing," Rick said with astonishment.

"Just think we have a chance to fly it, maybe in a couple of months."

Mr. Wright walked over and said, "Well, boys, what do you think of the Flying Fortress?"

Sean said in reply, "I was just telling Rick that we might be flying this someday soon."

"That is a serious possibility. Flying the B-17F is an experience a lucky man might have only once. You two may have a chance to fly it many times," he said admiring her curves and aerodynamic features resembling the lines of a beautiful human female.

"She is a beautiful plane, none more beautiful in the sky and one of the few that looks just as beautiful sitting on the ground. Notice how her nose points to the air as if proud and praying to fly. Notice how the twelve .50-caliber (cal.) machine guns peer from every surface daring anyone to approach her without invitation. She means business, boys," tapping her side. "She will win the war for us."

"I hope I get the chance to fly her," Rick said.

"She is the safest plane ever built and will bring you home with even two engines out. We have records of the tail being almost severed from the empennage and still flying home. We have a personal account of the nose being blown clean off and still flying 700 miles. We have testimonials of some planes having sustained so much battle damage from flak and bullets that only after landing would break in two; only after she knew her crew was safe. This is a machine that has a true heart; a heart that loves the men aboard her."

Rick thought of his words as he continued to speak and was reminded of another place and structure that also loved. That was home and Bodie. He thought for a while looking at that bird of war, built for victory by men who, no doubt, had sex on the brain because of the grace and smoothness of her design. He thought of a plan, something he would like to do when or if he returned back home. He vowed that if the chance was afforded him he would try to do it. "Bodie," he thought, "has to meet her, one lovely lady to another."

Rick looked over at the four-engine B-29 Super Fortress, a silver giant of a plane much bigger than the B-17. The B-29 was built to reach deep into enemy territory with twice the range of the B-17. He noticed the Boeing guys and his friends looking her over and talking to a man who just emerged from her silver belly. Mr. Eddie Allen, Boeing's chief test pilot for the B-29, was one of several Boeing representatives to come over and see Mr. Wright and Powell. Mr. Allen also noticed the muscular man that emerged from the B-29 and said, "Hey, E.J. How she look?"

E. J., having been busy inspecting control linkages and cable tensions for the past hour, said, wiping his brow with his handkerchief after removing his green and white John Deere hat, "The pulleys are secured and safety wired and I gave the rudder a couple of more degrees right deflection like you wanted."

"Great," said Mr. Allen. "Gentlemen, I want you to meet our chief inspector on the B-29 line, E.J."

E.J. was a tall hulk of a man. Tan from years working on his two farms west and east of Wichita and maintaining the equipment he needed to plant and harvest crops of wheat and milo. His forearms were like telephone poles which led to hands that could grip a basketball. But most remarkable was his smile. His straight white teeth and masculine features showed that he was as gentle as any man could be. He was the epitome of the Boeing aircraft worker, an American of power and determination, to defeat a ruthless enemy hell bent on taking away liberty from free men. His power was his mettle and that was concentrated to provide the best resources to the American fighting man so they could accomplish their mission.

After the introductions, Mr. Allen asked E.J. to tell the cadets about the differences between the two aircraft.

"This is Number One XB-29, guys, the first B-29, and it stands at about thirty feet high, has a wing span of 141 feet, and has a length of nearly 100 feet, which equates to being, on average, about twenty-five to thirty percent bigger than the B-17. But with that minimal difference it can carry a 20,000-pound bomb load, which is 14,000 pounds, or three and a third times more than the B-17, over 3,250 miles, which is twice the distance. The biggest technological difference is that now the crews can fly in a pressurized cabin over 31,000 feet without being attached to an oxygen system, not to mention the computerized gun sights."

Rick thought she was an interesting plane with a round nose and plenty of glass for the pilots to look through but it lacked something. After some comparison between the two he noticed that the B-29 stood level because of her tricycle gear, that the round shape of the nose continued all the way back to the tail and she had long narrow wings, whereas the B-17 was olive green with a light gray underbelly. She was a four-engine tail-dragger with her nose pointed to the sky with a thicker wing and a cockpit that resembled the nose of a beagle. "She looks...softer," he told E.J. pointing to the B-17.

E.J. said, "She is my favorite too." Taking his John Deere ball cap off again and wiping his brow with his forearm he began to laugh a little, saying, "She reminds me of my wife, Margaret. Clean and smooth to the touch. Pretty to look at but frisky and wild when riled up and can hit you hard when you least expect it." He slapped his cap on his thigh and said, "Yep," with a big smile adoring the thought of her.

The B-17 and B-29 were posed to attack with pledged victory with every rivet. Each plane was exquisite in its own personal way, color and style. Rick tried to put into words what he was feeling when he looked at each bomber.

"Romance," Rick said to E.J. "The B-17 is romantic. You can see the love that went into her design. The love and respect that her crews have for her and the promise that the Fortress gives in return, to bring her crew back home or die trying."

"Her crews swear by her, that's for sure, and her crew," E.J. said pointing to the nose of the B-17, "named her *Danny Boy* after the pilot's son. Everybody on the crew is tight like a family because they know that is critical that they fight like one."

"That's good enough for me," Rick said.

One week later on February 18, Rick was told by Mr. Wright that Mr. Allen and Boeing's top flight test crew were killed when Number Two XB-29 crashed during a test hop. As it was explained to him, an engine caught fire, which the B-29 had problems with because of the double rows of cylinders overheating, catching the magnesium gear box on fire which, in turn, melted the main wing spar breaking the wing off in flight. Everybody died along with eighteen people on the ground when it hit a meat-packing plant outside the city limits of Wichita.

This was Rick's first encounter with the death of a person that he knew, albeit not very well, but knew just the same. It impressed him and made him realize even more that he was in a serious and deadly business. Sean and Rick went to Mass the following Sunday and prayed for their souls and the security of families. Afterwards they wrote home explaining what happened and not to worry. They reassured their parents that the training was the best in the world and that they were proud to serve. They explained that each guy was watching over the other, now more than ever.

Rick and Sean finished their basic training by flying acrobatics, multi-plane formations, night flying and plenty of cross-country and solo flying. By the end of their stay at Perrin Field, Rick and Sean had accumulated a little over seventy hours of flight time including over fifty hours of solo and ten hours of night time.

On March 26 they graduated from basic training under a blue sky and cool temperatures. After heartfelt farewells to friends and flight instructors, they packed up the bus that was to take them to Lubbock Army Flying School in Lubbock, Texas, for the last phase of training. It was considered advanced because they were going to fly the twin-engine Cessna AT-17.

The AT-17 was similar in appearance to the DC-3 but much smaller as it was also a tail-dragger and had two engines. The cockpit was side by side which allowed for more up-front and personal instruction. The cockpit layout allowed instructors to introduce students to a crew concept, of working together, of accomplishing a mission as a team.

Upon checking in, Rick was assigned Mr. Richard "Dick" Weldon as his flight instructor. A thirty-year-old pilot with over 1,500 hours in multi-engine aircraft he was a recent acquisition to the Army Air Corps from National Airlines. Soon after he was hired by National, he volunteered to serve for one year as a flight instructor. Mr. Baker, understanding the need and urgency for qualified pilots in the service, gave him the leave of absence without any loss of seniority.

Rick enjoyed the AT-17 because he felt, for the first time he had a real airplane and did not feel the threat of attrition. It was well known that if you got this far in the training, you were probably going to get winged and that was a day Rick was looking forward to. Mr. Weldon taught Rick everything he knew from radio navigation to landing in a stiff crosswind. Mr. Weldon would find an auxiliary field with the greatest crosswind component and demonstrate a landing on it. He would then give Rick the controls so he could try.

On one approach Mr. Weldon chose a runway with a twenty-five-knot crosswind, sixty degrees or more off the nose. Calling for "Gear, flaps…landing checklist," the approach included a twenty-degree right-wing-down, left-rudder approach to about twenty feet above the ground, straightening out the aircraft to runway heading and greasing on the landing. Rick's first experience with this demonstration was scary to say the least but after a while he thought the approaches were fun and they didn't faze him a bit.

One night while doing instrument flying, Mr. Weldon showed him tricks that were not in the instrument flight manual and involved a deeper study and understanding of partial panel flight. Mr. Weldon explained how if the flight indicator, which is the instrument that shows aircraft attitude in relation to the surface of the earth, and if the radio compass, which shows heading and position on a radio navigation beacon, failed due to a DC electrical problem, you could still fly and navigate an airplane safely. He explained how by using the instruments powered by ambient atmospheric pressure such as the altimeter (altitude) and airspeed indicator combined with the use of the turn-and-bank indicator—also known as the turn-and-slip indicator—clock and wet compass you can fly, with practice, a general course or direction. He told Rick that if the compass is turning you are obviously turning. Your turn indicator can help you in this determination. If the airspeed increases and you have not touched the throttles you are descending; conversely if you are slowing down, you are climbing. All instruments have to be cross-checked to verify the flight condition. So a good instrument scan had to be established early in training so an advanced scanning technique could be taught and mastered.

They would practice this for a while; then Mr. Weldon took even more instruments away. He explained how sometimes in combat the cockpit could get so badly damaged that even the basic instruments won't work. He reached over around his neck and removed his dog tags and hung them from the center of the glare shield so they could hang freely. Placing cards over the wet compass and the turn-and-bank indicator and with the flight indicator and radio compass already disabled, Mr. Weldon began simple turns, climbs, and descents and told Rick to watch the dog tags as he maneuvered the plane. Rick watched, in amazement, as the tags moved to the laws of Newton, that being, "For every action, there is an equal and opposite reaction." Mr. Weldon would have Rick close his eyes. Mr. Weldon would then maneuver the plane then tell Rick to open his eyes and look at the instruments and the dog tags and identify the flight characteristics of the plane. Rick made mistakes at first but got good at identifying turns, climbs and descents with just the altimeter and dog tags. That demonstration was remarkable and, with the flight being flown at night, with the light from the moon and the stars being seen from the window above Rick's head, the lesson made it just that much more memorable.

Through letters home, Rick arranged for Kelly to surprise Sean at the winging. Kelly arrived the day before and stayed out in town with her mom. Rick met them at the train station without Sean knowing.

The first meeting in ten months was as heartwarming as the meeting between any two close friends could be. Before the train even came to a stop, Kelly was screaming at Rick through her window. As soon as the train stopped and through the steam between the two rail cars, Kelly emerged running at full gallop and jumped into Rick's arms. Her mom gracefully got off the train and stood there watching the two embrace. He acted as if she caught him off guard with the emotion but the reality was he expected every bit of it.

After she was done kissing his cheek and with a breathless pant she said, "First, I promised I would kiss you for your mom," kissing him sweetly on both cheeks, forehead and over each closed eye, like his mom did when he was a child.

"You look great, Rick! You look older and manly. Oh my God, Mom, look at him!"

"Hi, Rick," Mrs. Stewart said standing looking at Rick with the biggest smile imaginable.

Taking a good look at Kelly's mom, Rick was taken by her mature beauty. He walked to her and gave her a respectful kiss on the cheek saying, "Thanks for coming. Sean is just going to die when he sees you and Kelly. Die, just die."

Stepping back to look at the both of them, he said, "You have to be tired."

Putting his arm around each lady on either side of him he said, "I have made reservations in a quaint little motel just outside the main gate which is shaded by beautiful trees. I have covered all expenses so don't worry about a thing."

"What is Sean doing today and what are the plans?" Kelly asked.

"Sean is getting his uniform ready. We will be wearing full uniform and ties for the winging ceremony tomorrow. You will think he looks 'manly' too." Kelly punched Rick in the arm but followed it up quickly with another kiss.

He continued, "He, of course, has no idea that you are in town. This will be the biggest surprise of his life."

"How was the training, Rick? It appears to have agreed with you," asked Mrs. Stewart.

"It has been a life-altering experience. I feel much different and I know I look different. The people and the instructors I have met are the most professional anywhere and I have learned a lot from them. I have traveled to places and done things that I only could have done in the Air Corps. Flight training was challenging and there were times I wondered if I had what it took to do this. Sean had it a little rougher than I did but I was there for him and he was there for me. Flight school teaches team work, friendship, and support. Everybody on that line, you will see tomorrow, is family. We all owe our successes to each other."

"I can't wait to see Sean!" said Kelly.

"Sean has changed too, Kelly," Rick said. "He has grown up a lot through his experiences. Sean, as you know, has a serious side to him. He takes this new job very seriously because so many people will depend on him. Aviation took him to a new level of concentration. He never studied harder in his life. Don't get me wrong. Sean is Sean and will always be playful and love you. He has just grown up here. We all have."

After getting the girls checked in and after he took them to dinner, Rick returned to base so he would not raise suspicion from Sean.

June 26 was the big day. Being commissioned a second lieutenant in the Army Air Corps and getting winged on the same day was an accomplishment that less than one percent of America's best young men are capable of doing. Half of the guys that started training ten months ago were reassigned, doing something else such as serving as navigators, bombardiers, maintenance officers, supply officers or some other job within the Air Corps.

The commanding officer pinned the gold bars of second lieutenant on the shoulders of Sean and Rick and on the shoulders of each cadet in line. He then gave them the oath which they all said in unison raising their right hand. He then went back to each officer to ceremonially attach the wings of aviator if the officer did not request anyone in particular to do it.

Sean was, of course, at Rick's side when Mr. Weldon winged Rick, at his request. When the commanding officer stood before Sean, he asked him who he had chosen to pin his wings on. Before Sean could answer, Rick said, "Excuse me, sir, I believe she would like to do it," as he pointed to Kelly standing behind two big Army officers in the audience.

The commanding officer stepped aside and Sean saw her poke her little head from behind the two gentlemen who were involved in the plot. Mrs. Stewart also appeared from a different portion of the audience after Kelly started walking towards Sean. Sean was aghast and immediately got weak at the knees. He began to break formation to run to her when he regained his composure, remembered where he was, and just stood at attention with a smile and a joyful tear in his eye. Upon reaching him, the commanding officer gave Kelly the silver wings. Holding them in her precious little hands she looked at them, kissed them, looked into Sean's eyes, and put her left hand in his jacket behind the upper portion of his left breast pocket and pinned them on perfectly straight as if she had done it a hundred times before. That was all Sean could take and hugged her and kissed her in front of all of his buddies, their families and officers and men of Lubbock.

"I love you, Kelly," he said.

"I love you, Sean, and I am so proud of you. I'll see you when this is over."

Kelly turned and walked to her mother where they both embraced knowing how important that moment was to everybody present.

Rick looked over at Sean and elbowed him. Sean, visibly touched by Rick's friendship and the efforts that so many people made to make this surprise happen, said, "You wait, my friend. I will get you back. I can promise you that and it will top what you just did here today."

Rick smiled, knowing that his boast was not possible but loved his friend for saying it.

Of the twenty pilots in that line five were going to join Fighter Commands; one was going to Air Transport Command. The rest were going to Bomber Commands. Rick, Sean, Tab and Bunky were going to Salt Lake City, Utah, to be part of the Second Air Force, 18th Replacement Wing, reporting for duty July 17. This would be the first break in ten months of rigorous training, a break that everybody was looking forward to. Especially for Sean, now that Kelly was there.

After the ceremony Rick and Sean walked to where Kelly and her mother were standing. Sean immediately hugged Kelly's mom whispering in her ear, "I can't possibly ever repay you for bringing Kelly here today."

She whispered back, "*You* are a repayment…more than you know," and with that she kissed him on the cheek.

Mrs. Stewart just stared at Rick and Sean.

"I never saw two more handsome men in my whole life," she said. "I swear if I was twenty years younger neither one of you would be safe."

"Excuse me, ma'am," Rick said. "I dare say, I am the war fighter here and that it is *you* who would be in grave danger."

"Oh, you are so fresh," Mrs. Stewart said waving her hand.

Sean, taking Kelly into his arms, reached across his chest and removed his wings and pinned them on Kelly's pink cashmere sweater. "They look much better here, in fact pretty, on you."

Rick, eyes wide, open mouth and a smile of surprise said, "Hold on, cowboy! You know what you just did?"

Kelly and her mom, not sure what Rick was talking about, just looked around as if looking for someone to tell them what had happened.

"What…what did he do?" said Kelly in amazement.

Sean, knowing exactly what pinning his sweetheart meant, took Kelly by her left hand and holding it in both of his, said, "Kelly, make me the happiest man on earth and marry me."

Kelly's eyes filled up instantly, her mom's almost as fast. Rick was not far behind. Kelly instantly hugged him saying, "I loved you from the moment you and Rick faked that stupid fight. I *will* marry you and promise to love you always."

"Congratulations, Sean," Rick said shaking his hand. Turning to Kelly he gave her a kiss on the lips to let her know that he approved.

Upon seeing the commotion and the wings on her chest, the other members of Class 43-F came over and gave congratulations to the both of them.

Rick just stood back with Mrs. Stewart and took in this most blessed scene of deserved happiness.

Mrs. Stewart said, "This is a day that shadows the best of dreams. I wish her father could be here to see this. He would have been so proud of her and both of you boys."

"Sean has a great lady. Much like her mother, I feel," Rick said looking at Kelly's mom.

"You are a sweet man, Rick. I know how you and Kelly feel about each other, the dearest of friends, and we both know how you feel about Lucia. Things will work out for you. It is a woman's instinct, strong, true and sure as life and death but you and Lucia will be together. I don't know how or when or by what means but I feel it."

With a distant stare, Rick said, "It seems ages ago that I held her. I can still feel her kiss and the smell of her hair," he said inhaling. "I remember her smile when I gave her that lighthouse pendant and the tears that fell off her cheek when she told me she had to go back to Italy."

"I remember the pendant," she said. "It was beautiful. She never took it off."

Then looking back at Mrs. Stewart, Rick said, "I have an intuition too, Mrs. Stewart. I feel I will see her again." Then, repeating what she said a minute before, he said, "I don't know how, when or by what means those events will happen but I feel it is inevitable."

Both smiled, certain in the feelings for the other and of their future.

Sean walked over and said, "Rick and I are going to get out of our uniforms and we'll get out of here. We know of a nice place by the lake in town where we can have a nice lunch."

"OK, that is fine but I'm buying dinner. No arguing. I'm still the adult here," said Kelly's mom.

After a fine afternoon by the lake catching up on things, they all went to a fine dining restaurant near the edge of a grove of trees in town. Rick was told that Bodie Lighthouse was being used by the military as a lookout for German U-Boats which were known to patrol the water off the shores of the Outer Banks.

"Because of the patrols the light has been extinguished," Mrs. Stewart said.

"Not forever, right?" Rick said with some concern.

"No, of course not, but right now Bodie is marking the American shore and we don't want to help the Germans in their navigation. You knew of the seven ships sunk in January '42. Every month since then you can see fires out at sea. It really was just a matter of time. It's pretty scary seeing the Germans that close."

"Yeah, I know," Rick said. "I just hope the coast watchers don't trash the place up. I'm sure they are in the caretaker's house. I have some sentimental things there."

"I know you do but there is absolutely nothing we can do about that."

Kelly interjected, "I will go over when I get back to take a look around."

"That's fine, Kelly," her mom said, "but you will not go alone." Then turning to Rick said, "We both will go over and let you know how it's going."

Rick just nodded.

The announcements for the wedding were sent out via Western-Union telegram to Rick's parents and, of course, the Ryans. Kelly sent one to Lucia addressed simply "Lucia Bellamonte, Bellamonte Vineyards, San Gimignano, IT." Kelly was hopeful that it would reach her but, like Rick, hoped it would not draw too much attention to her by those who would threaten her security. She certainly did not expect a response but hoped that the note found her well.

The wedding was to take place on Saturday, July 10 at the base chapel. It would give time for people to make arrangements at home, get transportation to Texas and for visits with family. It would also allow time for Sean and Kelly to be together as husband and wife before reporting for duty in Utah.

Rick's parents arrived a couple of days prior to the wedding and were overwhelmed with emotion when they saw Rick and Sean, who eleven months previous were boys running around on the beaches of North Carolina. Now they were wearing military uniforms, commissioned officers, and ready to lead men into combat. Rick's mom never let Rick out of her sight. Rick was elated to have her there. The families from Manteo who meant the most to Rick and Sean were there. It was a fabulous week with picnics and tours of the base. They showed the airplanes they flew, introduced their family and friends to new friends, and went on country drives. Rick's parents were never prouder of their boy and his far-reaching accomplishments.

The wedding had a small quaint service since many of their classmates had already left for their next duty station and training. Tab and Bunky stayed back as did a couple of other guys in their class who had orders to Salt Lake City. Mr. Weldon let Sean borrow his car for the trip to Chaprock Canyon less than 100 miles northeast of Lubbock for their honeymoon. The officers of

Class 43-F pitched in and rented a cabin for a week in the canyon by the lake owned by the mayor of Lubbock. Beautiful and pristine, it was the perfect getaway for Sean and Kelly; a great place for a new start.

Everybody had left after a great week vacationing in Texas. It was decided, because of the uncertainty of Sean's training schedule and the rigors that were certain to accompany him, that Kelly should return home to Manteo and try to find a house for the two of them to live when he returned from the war. Besides, Kelly's mom needed help managing the business which was taking off and making money. The business expanded because of the company's reputation at Bluethenthal Field at Wilmington. There, they were building barracks, administration and operation buildings for service members in the defense of the North Carolina shore line and for the training of P-47 pilots.

Rick and Sean along with Tab and Bunky left by bus to Salt Lake City where, upon arrival, they were told that they have been categorized as "1022," meaning that they were now twin-engine certified pilots and that their orders have been updated, having them report to the 463rd Bomb Group (BG) at Rapid City, South Dakota, by August 19. They were also told that the 463rd was the newest Bomb Group being activated August 1 with four squadrons of B-17s. "You guys will be some of the first reporting in because of your graduation date. You will be assigned a squadron when you get there," said the staff non-commissioned officer in charge of the orders-processing section.

"That's it," the new second lieutenants thought. "We are really going to be bomber pilots and fly the B-17."

"All of the hard work has paid off, Tab," said Rick.

"Yep, now all we have to do is study a little harder and learn to survive," Sean said to the others.

Bunky said to Sean, "Don't get too caught up in surviving. Just fly the plane. Survival will come if you just do your job. Stay in formation, keep tight and keep your head. If you worry too much about surviving, you will go crazy."

"He's right," said Rick. "Let's just concentrate on the task at hand. Fate is out of our control now. What happens, happens."

While in Utah, all of the officers qualified on the .45-cal. pistol. Classroom instruction continued with practical experience with malaria control, flight crew discipline, and flight training in the altitude pressure chamber. Being able to detect and recognize hypoxia, which is the lack of oxygen to the brain at altitudes above 10,000 feet, could save a life, even your own. Hypoxia training continued with the use of the oxygen mask (O_2 mask) which every crew member was required to be completely proficient and comfortable with by the time they went flying. Their first flight in the B-17 was to occur at Rapid City.

Training was fast and furious as they were in their last stretch before shipping overseas. Nobody knew for sure, just yet, where they were going because simulated map missions were planned over European and Southwest Pacific targets. Mission planning was critical as it gave the pilots, navigators and bombardiers an appreciation of how each position in the crew had an important and crucial role to play in the successful accomplishment of the mission and survival in the skies. Each member of the crew intricately depended on the other. Without the navigator they could not find the target. Without the bombardier the bombs would miss the target; and without the radio operator, communications would not be possible. That became vividly obvious when mistakes were made in training.

While in Camp Rapid everybody was assigned to one of four Bomber Squadrons (BS), 772nd BS, 773rd BS, 774th BS and the 775th BS. Rick and Tab were assigned to the 772nd and Sean and Bunky were assigned to the 773rd. Sean and Rick were disappointed that they could not fly together but counted their blessings that they got this far without splitting up.

"Besides, as tight as we will fly formations anyway you might as well be in the same cockpit," said Tab.

After a month in South Dakota the group moved to the Army Air Force School of Applied Tactics at Orlando, Florida, from which, after a month of more ground school, moved to Montbrook, Florida, which was about 130 miles north of Orlando where they started actual training in the B-17.

Tab and Bunky were selected to be part of the "model crew" to pick up the first B-17s for the group and train in the model to become flight instructors for the rest of their respective squadrons. They were asked to recommend who they would want as their crew and, of course, Rick and Sean were chosen. Rick and Sean were elated that they were going to be some of the first to fly in the new 463th BG. Days later they began the swift and intensive flight training.

The commanding officers, Captain George D. Burges of the 772nd and Captain James W. Patton of the 773rd, signed off on the assignments because they knew of the close relationships the four of them had and of their fine performance in basic and advanced flight training. Each commander knew that a model crew had to mirror Colonel Kurtz's accurate guidance that "Only through close and harmonious cooperation could the group accomplish its mission" and that began with crew cooperation and coordination. Being the best of friends was a reliable step in the right direction.

LUCIA
WHERE YOU ARE

With each squadron getting one plane each, every plane was scheduled to fly as much as the maintenance crews could allow. Familiarization flights led to the more complex formation flying. Close is close but when you are flying a big plane like the B-17 close seems too close. Along with time in the aircraft comes familiarity and after a while everybody got comfortable with the positions and distances required to be maintained by each bomber in the flight.

Missions were planned to cities of the southeast United States, training each model crew until "proficient." They returned back to Camp Rapid on September 29 to train the rest of the group that had been accumulating personnel for flight crews. Rick and all the others who had ventured forth from Rapid City were now poised to train an entire group of pilots and aircrews.

October came and went fast as being mentally occupied will make time short. The entire group moved to MacDill Field in Tampa, Florida, to continue flight training. Once they reported to MacDill, they found that it was a makeshift twin-engine base which was quickly modified to accommodate the massive B-17, their crews, and support personnel. Without missing a beat, the men of the 463rd unpacked their gear and made themselves comfortable in their little olive-green canvas homes away from home. Green tents were everywhere. They had an indirect purpose though; as they helped the new crews get acclimated to the weather and the hardships that were ahead. Nobody really complained of the conditions as they knew that the situation could be a lot worse than it was and could certainly, in fact most probably, be worse where they were going.

On November 10 the group has its first accident and fatalities. The 774th had a midair while flying formation near Tampa, killing all members of one crew. The other plane returned safely to base despite major damage to her wing. Rick and Sean knew all the crew members and grieved over their loss. Both solemnly knew that this was just the beginning.

Crews were checking in by the dozens every week, some with B-17 experience and some brand new from other training commands. The senior crews served as flight leaders, which the rookie pilots were pleased to see. Their experience and professionalism proved comforting and instilled confidence in the new crews. It proved, by example, that hard work and respect for the dangers that are innate with the profession can serve as your lifeboat when called upon in a crisis.

Simulated bombing missions were conduced with large formations to

Columbia, South Carolina, and Brunswick, Georgia. Those missions included P-47 fighters to serve as cover and aggressor aircraft.

"The training was remarkably realistic," said Captain Spearman flying the lead aircraft of the formation at the debriefing. "Imagine them trying to kill you and you still won't feel the fear that you will have facing down the gun barrel of a Me-109 shooting white lightning right at your head. Seconds seem like eternity and home seems like a million years ago."

The debriefing was silent.

"Start getting used to it. On this mission everybody came back. Over there," pointing to Germany on a huge map hanging from the ceiling, "expect losses to be as high as thirty percent. That means that the chances are good that thirty percent of you who enter a flight briefing won't be there for the debriefing. Fear is good. We all have it regardless of how many missions we have under our belt. It is fear that will keep you alive and sharp. But don't under any circumstance let it cloud your judgment. You will develop habits when you train. It is the habits that will take over when your brain freezes from fear and shock. It is the repetitive training that will save your ass. Train hard and live. Fly straight and level and for God's sake stay tight. There is strength in numbers. That is how we get bombs on target and that, gentlemen, is our sole purpose to even exist."

Colonel Kurtz walked to the front of the group and said, "Gentlemen, nice mission. Next month we will be inspected by the Third Air Force after we arrive at Drane Field in Lakeland. I expect the mission they will assign will be similar to this one but be ready for anything and anywhere. One other bit of information I want to share with you now, that I got from HQ about an hour ago We are to join up with the Fifteenth Air Force between mid to late February. As some of you might already know the Fifteenth is a new Air Force pieced together from units of the Eight, Ninth and Twelfth Air Force in one way or another. It is hoped that by flying out of Foggia, Italy, Celone Airfield to be exact, we can help to bring this war to a speedy and noble end. Attacking targets from bases in Italy we can open a new air front. We can fly when English bases are socked in. When they can fly we can combine our efforts through coordinated attacks and hit them from two sides vice a predicted and expected westerly one. OK, that's it for now. Squadron commanders, get 'em moving."

With a small turn of his head Rick faced Sean after being called to attention and being dismissed. A slow thoughtful smile appeared on Sean's face. Rick had a stoic appearance.

"Can you believe what I just heard," said Sean in total disbelief.

Rick just stood there. Not a word.

"We are going to Italy, Rick. Did you hear me?"

Rick began a smile but slowly retracted it when concern came over him.

"What the hell is the matter with you?" Sean asked.

"I want to be her life, not her end," said Rick. "I never really thought that I might be bombing her home!"

"We are being based in Italy, partner. Italy surrendered in September. We are not enemies anymore."

"I know that, but the Germans are still there and we have to push them out, which means bombing them and destroying where they are."

"Relax, Rick. Let's get a map and see just where everything is. That will put things in perspective."

After finding a map in the operations tent they opened it and found Foggia near the ankle of Italy off the Adriatic coast.

"I know we have been bombing the crap out of this area from the intelligence briefings we have been getting. We must have the area secured now if they are considering putting us there," Sean said pointing to Foggia area.

Tracing the map with his finger he searched intensely for San Gimignano. "How do you spell it?" Sean asked.

"Man, I don't know. Italian is spelled just like it sounds. S-a-n G-i-a-m-a-n-o."

Getting frustrated, Sean said, "I can't find it anywhere. Did Lucia ever say or give a hint as to where it is near, any clue at all?"

"Yeah...yeah, she said it was south of Florence."

"OK, that's good. Here is Florence. Damn, no wonder we couldn't find it. You spelled it wrong first of all. It is just a little speck on the map. A little bit of nothing. I don't see any tactical significance to that area at all."

Rick thinking a bit more said, "Find Sienna."

"Sienna? Why?"

"Just find it."

"Any idea where *it* might be?"

"I don't think it is far from San Gimignano."

"You're right. Here it is. Just southeast. It is a bigger town. Why are you interested in Sienna?"

"Because if she got married like she said she had to, she might be living *there* with him," Rick said as a matter of fact.

"Wow, Rick. This complicates things a bit."

"How do you mean?" Rick said just to get Sean's interpretation of the situation. Rick knew immediately the gravity of Lucia's geographical position after finding it on the map.

"Germans are sure to be in this area," Sean said pointing to the Tuscany region on the map. "It is too far north of Salerno or Rome, for that matter, for them not to be. We know for a fact they still occupy the western coast of Italy, because Patton pushed them there from Sicily. Rome and north," Sean said pausing, "and Sienna and San Gimignano are in the middle between Rome and the Alps."

The look on the two faces told the story of their feelings better than any novelist could ever attempt. Rick folded the map and placed it in his pocket without another word being said by either of them. Rick knew from reports that the Germans were notorious for wanton destruction when they withdrew from a city or town.

Walking back to their tent Sean said, "One good thing runs in our favor and in Lucia's. If she is in San Gimignano it is unlikely she is being harassed by the German's because she is in the country away from industry and government. Because of that very reason *we* should not be interested either. If she is in Sienna there is more risk but it still seems to me to be an insignificant place, tactically speaking."

"Agreed but we need to get more information to be sure."

"It would be helpful if we knew where for sure she is and what she is doing, married or not."

"I know, Sean, but her situation is difficult because of me and her feelings for me. Before she left we both agreed that communication would have to stop as she could not risk having anybody find out about us. We both feel that something will happen that will allow us to be together. We just cannot push things to happen, they just have to."

"Understood. With that said, let's just keep our eyes and ears open and find out all that we can."

Sean was completely committed to Rick and his mission. Best friends owe it to each other to help, support, and comfort the other when needed. Sean knew that Rick was troubled and that there was not much that he could do that would affect a positive outcome now. A faith in God and the righteousness of the American cause was all both of them had and for now it had to be good enough.

8

On February 2 and 3 the ground crews, support and administration staff left for Camp Patrick Henry in Newport News, Virginia, to begin their long trip by ship to Foggia, Italy. The bomber crews with some maintenance crews and spare parts flew from Florida to the Caribbean then on to Brazil. After a night's rest and some repairs to the aircraft they continued their longest leg to North Africa with an intermediate stop in the Azores for refueling. From North Africa they flew to Sicily then on to Foggia. Acceptable losses by the Air Force on ferry flights were ten percent but the 463rd made it over without the loss of a single plane.

Everybody within the 463rd met up at Celone by the beginning of March. They quickly assembled working parties to repair the damage sustained to block buildings and runways by the concentrated allied bombings of '43. The Foggia airfields were used by the Luftwaffe and the best way to make any airfield untenable is to put craters in it and destroy every aircraft and support building possible. Allied bombers did just that but now what made the airfield unusable to the Germans made it unusable to the Americans, so it had to be repaired. Fortunately, much of the runway repairs at Celone were done prior to the arrival of the 463rd bombers by local villagers looking for work, and army personnel assigned from other squadrons already in the Foggia area.

Tents became living quarters for most of the airmen until makeshift wooden barracks could be built and stone buildings on and around the field could be repaired or modified for use. Some of the senior staff found accommodations in renovated barns but most lived and operated in what was constructed by them.

Most notably about Celone were the destitute living conditions of the local people. The absolute innocence of the children, and helplessness of the parents, would make the strongest man weep and on occasion did. Among the destruction, and crumbling rubble that years of war and deficiency would bring, was the strongest sense of family Rick had ever seen. Everybody worked for the other and everybody shared. At first the Italian people were cautious about the neat, clean, and generous Americans but they quickly warmed up to them to the point that it became a problem with security. The Americans, knowing the cruelty and abstinence they had to endure under Mussolini and under German occupation and the Allied bombing, didn't have the heart to deny them anything, so when conditions allowed they would give them what they could.

Basic necessities such as food were scarce for the Italian people. The American mess tents and the dumps surrounding them were a hive of activity. It was heart-wrenching to see kids of every age, and some elderly women, going through the garbage to find some morsel they could take back to their meager homes to begin soup, or spice up a potion of marinara sauce. The Italian people are ingenious and made the best pasta with nothing more than tomato sauce, a chicken breast and some herbs they would find in their desolate garden. Once rapport was established with the locals, airmen would be invited to an Italian family's home for a simple yet joyous and generous supper. It was obvious that the effort to put together such a meal in light of the scarcity of food took great effort from, oftentimes, a community of families. This did wonders to establish a trust and love for cultures so different and separated by thousands of years of history.

Young, healthy American boys met old-world and traditional Italy. The Italian people around Celone were not uncommon in their warm spirit and hospitality. This story was told everywhere that Americans stayed and interacted with the culture. The smiles and warm touches which were often accented by a kiss on the cheek by the mothers and grandmothers, defined a genuine appreciation that came from the deepest part of the soul that when felt by the young naive heart of America's finest children anodized their hearts forever.

Generosity and graciousness was introduced to the men of the 463rd in March '44. They came to liberate but what they didn't expect was to be themselves liberated from the confusion that was often born from hate and bias. The men realized quickly, while in Italy, that the killing that they would be called to do was not prejudicial in any way but a call to duty, to do the right thing for the world, to help others who could not help themselves. If for nothing else, the 463rd was there to show the helpless people of the world that there was hope and it lived upon the wings of their Flying Fortresses and within the hearts of the crews flying and supporting them.

On March 22, Mt. Vesuvius erupted destroying eighty-eight B-25 Mitchell twin-engine light bombers of the 340th Bomb Group located near Pompeii. The men of the 463rd hoped that a reconnaissance of the area could be made so they could see it but that idea fell quickly to the side as they readied for their first combat mission. There was still much work that had to be done.

Rick was flying as co-pilot on his first mission on March 30 until he got at least five combat missions under his belt. He flew with Captain John Schuler, who had twenty combat missions with the Eighth Air Force before being reassigned to the Fifteenth. Most crews had an experienced combat pilot flying with them for the first several missions because of the certain fear the novice crews would experience. Having a combat veteran in command helped to calm nerves and on the first missions any calming effect was welcomed.

Rick's crew was established and was flying with him on the mission to Imotsky, Yugoslavia, to bomb an aerodrome (airfield) there. The briefing did not spell out any real intense threat such as fighters or flak but they always prepared for the worst. Rick's crew was the same that flew over with him to Celone from Florida a month ago, minus Tab, who was sick with the flu. It would have been Rick who would have sat out the first missions but as fate would have it Tab was the one who got sick, which made selecting the first pilot easy. It was decided by the crew that they would not name their plane until after their first five missions and as tradition would have it, the pilot, Second Lieutenant Rick Hamilton, would have the honor.

Everybody got along and worked well together as a team. Communication was key and the men exercised it freely within the confines of procedure and necessity. Nobody had any problem communicating to the other, regardless of rank or position on the crew. The first mission was tense. Everybody was anxious to get airborne, get there and get back so the countdown to twenty-five or thirty-five missions and a trip home could begin. The number of missions required to get home depended on when you flew your missions, your responsibility and position in the flight or formation. The more important the role, such as flight leader, the sooner you got back stateside.

The crew consisted of ten men, four officers and six enlisted. The officer positions were Captain John Schuler, pilot; Second Lieutenant Rick Hamilton, co-pilot; Second Lieutenant Jim "Jimbo" Titus, navigator/flex gunner; and Second Lieutenant Artie "Boom" Powell, bombardier/flex chin turret gunner. The enlisted crew members were Staff Sergeant Ned "Tweak" Turner, flight engineer/top turret gunner; Sergeant Eddie Hill, radio operator/flex gunner; Sergeant Glen "Lieutenant" Brisco, ball turret gunner; Corporal Robert "Hambone" Hammer, left waist gunner; Corporal Bill "Billy" Cody, right waist gunner; and Corporal Joe "Link" Anderson, tail gunner.

Rick's plane was the lead plane in the third flight of four flights so he would be just below and to the left of the lead with just seventy-five feet of separation between planes. "Practice the way you fight" was all he heard for five months and now he was used to the close proximity and being boxed in.

He was the seventh plane to take off; thirty seconds after the plane ahead of him began his take-off roll Captain Schuler began his by advancing the power levers to full take-off power that Rick finally set as his co-pilot. He lifted off the runway feeling the roughness of the ground being replaced by the softness of the air. He began the gentle turn to take his plane's position in the formation while executing join-up procedures in a left turn. Rick was flying in the right seat on this mission taking mental notes of every maneuver and studying everything that Captain Schuler did. Rick was setting power, adjusting prop RPM and manifold pressure. He was backing up the pilot by verifying flight and join-up procedures such as indicated airspeed (IAS), 150 knots (kts); rate of climb (vertical speed indicator, VSI), 400 feet per minute (fpm); climbing to a join-up altitude of 2,000 feet. All this, while cross-checking engine instruments such as oil pressure, cylinder head temperatures and hydraulic pressure.

Join-up was errorless and the flight was impressive. Thirty nine B-17s fully loaded en route at 20,000 feet, hopefully, to an unsuspecting enemy. Air cover was provided by P-38 Lightnings, which were twin-engine fighters from the 305th Fighter Wing (FW). The P-38s broke off their escort just prior to the flak, which was a serious education in man-made turbulence. Shrapnel was flying everywhere hitting and ripping through all parts of the aircraft. Every plane would experience damage of some kind but most could be patched up quickly.

"Flak has an advertised killing radius of thirty feet," Rick recalled, "but I would bet it would kill at thirty-one!" he remembered telling Tab.

Weather was fair with the target being only partially obscured by clouds and because of that the hits on target were not as effective as they would have liked. One airplane returned with an engine feathered, which meant the engine was failing and the pitch of the props was placed parallel to the airflow. If the engine was allowed to stop without setting the prop to the feathered position drag on that wing would be so great that flying the aircraft would be difficult and if the other engine on the same side was to quit, a descent to mother earth would most probably result. Controlled flight was possible with an un-feathered engine depending on the weight of the plane, battle damage, if any, but it was difficult, so feathering a failing engine before oil pressure dropped below thirty PSI was critical (the prop feathering mechanism was operated from engine oil pressure).

One crew member from 774th BS was injured on the raid but returned to flight status a couple of weeks later. The first mission was exhilarating. A debriefing was conducted by each individual squadron to get a Battle Damage Assessment (BDA) of the target. Weather, formation integrity, and enemy resistance were all points that were thoroughly debriefed and analyzed by operations and intelligence personnel. To sum up the entire day, the group came together to debrief and critique the mission from takeoff to landing.

Colonel Kurtz said, "The target was hit, and they knew we were there but we left sixty percent of the airfield intact." He said that, "The group dropped 117 tons of bombs with no losses of our own."

He was happy about that but also stated that "We have to get better because you never want to go back and revisit a target that knows you are coming."

Captain Schuler said that it was a "milk run," meaning that it was simple and not threatening but a "good introduction to flak without being costly."

Rick went back to his quarters with Sean. Both were quiet about the day, partially because it began at 0400 and they were tired, but mostly because of the adrenalin that was coursing through their bodies for the past ten hours.

Sean looked at Rick while they were walking to get some chow and said, "What do you think?"

Rick shook his head as he said, "I'm sure glad that Captain Schuler was there."

"It's going to get worse. You know that, right? Soon you will be the pilot and will have to take that crew to hell and back and never letting them see you're scared to the point of pissing your pants!"

Rick turned to Sean and said, "What did you think about today?"

"Hell, I was scared shitless. I'm not going to lie. But I never felt prouder in my life. My crew did a marvelous job, every one of them. I just hope I can be the leader they deserve."

"You will, Sean. You are a natural leader and a good pilot."

It's going to take more than good piloting skills to get us through this. You know that, right? Luck is going to have to play a large part."

"And a prayer."

"Yeah," Sean said. After thinking for a moment he said with some excitement, "You know, I think that is what I will name her."

"Name what?" asked Rick

"My plane, *Luck and a Prayer*. No, how about *Kelly's Lucky Prayer?*"

"I like it," said Rick.

"And you? Have you thought about your name?"

"No, not really, I'm too busy thinking about other things right now."

Putting his arm around Rick on the walk he said, "I'm hungry, I hope it is Spam."

With a chuckle, they both went in and devoured a delicious army meal of corn bread, Spam, peas, and powdered mashed potatoes.

The following week began with a mission on April 2 to Brod, Yugoslavia, to destroy the marshalling yards there. Thirty-four planes took off from the 463rd and all returned with the usual damage and combat injuries. Again the results were "poor" but everybody was relieved to be back to terra firma and to get a hot meal.

Rick went to the base infirmary after the debriefing to check on Tab, who was recovering but got a serious ear infection because of the flu. The flight surgeon said he would probably be out for at least a week to ten days.

"He has to have clear ears to fly, you know it and he knows it," the doctor said.

With the B-17 being un-pressurized, having a clear head was an absolute necessity. There were few things more painful than an ear block when descending from high altitude. The pain could render a pilot unresponsive to carrying out even the simplest of procedures. If the pressure did not equalize between the inner ear and the atmosphere a rupture of the ear drum would occur and that could make the pilot a permanent causality, a loss to the squadron.

When Rick got back to the barracks he was told by one of the operations clerks that they would be returning tomorrow to Brod to re-bomb the target. He went to see Captain Schuler, who was in the operations shack looking over the route.

"Hi, excuse me, Captain Schuler, I came over here to see if you knew about the mission tomorrow, but I can see that you do."

"Yep, sure do. I'm glad you are here. You can help me plan the route."

Pointing to the map he said, "We know of 88s here, here and here because they hit us today. If we fly west we put ourselves at risk from 109s and 190s based here and here."

Captain Schuler looking at Rick said, "What do you think, Rick?"

"Since we know where the 88s are and the other routes are more risky, what if we send in P-47s to knock them out before we get there."

Captain Schuler and Major Daye stood there looking at the table for what seemed like ages and called the ops clerk over.

"Call Wing and request the mission. Ask if the Thunderbolts are up to the challenge. We will need the targets silenced by 1100 tomorrow."

"Yes, sir," replied the clerk.

Major Daye looking at Rick said, "It is your flight, Lieutenant. Captain Schuler, let Lieutenant Hamilton brief the mission to his flight tomorrow morning."

"Yes, sir," replied Captain Schuler.

"Let him sign for the aircraft too. This will be your check ride, Lieutenant, for aircraft commander."

"Damn, sir, I just came in here to see if Captain Schuler knew of tomorrow's mission. I'm not sure that…"

"You made an aggressive, and I believe, a sound decision, Lieutenant, a sign of a good leader. That will be all."

Captain Schuler just smiled and walked out to the briefing room with Rick.

"Just relax, Rick. I know this is early for you. Hell, it would be early for anybody, but I will be there with you tomorrow and for the rest of the week."

"What if my decision doesn't work and we lose airplanes and crews?"

"Command is hell and a huge responsibility but decisions have to be made. Don't worry about it though, Rick. Fact is the major and I came up with a similar decision just before you came in. You just validated it."

Rick briefed the mission to the flight with authority and confidence. The weather officer described the weather over the target area and en route. The operations officer described the target and what resistance could be expected. Soon afterwards the bombardiers, navigators, radio operators and gunners went to their own separate and detailed briefings.

After all of the briefings the crews climbed into trucks that would take them to storage sheds where their flight gear was stored. At altitude, temperatures reached minus 10 to 40 degrees below zero Fahrenheit. So crews had to dress appropriately. The men would begin the long ritual of first putting on their long thick winter underwear, wool socks, wool-lined flight boots, dark olive-drab wool trousers and shirts, sheepskin-lined leather B-3 jackets, wool trousers and flight gloves. Pilots would strap on a shoulder holster with an —1911, semi-automatic Colt .45. Once at the plane pilots would strap on their parachutes. Other crew members would stow them in the airplane near their station and put them on if needed. Once on board, the crew would also put on wool-lined leather head and communications gear. With all this winter equipment on and at minus 40 degrees, you could still sweat because you were scared to death. There were two problems associated with sweating at altitude. One was the freezing that comes afterwards in their clothes and second was the frost from the condensation on the crewmen's goggles making them opaque. Aircrew had to deal with these issues every time they flew, and got good at it after a while. Gunners even had to practice assembly, disassembly, loading and clearing their .50 cal's with gloves on; a near impossible task but necessary in order to keep them firing.

The group took off with thirty-nine planes and returned with thirty-nine planes. One bomber flew under a flak burst and had debris penetrate his number one and two fuel tanks, resulting in a landing with minimum fuel for number one and two engines. A slow leak was still seen dripping from under the wing after landing, so it was parked down the field and away from all other aircraft in case of fire. Flak was minimal with only a few German fighters attacking the group.

P-47s were nowhere to be seen as their attack was low and earlier in the day. Rick was looking forward to seeing his first P-47 in combat, especially since he requested their help.

Rick passed his command ride and was initiated by his crew and Captain Schuler upon arrival by having a cold Pabst Export Beer poured over his head. Rick was the first to make aircraft commander under combat conditions in the 463rd. Colonel Kurtz was on the apron when Rick's plane arrived to be the first to shake his hand. Fact is, however, Colonel Kurtz was the second because Captain Schuler shook Rick's hand after the battery power was secured in the airplane on shut down congratulating him on a great flight.

After Rick eased himself down from the nose of the bomber through the small hatch just under the cockpit he walked over to Colonel Kurtz.

"Congratulations, Lieutenant," said Colonel Kurtz with a strong handshake. "Nice mission."

"Thank you, sir, I hope my crew is ready for me."

"They are ready, Lieutenant, or Major Daye, Captain Schuler, and Major Patton would not have made the recommendation that you get the ride so early. How do you think the mission went?" asked Colonel Kurtz.

"From where I was sitting I know we hit the target. Tail End Charlie had the best view."

"Don't weasel around the answer, Lieutenant," Colonel Kurtz replied with playful amusement. "How do *you* think we did?" he inquired again looking for a more direct answer.

"Good, sir. The results will be better than the day before. We had a better spread over the target area and had some pretty impressive secondary explosions."

"Now that is an answer," the group commander said, giving Rick a firm pat on the sleeve of his right arm. He returned Rick's salute and walked down to the next B-17 to meet Major Patton, who was just securing his engines.

On April 6 a mission was planned to Zagreb, Yugoslavia, to hit another aerodrome. It was to be Rick's last flight with Captain Schuler and he was not anxious to see him go. Rick was the pilot since it was his plane and his crew. Captain Schuler knew Rick needed the command experience so assumed all of the co-pilot responsibilities. He was glad to do it for a number of reasons. First, because by right, Rick would be there for the long term. The 772nd was his squadron and this was his crew. He would have to lead these men. Second, because he needed to show the crew that he had every confidence that Rick had what it took to take these men into harm's way and back again, day after day. Rick's crew had a lot of faith in Rick but he had yet to be really combat tested. No one in the crew had. Seeing what they had seen so far, no one was anxious to see an Me-109 up close.

In the morning briefing the crews were told to expect more enemy resistance than in the past so everybody tightened their boots a little tighter and did a better job inspecting their Browning .50-cal. machine guns. Rick was going to be the right wing of the second (high) flight. He knew it was one of the most vulnerable positions but everybody had to take their turn. Now was as good a time as any.

Soon after take-off the gunners test fired their weapons and did their last area inspections before entering "the box," which was where the Germans pre-aimed their anti-air (flak) batteries, the worst of which was the dreaded 88mm shell. The box was a mile square by 2,000 feet deep piece of sky that the B-17 and B-24s were expected to fly into. Just prior to entry into the box the

Germans would open up with everything they had. Fuses in the shells were set at or above the predicted altitudes but usually no higher than 20,000 feet, which was the maximum range for the 88mm. After a shell exploded, if the force of the explosion didn't do any outright damage the falling metal shards of debris formed a deadly metal shower that the bombers had to fly through did. Flak was feared the most by the crews because it was an indiscriminate killer and nearly impossible to defend against except by avoidance. There were only two things an aircraft could do to avoid being hit by the flak. First, was to fly over the maximum exploding altitude, which was not always possible. Second was to avoid overflying the anti-air emplacements all together. Problem was their position was not always known and sometimes you had no choice.

It was felt by General LeMay of the Eighth Air Force that it would take over 370, 88mm shells to kill one bomber. The Germans estimated 4,000, but in either case it was the basis for the creation of the procedure to just fly straight and level through it as you are just as likely to evasively maneuver or "jink" into a shell.

At a hundred miles out from the target area a flight of bandits were spotted from the northeast. They came in a swarm that hit the left side of the formation first. Concentrated .50-cal. fire from a group of B-17s was the most effective deterrent. The Germans practiced the same massed fire on a target procedure as the gunners in B-17 formations did except they did it as they swarmed into the tight formations. Two bombers were noticeably hit as smoke began to trail from their wings. After they flew past and through the formation, like pesky flies, some attacked the right side while others attacked the rear of the formation, namely "Tail End Charlie."

Tweak saw a section diving in from the right side high from his top turret.

"Bandits, three o'clock high, yours, Billy."

"I see 'em too," said Eddie from the radio flex gun.

"Got 'em," Billy said beginning his burst of 600 rounds per minute from his black sixty-four-pound beauty.

"He's going under, Lieutenant!"

While he was saying it, Glen "Lieutenant" Briscoe had already begun is twin .50-cal. burst swinging and rolling the ball turret as he flew by.

No sooner did the fighter pass to Lieutenant than Link broadcast through the headset, "I have one doing a dead run at our six," as he was blasting the Messerschmitt with his twin .50s.

Rick's plane took hits in the left wing and number two engine from the Me-109's 13mm guns.

"She's coming under!"

Lieutenant caught him, guns blazing from the underside.

"Passing to you, Boom!" Lieutenant said.

"Finally I get a shot," Boom said shooting his twin .50s as the Me-109 scatted away.

After their first run with the enemy Rick did a radio check, "Is everybody OK? Link, you back there?"

"Yes, sir, skipper, whew!"

"Lieutenant?" Rick called.

"Ball's good," Lieutenant said.

"Billy? Hambone?"

"Good here, skipper," said Hambone. "You might want to look at number two though. She is smoking a little and it looks like we are leaking fuel and oil."

Captain Schuler tapped on the oil gage for number two and said, "Right now pressure is good, RPM is good, number two tank is lower than the rest."

"Keep an eye on number two and adjust power as necessary to keep her up with her sisters. Let me know if oil pressure drops below thirty-five. We won't transfer fuel unless we have to."

Rick, talking to the crew, said, "Nice shooting, guys. Great passing commands. Keep an eye out in case they are out there waiting for us when we fly back."

"Boom to pilot, flak ahead," the bombardier called from the nose of the airplane.

"Hold on, guys. This is going to be a rough ride."

Captain Schuler, looking straight ahead then looking at Rick, said, "Now this is flak. This won't be a milk run. You are going to be baptized today."

The flak was thick. Black deadly puffs of shard steel flying everywhere and hitting everything. Maintaining formation without hitting another airplane was a challenge even in smooth air. Keeping within seventy-five feet of another B-17 with razor-sharp steel flying through your thin-skinned airplane, missing your nose by inches, and the pounding of the airplane as it forced its way through exploding air making her jump plus or minus twenty feet in altitude took pure guts and determination.

"We're coming over the target, Boom," Rick broadcasted.

"Hold her steady, Rick. Bomb-bay doors open," called Boom.

"The airplane is yours, Boom," Rick said as he threw the autopilot switch to bombardier. "Don't make us have to come back here tomorrow."

"Almost there," Boom said with concentration guiding his muffled voice.

"Bombs away!" Boom said.

As soon as the call was made, the bomber leaped into the air, becoming 6,000 pounds lighter at an instant. The plane immediately became more maneuverable and playful as Rick took the aircraft back from the bombardier by flicking the autopilot switch to begin the left turn back to Celone. They all knew that the flak was just as deadly going home as it was going to the target. Going through the flak the first time was for country. Going through it the second time was for them, which made it more frightening. Usually the Germans had time to readjust the timed fuses within the shell to the altitude at which the bombers were suspected to be flying at on their return. That made detonations within the formations more frequent so the bombers climbed to 25,000 feet. The egress route was always different from the ingress route to keep the enemy off guard, but that did little to lessen the worry of the crews.

"Link to pilot."

"Go ahead, Link"

"773 has a bomber dropping back. It's trailing smoke pretty bad from number four. From what I can see number three is already feathered."

"Can you tell whose plane it is?" inquired Rick.

"Can't tell for sure because she is out of position but I think it's Whitey's."

"If he can't keep up he will be jumped and finished off if the 109s are out there," said Captain Schuler. Just as he said that two 109s jumped him.

The intercom erupted with chatter.

"Here they come, three o'clock level. Diving right," said Billy shooting.

"Another one, three o'clock off the nose. He is going after the lead," said Tweak.

"Twelve o'clock high. His twenty is shooting!" said Tweak as one round penetrated the aft portion of the right wing.

"Somebody get that son of a bitch!" yelled Billy, catching him as he flew by his gun port at a closure rate of 600 MPH noticing the damage on his side of the aircraft.

"Coming up from below. Your side, Hambone," said Lieutenant over the roar of his guns.

"I see him," said Hambone taking dead aim leading the Me-109 perfectly.

"Nice shooting, Ham," said Tweak as he got his target acquired and let out a twin burst of his own.

"There goes Whitey," said Link.

"Another one is falling away too from 774," said Jimbo.

Captain Schuler said over the radio, transmitting in the blind hoping the 774 crew could hear him, "Get out of there, guys!"

"Any chutes?" said Rick hoping.

"Nothing from Whitey's yet. It is starting to burn. Jesus Christ!" said Link.

"I count five from 774. I don't know who it is," said Jimbo.

The fighters broke off their attack and the usual intercom check began. When the call went to Eddie in the radio compartment there was silence.

"Eddie, check in," called Rick.

Then again, "Eddie, check in, damn it!"

"I'm OK, Skipper. Through all of the excitement I didn't notice I was hit."

"How bad you hit?" Rick asked.

"Not sure."

"Jimbo, check on him," ordered Rick.

After several minutes Jimbo answered back, "His jacket has a big hole in it from the back right side to the front. I can't really tell too much with all his gear on and I don't want to take it off or he will freeze."

"Right...OK, do what you can. Is it serious you think?"

"I don't think so, Skipper."

Approaching Celone, Rick ordered that a red flair be shot to indicate to the ground that they had a wounded crewman aboard. The number two engine operated roughly all the way back but was producing power so they kept it running. The landing gear operated, which they were happy about since the wings and tail sustained some damage. There was aileron or roll-control challenges but nothing that endangered the plane or her crew.

Upon landing they noticed airmen being taken from some aircraft on stretchers. He saw everyone loitering around their airplanes assessing the damage and occasionally looking at the sky seeing who was returning but more curiously asking themselves who wasn't. They knew that two bombers were not coming home and with them were twenty men who would not be having dinner with them that night, twenty bunks that would stay cold and twenty letters that would be written home notifying loved ones that their sons, fathers, husbands, brothers or any combination thereof that constituted a family were missing in action.

Eddie was placed on the stretcher with a bandage wrapped around his waist. He was grazed by a 13mm shot by one of the passing Me-109s. It was mostly a flesh wound but it would require stitches and bed rest for a couple of days.

Rick and Captain Schuler walked around the plane with Jimbo and Boom, who took in the sights and smells of combat survival: leaking fuel, hot engines, hydraulic fluid, oil, soot, and gunpowder filled the air. Holes punctured the aerodynamic surfaces taking the irregular sharp shape of the exploding steel that put them there. There was a shard of loose material on the rudder flapping in the breeze like a little flag.

Captain Schuler looked at Rick and said, "We were lucky today. As odd as it might sound I'm glad I was able to fly with you on this mission. You did really well. Better than some, I have to say," and shook his hand.

"Thanks. Thanks for everything. Thanks for your mentorship and leadership. Hell, thanks for just being there with me," Rick said. Then turning and looking at his crew he said, "We all owe you, I owe you."

Captain Schuler looking up at the nose said, "Well, what are you going to name her? She has a good crew, now she needs a name to fly into combat with."

"I have been giving it some thought and something you said a minute ago gave my thought the finishing touch. How about *Lucky Irishman?*" Rick said. Pointing to the nose, he traced with his finger a four-leaf clover.

"Perfect," Captain Schuler said with a pat on the back. "Who are you going to get to paint it?"

"There is a guy in the mess tent who is a tremendous artist. I will ask him."

"You might want to get him right away. Many planes will be named today and painted."

"I will do it tomorrow," said Rick. "Where are you off to now?" Rick said knowing that Captain Schuler would be reassigned.

"There is always a crew that needs training somewhere," as his eyes panned the airfield. With that said Captain Schuler picked up his parachute and bag, smiled and said with a tilt of his head, "See ya around," and walked towards a truck to give him a ride back to the flight equipment shed.

The next morning after checking on Eddie at the hospital, Rick went to the mess hall for a little breakfast. While in line he saw Private Scot Lowry serving the meal.

"Hey there, Scottie. Want a job?" Rick said in a good mood.

"You finally have a name, sir?" Scot said.

"Yep, sure do, and a little drawing to give you an idea what I want. How about meeting me at my plane, trip seven, after you get done here, say about 0930?" Rick said. "Trip seven" was the last seven numbers on the plane's tail, 231777.

At 0930 sharp Scot arrived at the plane. The flight crew and maintenance ground crews were busy working all over the plane, changing the engine, patching holes, draining the fuel tanks and many other maintenance items that were routine and some not so routine.

Rick was standing by the nose and handed Scot the drawing.

"I want a large four-leaf clover with the words 'The Lucky Irishman' written across the top. At the four o'clock position of the clover I want this painted."

Rick handed Scot the picture of Lucia sitting by a rose bush at Tryon Palace.

"Wow, sir," Scot said lustfully.

"Don't give me that wow crap. Can you do a good job putting her picture there?"

"I'm better than most. It will look like her when I am done."

"Great. I've seen your work and you are good. That is why I chose you. Also paint on five bombs."

"It will be ready before you go on your next mission. Now, about payment," Scot said looking at the nose gun.

"What would you like?" Rick asked.

"I want a ride…on a combat mission," Scot said seriously.

"Hold on there, Scottie," Rick said, not being anxious to bring a non-combatant into combat. "How about cash? Combat mission? That's dangerous. I don't know…"

"Come on, Skipper. I will never get to fly in one of these things as a cook and I want to be able to tell my mom, dad, kids one day that I went on a mission over Germany."

Rick, being very hesitant about this risky deal but understanding his enthusiasm said, "OK, but I choose the mission. Lucky for you, you can't weigh more than 120 pounds, otherwise there would be no way. But I could probably swing it…as replacement aircrew…but only if you do a great job on the painting!"

Scot did do a great job. Fact is, it almost looked exactly like the photograph. Rick was very happy with it and the crew loved the fact that a beautiful lady rested her head on the nose of their plane.

Tab joined the crew for their next sortie on April 20 to Vicenza, Italy, which was far from where Lucia was suspected to be. Weather being what it was, it overcast the target so all the airplanes kept their bomb load until over the Adriatic Sea, where they dumped their loads and returned to base. American crews almost never dropped their bombs unless they could positively identify the target. Collateral damage to civilian sites was always avoided when possible. The flight turned out to be nothing more than a refresher for Tab, which he was grateful to have had.

April, May, June came and went with thirty-four aircraft losses and 340 men from the 463rd. Rick and Sean were seasoned bomber veterans now, living through several more flights over the expected survival average of fifteen missions for a bomber pilot, crew and airplane. They had seen death up close and personal by witnessing mid-air collisions between B-17s in tight formation, exploding B-17s and B-24s after a direct hit from flak, collisions with enemy fighters out of control after being hit by gunners aboard the bombers, and B-17s having their tails and wings shot off by the 20mm canons from Me-109s and flak. They even saw a B-17 stray into the path of dropped bombs from an aircraft in a higher formation.

Horrific sights of human carnage impressed mortal memory. The crews would never forget watching airmen fall from torn burning wreckage, some with parachutes, some without, some on fire from altitudes of over 25,000 feet. Rick lived through an incident which involved an aircraft in a formation several flights in front of him blowing up suddenly. The crew no doubt had no warning as the nose and the wind screen of *The Lucky Irishman* could testify because she was bloodied with the entrails of her falling crewmen. The serial number from an engine block of the exploding plane was pulled from a leaking fuel tank of Rick's plane two days after they landed.

Flying missions that involved this level of destruction would harden any normal human being. But the airmen of the 463rd were not normal, nor were the airmen of any air force. They were able to categorize and store memories and feelings so they could do their job the next day. They would all distantly remember the events of Polesti, Romania and Wiener-Neustadt, Austria, where the losses on those four missions alone accounted for over fifty-five percent of their total losses up to July 6. They would not purposely recall those vividly dreadful missions because it would cripple their thought processes with cogitations of safety and home. That would jeopardize the mission and their safety and they knew it. Only when it was over, the war was won and the last B-17 had landed would they be able to sit and recall the times from their youth through the nightmares of their dreams and tears from their reunions.

One afternoon in early June after an excellent raid on a submarine base in Pola, Italy, and two days after a good friend from 772 was killed along with his crew over Belgrade, Rick took a quiet walk along the perimeter of the airfield. It was a good time to sort things out, to get in touch with his thoughts and not be bothered with the hustle of the squadron. A lot had happened during the past week and he needed to be alone for a while; everybody does from time to time. He thought of his lost friends and the missions to come. He thought also of Lucia, hoping that she was safe and was thinking of him.

While on his stroll, and on the opposite side of the airfield, he came across a little Italian girl about three years old sitting on a discarded crate just playing with some little beetles. She was wearing a little white dress soiled from a week's activities with little white socks and little brown leather shoes. Her hair was curly brown that fell to the top of her shoulders. Her face was a little dirty, as were her arms and legs, but her cute tiny cherub features were cleanly seen. Rick carefully went over to her so he wouldn't scare her.

Since Rick took one year of intensive Italian his last two semesters in Richmond, he knew just enough to get in trouble but said confidently, "*Ciao.*"

The girl did not acknowledge him right away except by saying and still looking down at her little playmates moments later, "*Ciao,*" right back.

Rick said slowly, "*Che cosa è il vostro nome?*" which is, "What is your name?"

The cute little girl still not looking up said, "*Cara.*"

Rick still trying to search his mind for Italian vocabulary, not practiced for over a year and a half, said, "*Cara,* aaahhh, *quello è un nome grazioso,*" which means, "That is a pretty name."

The girl looked up for the first time and said with a three-year-old's diction and with eyes so blue and clear, "*Desiderate giocare con me ed i miei scarabei?*"

That was about it for Rick's attempt at Italian and he just knelt down beside her knowing she said something about "wanting to play."

Rick looked at her and was curious about where she came from and wondered where her parents were. He stayed there a while practicing international communications with play as the ambassador. She laughed when he picked up a beetle and pretended it was dancing with another one. "What a darling laugh," he thought. It reminded him of Lucia so much.

"*Vivete intorno qui?*" Rick said meaning, "Do you live around here?"

"*Ciao,*" was her cute response pointing to a group of houses about 150 yards away.

"*I vostri genitori sanno dove siete?*" Rick said meaning, "Do your parents know where you are?"

Looking back down to the ground holding her beetle she said, "*No. Il nonno dice che sono andato via.*"

Rick, not catching all of what she said, understood something about her grandfather and her parents being gone. Rick's heart just sank. He had a credible feeling that her parents were dead and she was living with her grandparents. Rick wanted to help immediately so he asked her if he could meet her grandparents. She agreed to take him to where she lived.

"Attesa qui. Sarò giusta parte posteriore. Non si muova," he said which meant, he hoped, "Wait here. I will be right back. Don't move."

Rick ran to the mess hall and grabbed all of the canned goods, meat and vegetables he could carry. Private Lowry helped him pack and carry the box to Cara's house.

Walking to Cara's house he noticed the carnage that war brought up close. Debris and broken walls were everywhere but, in light of all that the villagers have been through, "Not too bad," he thought. "Other than some rubble the place is clean." The dwelling could hardly be considered a house but it was certainly a home because love filled the space from wall to wall. Cara's grandmother was shocked at first by the arrival and appearance of Rick and Scot with her granddaughter, but the smiles on the faces of Rick and the way Cara was holding Rick's finger indicated that the visit was respectful and friendly, which immediately put Cara's grandmother at ease.

"Hi, please excuse the intrusion. I mean no disrespect..." Rick said, stopping suddenly realizing that Cara's grandmother did not understand English. Rick's brain was working at maximum capacity since he saw Cara, trying to recall the Italian linguistic processes. Being so excited, confusion garbled his thoughts. He took a couple of slow indiscreet breaths and looked at Cara to calm down. He found remarkable calm in Cara which served to sooth his mind. He found the words and their arrangements surprisingly easier after composing himself.

Rick tried again saying, "OK, ah, *Buona sera. Ho visto Cara giocare dall'aerodromo ed ho desiderato portarvi questi. È una ragazza piccola molto graziosa,"* which meant, "Good evening. I saw Cara playing by the airfield and wanted to bring you these. She is a very pretty little girl."

Cara's grandmother was very appreciative of the box and his attempt to speak Italian and said, *"Grazie."* Then looking down at Cara, who was by now at her grandmother's side said, *"Cara, non dovreste andare là. È pericoloso."* which meant, "Cara, you should not go over there. It's dangerous."

Rick did not want the little sweetheart to be in trouble, and said with a big heart, *"Non era in alcun pericolo affatto. Era una signora piccola perfetta. Spero permettiate che me ritorni e visiti."* which meant, "She was not in any danger at all. She was a perfect little lady. I hope you will allow me to come back and visit."

Cara's grandmother nodded in approval. After a short visit and not wanting to overstay their welcome, Rick gestured that they had to be going and showed their respects. The grandmother gave Rick and Scot a lovely hug then placed her hands over her heart. Rick was touched by her warm affection and the elegant class of their customs.

Rick would return on occasion, always bringing food and soda pop. Sometimes Rick would swing by the Amicis' and ask if he could go on a walk with Cara. The first time he asked the Amicis if he could take Cara for a walk he took her to the base and showed her off to his friends and fed her. The Army nurses took an instant liking to Cara. Cara was always smiling and skipping like a little girl should, with her little white garment dressing the dance of her moves. She had an adorable round face and tiny hands. She was a living doll and everybody made a fuss to see who could hold her or talk to her next. Cara never complained and was never seen crying. She was a living example of the innocence lost in the war.

On one occasion, when the nurses heard that Rick was going back to visit Cara, Rick received a doll the nurses at the hospital made from bandages and sheets. It was a beautiful rag doll with hair, made from yarn from an old afghan blanket that one of the nurses had, that could rival any that may be found at Macy's. The doll was laid in a crib made from an empty wooden food crate that had notes from the hospital staff and patients which made a fine and unique mattress. The friendships made through her frequent visits warmed Rick's heart and gave him something to look forward to after a torturous mission where he was surrounded by worry and pain. Every crewman had to find refuge somewhere. Rick found his with Cara and the Amicis.

On another visit, the Amicis invited Rick to dinner and told him to bring a friend. Rick brought Sean and both officers brought gifts of meat, vegetables, milk, Nehi grape and orange soda, and Hershey chocolate for Cara. At dinner Grandpa Amici poured some wine from a bottle he pulled from a cabinet he had in the kitchen. He proudly poured each glass; Rick's and Sean's glass first then his wife and himself. Then he made a toast, *"All'amore degli amici e della famiglia ed all'amore troveremo in altri."*

Sean looked at Rick and whispered, "What did he say?"

Rick replied in a tone loud enough so everybody at the table could hear, "To the love of friends and family and to the love we will find in others." He raised his class toasted Sean's glass then each Amici, including Cara, who was holding a glass of milk that Rick brought over that day.

"That was nice," Sean said. "Did you notice the name on the bottle?"

Rick taking a hard look at the bottle that was next to Grandpa Amici noticed the label. On it was, *"Vigne Toscana Chianti Di Bellamonte, 1942,"* which translated to, "Bellamonte Vineyards Tuscany Chianti."

Rick's heart stopped. "She's alive and well," he thought.

Sean through the corner of his mouth said excitedly, "This is a sign."

Rick was certain it was a sign also. Time would tell. She was close and he could feel it.

July 7 began with the usual briefings. This day was going to bring Rick and most of the 5th, 47th and 49th Bomb Wings along with fighter support from the 306th Fighter Wing flying P-51 Mustangs together. The briefing room was a large barn with cinder blocks placed every five feet with a board lying across them forming a bench. In front was a stage raised about four feet off the ground so everybody could see the briefer and tactical map. Behind Colonel Kurtz was a large curtain covering the thirty-foot by ten-foot map. After the colonel discussed the group's bombing results, their navigation, formation flying, and gunnery from the previous mission he made recommendations to the improvements that had to be made. The colonel then began to talk about the mission the men were about to embark upon that morning. A hush came over the 260 men of the twenty-six bombers that were going to fly when the curtain opened revealing the target. The target was the oil refineries and shipping sites in Blechhammer, Germany, which meant heavy flak and strong resistance from enemy fighters.

"This will be a real test of your intestinal fortitude, men," the colonel said. "The flak will be the most intense you will see to date and many of you will not be here tomorrow for the next mission. There is no sense in sugarcoating this one. You guys better be ready. Put a couple of extra chocolate bars in your pocket. The fact is, if we can deny the enemy the fuel he needs to run his tanks and aircraft this war will end sooner and American lives will be saved. We have to score big today gentlemen. The Fifteenth is determined to take this target out so has committed much of its resources to this mission. Steady hands, aim true and stay tight."

It was going to be a real battle and every man knew it. The weather officer briefed the crews next. Weather was predicted to be fair en route and over the target. Dew point temperatures were narrowing because of a cold front pushing through so fog could be a problem late in the afternoon on the return flight but most likely only in the hilly regions in northern Italy.

After the ride over to the plane in one of the weapons trucks, Rick and his crew gathered under the nose by the beautiful four-leaf clover and painting of

Lucia and eighteen bombs. Private Scot Lowry was getting his ride today as the official photographer of the mission and to receive his payment for the wonderful painting on The Lucky Irishman. It was not Rick's choice of a mission for Scot to go on, but pictures of the target area had to be done and Scot volunteered to the operations officer when he asked if anybody had photography experience. Each received the last-minute briefing and tapped the clover with a boost up from Hambone, which was the ritual of good luck for each man.

Intercom checks were conducted as each man inspected his flight equipment, weapons, ammo and oxygen tank. Scottie took up a position in the waist because that is where the best pictures could be taken and not be in the way. The nose would give a nice perspective of the war but it was too cramped with the bomb sight, machine guns and the bombardier near the Plexiglas nose bubble. Scot was hoping the bomb-bay doors would be open long enough to get a good view from there but Rick would not promise anything. There were just too many uncertainties and he was not going to take any chances.

The July morning was surprisingly cool, which made the takeoff easier. Two hundred and fifteen B-17 and B-24 airplanes in tight formation was a sight to see; terrifying if they were coming your way with the intention of "Kicking Your Ass."

Join-up with the group took the usual hour or so and the join-up with the rest of the wing was made en route to the target. En route to the target area the formation was loose but still had integrity in the event they had to "close it up" in a hurry. The flight over the Alps was always a beautiful sight. They added an extra hurdle, however, if you were trying to get back home and were having engine trouble. Flying over them with three engines was not normally a problem. Getting over them with two, unless you were real light, was. Some crews would fly to neutral Switzerland rather than tempt the odds if the trip over the Alps was considered "too risky." Downed aircrews could find a way back to friendly lines if they landed at a friendly airfield or crash landed somewhere in Switzerland. Although the Swiss were considered neutral they did imprison Allied airmen. Most airmen would rather take their chances with the Swiss than with the Germans and some did.

Rick thought that no matter how beautiful something looked from altitude, unfortunately, there was some hazard attached to it. From 20,000 feet the countryside looked so peaceful, the mountains so clean and the water so smooth. He was glad he was a pilot so he did not have to see the gruesome suffering and destruction that war brought on land. He felt that he could help to correct the immoral and viciousness of war by helping Cara get a new and fair start. It was a small thing but in his mind Cara was the best thing that he had ever seen in this war. In her he saw hope and a happy future that was possible with an Allied victory. She was real and deserved a chance and if Rick had anything to do with it she was going to get it. That was his goal at Celone and did something for her and her family every day he could.

About 200 miles from the target area the dreadful words of "Bandits" filled the intercom. Boom in the nose, along with Tweak, alerted the crew of their aggressive approach. Everybody stood at the ready to defend *The Lucky Irishman*, one of the most senior airplanes in the group, like they had done eighteen times before.

"110 at nine o'clock high," called Tweak alerting Hambone. Guns erupted from *The Lucky Irishman* as well as from others in the formation. The Me-110, a twin-engine fighter, sent a burst hitting the *Ole Miss*, the bomber off Rick's right wing, setting her number one engine on fire. Lieutenant finished the 110's pass with a burst that sent the 110 smoking off into the distance.

"Nice shot, Lieutenant!' screamed Billy as he saw it pass under his window.

"That's one confirmed," said Jimbo.

"Two, ten o'clock coming in fast," screamed Tweak obviously excited.

A 110 took dead aim on *The Lucky Irishman* and raked the left wing with 7.92mm bullets clear over to and through the radio operator's compartment. White smoke filled the aft cabin.

"Skipper, Eddie has been hit," yelled Hambone seeing him hit the floor hard.

"Eddie…Eddie, check in," called Rick.

Tab looked at the engine instruments and about at the same time got an intercom call from Hambone yelling, "Fire! Number one engine!"

Rick quickly looked out his window saying to Tab, "She's on fire. Shut her down."

"Number one engine," Tab said asking for the required procedural confirmation.

"Confirm," replied Rick as Tab advanced the prop RPM to max after Rick secured the fuel. Rick then advanced the throttle to purge the engine of fuel.

"Hit the feather button," said Rick.

"Done."

"Generator power, secure."

"Off."

"Set fire selector to one and blow it. Finish the checklist," commanded Rick.

"Fire is out, Skipper," said Jimbo.

"Tweak, get off the gun and help us sort this out," Rick said.

Tweak made his way to the cockpit and looked between the two pilots assessing the situation then looked over to the co-pilot instrument panel where the fuel pressure and fuel quantity gages were.

"Tanks one and two are lower than they should be. Three and four look OK. Temps and pressures are normal. Just keep the power up on the other three. We can transfer if we have to."

"OK," Rick said. After clearing his throat and taking a deep breath he continued, "We can't lose another one if we are going to finish this," Rick said to Tab and Tweak.

"Keep those bastards off us," Rick said to the rest of the crew.

"Right-O, Skip," came the response from the crew.

"Nice job on the EP," said Tweak patting the shoulder of Rick.

"Check on Eddie will ya?" Rick said to Tweak.

After a minute Tweak came over the intercom, "Skip, Eddie is dead."

The plane went silent. It was the first loss of a crewman from Rick's crew. Solemnly Rick said, "Roger, get back to your gun."

"Bandits, six o'clock high," called Link, both guns firing. This time it was an Me-109 shooting fast at the tail of *The Lucky Irishman*. Other aircraft in the formation were firing at it also but the Messerschmitt had his sights on Link and the damaged *Irishman*. The 7.92mm bullets ran through the tail making Swiss cheese of the aft end of the fuselage. Lieutenant picked up the 109 as she flew under. The rest of the crew took notice of the silence from the tail of the aircraft where shooting should have been on the pass.

Billy bent over to look towards the tail gunners' position to see how Link faired in the attack. The sight, from his position, was gruesome with Link leaning to the right side in his seat. Holes in the tail section allowed round beams of white light resembling the bars of a deadly cage to fill the narrow tunnel from the retracted tail wheel to the rear of the wounded plane.

Billy called to the cockpit, "Billy to pilot, I am going to the tail to check on Link."

Rick confirmed the trip and asked him to check out the damage in the tail while he was back there.

After several minutes of trying to contact him over the intercom, Rick got the call from Hambone, who saw the shake of Billy's head as he emerged from the tail gunner's compartment.

"Skipper, Link is gone."

"Tighten up, boys," came a call from Boom. "Flak, dead ahead."

No time to mourn now as Rick held on tight to the controls trying to maintain position in the formation with only three engines and two dead crewmen. The airplane was flying OK. She was still in the game. She was just a little sloppy on the rudder.

Ten minutes from the target area the call "IP, ten minutes" was heard as the formation did a gradual right turn for their final approach tightening up to within seventy-five feet of each other so they could concentrate the group's bomb mass on the target. The American fighters broke off and loitered for the bombers to emerge from the flak on their return trip along the planned egress route. There was no sense in going into the "steel curtain" since the German fighters would not be going in. It was suicide, crazy and the bomber crews knew it which made them a little different from all of the other pilots in the war. The flak was thick as smoke. The briefing was not an exaggeration. A B-24 was seen bursting in mid-air just after entering the box. Another B-24 was hit; both wings immediately caught fire and broke back from the fuselage. It went down, falling to earth like a lit match. A B-17 was seen descending wings level, no smoke or fire from the formation, which would indicate the possible sudden death of both pilots. In a matter of two minutes the flight lost three bombers. Seconds later a single flak burst hit the wings of two B-24s flying close to each other. With the sudden loss of lift from their wings the two bombers flew into each other like the folding of a piece of bread, spreading debris and flaming fuel everywhere behind and below.

The turbulence was so bad Rick wondered how the plane was staying together, especially since his bomber sustained so much damage to the wing and tail. Falling shrapnel was hitting Rick's plane like hail except it was tearing fearful holes through the thin skin. He quickly remembered E.J. and how proud he was at the Boeing plant. "Pride and American spirit built her. She will stay together," were his thoughts. It was all he was flying with.

"Bomb bay open," said Boom.

"Your plane," said Rick as he threw the autopilot switch to the bombardier position.

On this mission Boom's job was easy because all he had to do was "toggle" the bomb release when the lead plane dropped hers. The mission was briefed that if the colonel's plane was unable to complete the mission that Rick's plane was to take the lead, which would make Boom the lead bombardier. Things being what they were, however, Boom just toggled on visual queue.

"Bombs away," Boom said with a sudden lurch of altitude by the plane.

"OK, let's get the hell out of here," Tab said as the flight took a right diving turn to return home flipping the autopilot switch back to "Pilot."

Flak was stronger than ever, at least it seemed that way. The 463rd formations had three planes smoking. Rick noticed that one was Sean's.

"Pilot to Hambone, confirm that it is *Kelly's Lucky Prayer* that is streaming smoke."

"Yes, sir, Skipper. I was watching her too. She is keeping up."

As soon as the flak stopped Rick heard, "Fighters below, three o'clock and climbing up fast. Here they come!" came the warning from Lieutenant.

The attack continued for a good portion of the trip through German skies. Prior to the Germans reaching the limits of their fuel, Rick heard Lieutenant say, "Two, 109s at six. They're yours, Link."

Then silence. Everybody knew that Link was dead. It was a call made by habit. Now, not having any real defense in the back, they had to rely on the poor aim of the German pilot or the gunners from the other B-17s or both. It was preferred that the 109 could be destroyed outright but it was hoped that at least enough .50-cal. fire was sent his way to discourage him from staying back there. Normally Billy would have taken up the tail gunner position but the condition of the compartment made it untenable.

One Me-109 saw that no fire was coming from the tail guns and that a P-51 had not spotted him yet so he just settled into a nice comfortable deadly position just aft and about 150 to 200 yards behind *The Lucky Irishman*. He let everything fly that he had, hitting number one engine again then number two. The German continued working to the right using his rudder to guide the horizontal path of the 7.92mm bullets. Once into the cabin he let the 20mm canon loose, firing several shots until his yaw pointed onto the right wing where he continued to wreak havoc on the plane. It was only the concentrated fire from other B-17s nearby that forced him to break off the attack but the damage was done, his battle won.

On board *The Lucky Irishman*, the rounds started to tear everything up, starting with Lieutenant, who was hit immediately without even getting off a shot. The 7.92mm rounds went clear through the fuselage from the tail through the nose. Hambone and Billy were hit and thrown forward. Scottie was cut nearly in two with his camera flying out the open waist window. Jimbo was shot through the chest as he was manning his .50-cal. With that same burst that went clear through the length of the cabin, Boom was thrown into the chin bubble, Tweak became a dripping bloody mass of flesh and shredded leather. One round came through the cockpit, shooting Tab in his left calf that broke his shin, nearly tearing it off from the knee down. Rick was cut under his right eye and stunned with flying metal and glass as several rounds penetrated the instrument panel, knocking out most of the instruments necessary for navigation and attitude flying. All of this happened in a matter of seven seconds.

Rick looked over at number two engine through his window and saw that it was running but losing RPM.

Looking over at Tab, who was in dire shape, Rick called out, "Tab, you OK? Hang in there. Hang in there!"

Tab said, "My leg is shot off. I can't feel it."

"You still have your leg," Rick said reaching over and grabbing a handful of femoral artery on the inner portion of his upper thigh to slow the bleeding. Struggling to fly the plane and holding Tab's leg he said, "Can you see the fuel quantity gages and the pressure gages? Come on, Tab! Stay with me!" Rick said as Tab was drifting away due to the loss of blood from the massive wound.

"We are leaking fuel in all tanks. One and two almost gone. Oil pressure on number two is thirty-five and dropping. All others, OK."

"The Alps are dead ahead," Rick said.

Meanwhile he was dropping back. The Mustangs were busy fighting the 109 and 110 onslaught off the main body. He could not communicate with the flight because his radio was torn to shreds but he knew that they knew he was leaving them. Procedure was such that a formation would never slow down for a crippled aircraft. Rick knew he was on his own. As the flight was pulling away he noticed that Sean's plane was still with the formation and that comforted him. "At least someone will survive this war from Manteo. Fly, my friend, and live," he thought.

The Alps were directly underneath so now he knew he could, maybe with luck, reach Allied-held territory.

Number two started to vibrate terribly.

"Tab," Rick called, "Tab!"

Rick lifted Tab's head that was resting on his left shoulder. It was limp and heavy. Tab died somewhere over the Alps. Rick strained to see the oil pressure on number two engine. Securing an engine that was producing power is a cardinal sin he did not want to commit, but he also did not want a dead, un-feathered engine on his wing either. Especially since he would need every bit of fuel and aerodynamic prowess to get him to Celone.

"Shit," he said. "Thirty psi."

Rick began the prop-feathering procedure from memory and secured the engine, afterwards trimming the rudder to full right rudder. "Number three and four were still strong," he thought. He had to crank in three hands full of left wing down aileron to compensate for the lack of fuel in the lighter left wing. The airplane was drifting right of intended course for some time before he realized he was out of trim. "The right fuel tanks were really leaking fuel now," he thought. "There is no way I'm getting to friendly lines."

He saw a cloud bank below him and he was losing altitude. He could not throw anything overboard which is procedure because there was no one alive to do it. "Damn it!" he said out loud. He did a quick analysis. Rick was thinking in his head faster than he ever had before, "Heading...unknown except from the sun's position going generally south-southwest. Altitude 4,000 feet and descending at 200 feet per minute. Airspeed 150 kts, just barely fast enough to fly and keep this rate of descent slow, fuel...forget it, just about gone. Landing gear? Not an option. Belly landing. Lieutenant!? Dead, if not, God rest his soul, he soon will be along with the rest of us."

Then he thought of flying through the clouds and the possible fog underneath. Seeing that his standard electric basic instruments were shot to hell or not functioning due to the lack of DC power he made a quick survival assessment. "If there is any chance of survival at all I will have to land wings level and hope there is no building or mountain between me and our final resting place after the slide." He remembered what Mr. Weldon taught him about using dog tags.

"Right!" Rick said out loud. "If this works I owe you a beer."

Rick pulled out his dog tags and chain with a religious medal of St. Joseph Cupertino (patron saint of aviators), Scapular and with the other half of the Bodie Lighthouse. He hung them from the number one engine feathering switch located just to his right in front of him. He remembered briefly the night he gave Lucia the pendant and how they spent their last night together but no sooner than he did the bomber left the clear skies and entered the nebulous haze below.

Rick fought the fear that was pulling at his muscles at every angle. A lifetime flashed before his eyes. Training turned into habit and instincts guided his hand. He thought of his life plan unfinished, to see Lucia again, to hold her one more time, Mom and Dad. Rick thought of the crew he loved like the brothers he never had, now, never to see home again. Rick fought the swing and tilt of Bodie hanging straight with a slight sway back and forth resembling the ocean she watched. Turn needle and ball centered. He recalled on the tactical maps the general elevation of northern Italy especially in the general area he thought he might be in. He remembered that it was about 1,200 feet mean sea level (MSL) which meant when he reached about 1,200 feet on his altimeter he would be dead or on the scariest slide of his life.

At 2,500 feet, number three engine started to sputter from fuel starvation. Having oil pressure left, he quickly feathered it. Knowing that number four was right behind, he went ahead and feathered it also. The bomber was now a glider. Sir Isaac Newton and luck had the lifeless bomber.

At 1,200 feet Rick took one last glance at Bodie pointing straight down. "Perfect," he thought, "as you always have been for me." He saw the ground just prior to impact. He saw that his wings were level. "Thank God," he thought. Instantaneously he pulled back on the yoke to initiate a flare to arrest the rate of descent and bleed off airspeed. Hitting the ground hard with his tail, the elevator went full up, which threw the control column violently into Rick's chest as inertia and the force of the falling nose threw him forward, knocking the wind out of him, hitting his sternum and breaking both of his hands which had a death grip on the wheel. His harness and thick flying gear served as a cushion.

The Lucky Irishman was on the ground in a slippery slide with the luckiest Irishman on board. The aircraft came to rest after a fearful eight seconds of flying brush, soil, thin trees and fencing. All motion within the plane stopped as the dust and debris that was suspended in the air from all the wind either settled or fell to the deck of the plane. Rick looked through his broken windscreen with the control column still against his chest and felt the peace that must exist before death. The air was still and quiet. "The fog is thick," Rick quickly thought, "but most noticeable is the absence of fire." If there was he could not have gotten out. The reason he was not toasted alive was because of the lack of fuel in the fuel tanks. The lack of friction and the moistness of the ground prevented sparks from igniting any residual fuel that was present. Rick's last memory was looking at the fog seeing grape vines and damp grass in the foreground. Rick slipped into unconsciousness but was alive.

9

It was early morning the next day when Gino Marzoli, a local farmer, wanted to check out the noises he heard late the day before from the eerie fog. He got a couple of his workers with their tools, ox, and cart and started out to the hills where his vineyards were. As he walked he thought of the chores that had to be performed and the order in which they had to occur. He thought the day would be just another day in the Tuscan hills. After a walk of about twenty-five minutes he noticed a tall green tail, with a white upside-down triangle with a big black "Y" in the middle of it. The fuselage was quietly resting like a wounded dog between the plush green tiny hills and vines full of grapes. The work crew was dismayed at the sight and ran to the wreck. Paolo followed leading the ox by his reins. Upon arrival they slowed their approach, looking at the carnage of the wreck. The aircraft was resting on its belly and wings between two small hills. The nose of the aircraft was partially buried in a soft mound of damp topsoil. The body of the plane was dented and mangled slightly from the rocks that were underneath. The tail broke off on impact with the ground that was at an elevation slightly higher than the landscape of the eventual slide and rested about 200 yards from the rest of the wreck. After the tail separated the forward portion continued its precocious course spewing debris and bodies along the way. One worker, Filippo, an older man of fifty, upon seeing a dead crewman in the debris field, walked away in a stagger and threw up.

Gino, after seeing Filippo get sick, quickly called the crew over to formulate a plan.

"Filippo, go to the tail section and check for survivors along the way. Gennaro, come with me into the plane. Paolo," he said to his ten-year-old son, "stay here and keep an eye out for strangers," Gino said squeezing the little boy's arm assuring him that everything was OK.

Each man went to his assigned place while Gino carefully entered the cabin through the large opening left by the detached tail. Moving forward he checked the body of each crewman of the aircraft. He negotiated around the tangled metal of the ball turret and ammo tracks, and into the radio compartment. Once in the empty bomb bay, he maneuvered slowly through the twisted metal along the narrow walkway to the cockpit, noticing the blood from the top turret gunner along the floor aft and forward of the cockpit bulkhead. When he reached the cockpit he first looked to the right and straightened the body of the co-pilot to check for life. He then turned to the left and looked at the pilot. He noticed that Rick was breathing laboriously.

"Filippo! Gennaro! I found one alive!" he yelled back through the cabin of the plane.

Gennaro was right behind him when Gino turned and told him to go get a knife so he could cut the pilot's harness away. Gennaro returned quickly with a large knife. Gino did all the cutting he could to remove wreckage and to push the steering column forward and out of the way. Rick came to when Gino tried to move him.

"Owww," Rick said, before biting his lower lip feeling the worst pain he could ever imagine.

"Take it easy," Gino said in broken English. "I'm going to get you out and take you back to the house."

The movement out of the cockpit was excruciatingly difficult with sounds of piercing pain every step of the way. Carrying a 175-pound, badly injured man through spaces that barely allowed an agile person, in peak physical condition, was a monumental task. The twisted metal and debris formed impossible obstacles along the way. The evacuation was accomplished by pure determination, and will. Finally they were outside with Filippo, with Paolo quickly bringing over the ox cart to load Rick into. Gino got in the back with Rick while Gennaro led the ox. Filippo and Paolo walked along the side. The trip was a rough one because the trail was just that, a trail with rocks, ruts and holes, but even with things being what they were, it was not as rough as the extraction from the bomber.

The Marzoli farm house was built with earthen blocks and stone for walls. The roof was made of clay tile. The outside walls had green vines growing along them complementing the earthen tan and gray colors of the stone and mortar in a way that only Fauna, the Roman goddess of the earth, could design. Along the front was a simple flower garden filled with purple flowers and a tin watering can in the corner.

Upon arrival, Gino yelled, "Mama, get a bed ready and tear a sheet for bandages."

Esta came out in a rush with an apron around her waist all worried that little Paolo was hurt.

"Gino, what happened!" she said.

"Not sure, but this American airman is badly hurt. Get the house ready and be quick," Gino said. Esta urgently ran into the house.

Gino, Filippo, and Gennaro carried the injured pilot gingerly into the house and laid Rick onto a simple bed prepared by Esta.

The Italians began to take Rick's winter flight gear and uniform off so they could attend to his wounds. Esta brought hot water to wash his face and body.

Gino had spent some time in the military and knew about first aid to some degree. He knew that Rick's injuries were serious but not life threatening. Rick was having trouble breathing but not bleeding from the mouth, which indicated to Gino that his organs were probably intact. The bruises he had were located around his chest and his thumbs. His lungs sounded clear so Gino assessed, from the position of the control column he found against his chest, his difficulty in taking a deep breath, and his bruises that his ribs are probably broken or cracked. They wrapped him tightly with bandages holding a wood strip that was placed on both sides of his rib cage from his armpit to his hip to prevent any unnecessary bending or upper-body movement.

In a mix between Italian and English, Gino explained his condition and Rick said, "*Grazi.* How is my crew?" noticing that, overall, his English was not bad.

Gino understood English as did many Italians but he did not practice it often because the opportunity was not there or necessity did not require it. Gino tried his best to communicate in English to his visitor.

"You are in my house about twenty miles south of Florence. I am sorry but your crew is dead," he said sadly.

Trying to sit up, which he immediately found out was impossible, he settled back into the bed.

"You have to be still, ahhh…" Gino said realizing he did not know his name.

"Rick. Lieutenant Rick Hamilton, American Army Air Force."

"You have broken ribs and sprained thumbs, Lieutenant Rick. You will be here for some time."

"Some time? I can't stay here. I have to get back to Celone."

"You are not going anywhere, Lieutenant. Not until you are well enough to move. Besides, Germans are in town and patrol around here on occasion. If they catch you here, well, let's just put it this way, they will not be as nice as we are. The SS will certainly interrogate you then probably kill you and us, so you keep quiet and we will all get through this."

Gino dismissed himself and went to his crew. He gave them instructions to get a pick ax, shovels, hammer, and some nails.

After making sure the house was secure and Esta was OK, Gino went back to where Rick was lying down.

"I am going back to your plane to bury your crew," Gino said. "I will be back shortly."

Rick, visually upset over the loss of his crew and wishing he could see them and help bury them, said, "*Grazi*. Really, I mean it," he said disturbed but thankful. "There are several first-aid kits in the airplane. Could you gather them and bring them back?"

"*Sì. Certamente*," Gino said, and with his crew and Paolo, they left for the plane.

Gathering the American crew for burial was a gruesome chore. They found nine bodies intact but only found parts of one other, Lieutenant, in the ball turret under the belly of the aircraft. He was spread over the entire skid of the airplane, 200 yards.

Gino wanted to mark each grave with a cross. He made each one from wood lying around a storage shed he had along the road to the wreck. All the boards were white which made the graves very visible. Upon each cross he nailed one of their two dog tags, leaving the other one on the neck of the body. Gino put all the parts he could find of Lieutenant in a grave, placing the dog tag on top. Ten crosses, all in a row. Other than it not being in American soil it was in a setting that no one could complain about.

Gino stood and looked at his sweating crew and counted the crosses again. "Ten," he said out loud. "The plane only has a crew of ten," he said, puzzled to his work crew. "Why did he fly with eleven? No matter, this will work in our favor if the Germans find the wreck. Gather what we can use, don't forget the first-aid kits," he told his workers.

"You want to take the maps and pilot notes?" asked Gennaro.

"No, we want the Germans to think that it was just uninterested villagers or farmers who buried the poor souls. Leave them here."

As Filippo and Gennaro were gathering their things, Gino went to the nose of the aircraft and saw the top two-thirds of the artwork that Scottie had painted. Being curious, Gino cleared the soil and rocks from the rest of the painting and just stared at it.

"Filippo, Gennaro, come here," he said with uncertain excitement. They came over with Paolo and stood by Gino looking at the painting of *The Lucky Irishman*.

"Lucia," said Filippo.

"Lucia. Lucia Pallanti?" said Gennaro. "You think?"

Gino, having his exact thoughts confirmed, said to Paolo, "Go back to the house and tell your momma to come out here quick. Stay with the American until we all get back."

"*Si, Papa,*" Paolo said and took off running.

Thirty minutes later Esta arrived by cart and pulled up near where they were standing.

"What is it, Papa?"

"Look at the painting on the plane," he said pointing.

After some curious study she went to the painting and touched it. "It looks like Lucia…but it has to be just a lucky coincidence."

"Yeah, I'm sure but she needs to see this. She is supposed to be in town in a couple of days. We will bring her out here then and surprise her," said Gino. Calling everybody over he said, "This is very serious. No one can talk about the American. He does not exist. Does everybody understand? Everybody died in the plane. The plane carries a crew of ten and there are ten confirmed bodies. No one ever needs to know about the lieutenant. OK?"

"*Si. Signore Marzoli*" was the response. Everybody knew of the dangers and risks involved, but they all wanted to protect the American.

Saturday came and Lucia went to the market at San Gimignano. The Marzolis were there also doing their shopping and selling some of their grapes and wine to the local stands and restaurants.

"*Ciao*, Lucia. How is my beautiful niece?" Gino said at a distance.

"*Caio*, Uncle. Aunt Esta. Well. Everything is good," she said with a hug. "*Caio*, Paolo. Give me a kiss," she said picking him up with some effort, giving him a hug also. "You are getting big."

"What are you doing today after you are through here?" said Gino.

"Nothing really, just going back to Sienna, I guess, unless you have a better idea."

"I do, actually. There is something I want to show you."

Lucia, being curious, said, "OK. I will meet you back here in an hour."

"*Grande. Arrivederci,* Lucia," said Gino and Esta.

Everybody met up an hour later and began the trip back to the Marzoli vineyard by cart. The road curved through the gentle hills where tall cypress trees guarded the road in long rows at times. They could all see that the green fields and vineyards were being worked by the families with centuries of traditions and toiled without complaint or need. The day was warm and the sun was high with spotted clouds going from hill to hill.

At the same place where Gino saw the tail for the first time Lucia saw the tail also. She gasped and looked at Esta and they both looked at Gino. At the sight of the wreck Lucia got down off the cart and looked at the devastation and the crosses that were in a neat, straight, long row at its side.

"When did this happen, Uncle?" Lucia said in a quandary.

"Late afternoon on the seventh. I did not see it until the next morning."

"Did anybody survive?" she asked as she was touching the wing.

"Come over here," Gino said standing at the nose of the plane.

Walking over she noticed the beautiful four-leaf clover painting and the words "The Lucky Irishman." As she got closer she noticed the image of the beautiful lady. She brushed away some dirt stuck to the art slowly with her hand as not to damage it. Gino, Esta, and Paolo were standing still in anxious anticipation of her reaction. She looked at them and looked again at the image. Kneeling down in front of it, she was awestruck. She looked at the picture, back at the Marzolis, and back at the picture where she adoringly touched it. Bewilderment was written all over her face and gestures.

"This is impossible. I think this is me!" she said in disbelief.

"That is what we thought, too," Gino said.

"This looks like the picture I took when I was in North Carolina with..." catching herself before she said Rick's name, "friends."

She glanced over her right shoulder and looked over at the crosses and ran to them reading each dog tag. After reaching the last one she took a breath and said to Gino, "I don't understand this. I don't know any of these men. Why..." She stopped suddenly in her speech. She began to walk with urgency towards the fuselage and entered the inside of the cabin of the plane. She worked herself forward looking for, she did not know what, for anything, something that would make sense. She saw the dried blood and began to cry. "Oh God no, let this all be a dream," she thought over and over again.

When she entered the cockpit her heart stopped when she noticed Rick's dog tags mistakenly left behind by Gino and his crew. In front of the tags, and being the first thing she saw, was Rick's half of Bodie Lighthouse. She was too shocked to even move, as tears started to fall one after another from both eyes. Through her distorted vision, she lifted Rick's necklace and held it to her lips and to her heart; remembering those wonderful years in America with Rick, the days and nights on top of Bodie and the love they shared so perfectly in the rain.

Gaining some composure she remembered that his grave was not among the ten. She quickly turned and left the plane through the wreckage of the bomb bay. She went to her uncle and said, "I suspect that there is either a grave missing or there is something you need to tell me, Uncle," she said with dusty tears trailing down her face holding out the dog tags she found in the cockpit.

They all loaded into the cart again and headed for the house without a word. Esta put her arm around Lucia as Lucia rested her head. Lucia looked up at Esta as they sat in the cart and just looked into Esta's eyes which were also filling with the moisture from the tragedy of the scene and the pain that Lucia was obviously feeling.

"There *is* something else, isn't there?" Lucia said to Esta in a tone that only the truth could calm.

Gino heard Lucia's voice and said, "There is much at risk, Lucia. I did not want to tell you anything more than that plane but I feel there is something more at work here than I care to know or understand. Do you know the American whose name is on those tags?" Gino asked.

Esta caressing Lucia's neck and back with tender strokes noticed her thumbing and holding the tags and the lighthouse. She observed the same lighthouse dangling from her neck when she was leaning forward. Esta's heart jumped. Time stood still for a moment in her mind as she took a moment to recall the conversation that she and Lucia had in the strictest confidence, about a boy she was seeing in America when she was in college. She never thought much about it in all these years but it looked like fate had taken a remarkable and unbelievable turn.

"Gino, stop talking and get to the house," said Esta knowing that a serious encounter was about to occur. Lucia was the first to jump from the cart and ran into the house suspecting the answer she was seeking was inside.

"Rick! Rick!" she screamed.

The yells woke Rick up from a restless sleep with a jar; not deciphering who or what made the startling sounds that made him grimace in pain when he suddenly moved. She barged into his room as he was trying to adjust himself in his bed.

She just stood there in the doorway with streaks of muddy tears on her cheeks frozen in time and emotion.

Rick, forgetting all the pain, said, *"Lucia! Il mio amore e la mia vita,"* which means, "My love and my life." He immediately felt dizzy and thought that the drugs and the pain were affecting his vision and hearing. "Seeing is believing," he thought, "but this is impossible, an unimaginable miracle."

"Rick," she said in disbelief, happiness, and concern in one breathless syllable then quickly ran and dropped on him crying and kissing him. All the while Rick was gasping for breath as the simple aspirin that was given him from the first-aid kit for pain became grossly inadequate for the pouncing that Lucia lovingly administered.

"Ooowwww, oooo," he said, trying to enjoy this moment of shock and thoughtful anticipation that over three years of dreams made a reality. "Lucia, honey, hold on, get up, babe, you're pushing my ribs through my back," he said painfully exaggerating but finally getting her attention.

"How did you get here? You OK? You look injured," she said looking at the cuts on his face.

About the time Lucia pounced on Rick the Marzolis entered the house.

Esta entered the room and saw Lucia lavishly asking Rick questions with the sincerity and concern that one of familiarity would make appropriate.

"Come, child," said Esta. "Lieutenant Rick has some broken ribs and needs to rest."

"Broken ribs? Oh my God and I just…" she said as she was getting ready to pounce on him again to apologize but caught herself along with Esta's strong grip holding her back.

"I'm OK, Lucia. A bit sore that's all," Rick said with his hands out to catch her painfully loving pounce.

Esta saw that their presence was going to hinder the real communication that had to occur between Lucia and Rick. Esta said, "Come, Gino. Help me prepare dinner."

"Esta, I don't need…"

"Yes, you do, and get me some cool water. Come along, Paolo. Leave Lucia and Lieutenant Rick alone," Esta said closing the door.

140

"Lieutenant? You became a pilot?" Lucia said in complete amazement and pride.

"It was a way for me to try to find you. I didn't expect to do it this way though. Crashing into your farm and..." he said sadly and in shock. "I certainly didn't expect to loose my crew," he said. Deeply reminiscing, his eyes went blank when he said, "That Me-109 just sat in on us. We couldn't get him."

"Yes. I saw their graves. Uncle Gino buried them beautifully. You will be pleased." Seeing that Rick was deeply upset at the loss she delicately said, "I'm sorry about your friends, Rick. They were very brave."

Rick, knowing all too well that war had a terrible price, said, "They were the bravest men I ever knew. I flew nineteen combat missions with them. I trusted them with my life and they gave me their trust right back. They were my family in Italy, my responsibility...damn! I can't believe all this. Lucia, I did not want to see you again like this. Not with this price," he said, lying back on his pillow gingerly, feeling the pain in his chest. "I can't believe you are here. God does answer prayers in ways that are...unexpected. I can't believe this," he said closing his eyes as if he knew when he opened them again all of this would be gone.

Changing his thought pattern he said, "How did you know I was here?"

"Your plane crashed on my uncle's vineyard. He wanted to show me the painting on the plane."

Remembering the nose art, and with a look of emotional manifestation and enlightenment Rick said, "Your picture on the clover. This whole thing is just unreal," he said joyfully bewildered. "Everything I did, since you left, directed me to this place. If I had not done one thing in all of the things I have done you would not be here now."

"You being here is an answer to many prayers. The truth, that you survived the attacks and crash, is evidence that God is watching over you."

"Look, Lucia, your uncle and aunt are taking a big risk keeping me here. I should leave and soon, but I don't know how to do it being so banged up and all."

"The best thing you could do right now is do *exactly* what they say, Rick. There are German patrols out there and they come by every so often. Not so much now but...promise me. Uncle Gino is very smart and knows how to keep you safe. You must do exactly what they tell you and don't ask questions. There is a reason for me saying that that I cannot tell you right now. Just trust me and them."

"OK, Lucia, whatever you want. Are you living around here?" he said clearing his throat. "Close by maybe?" Then, reaching deep within his broken body, he asked the dreaded question that was heavy on his heart, "Did you ever marry Barone?"

Looking down at the bed but away from his eyes, she said, "Yes, about a year ago. He is a good man, Rick, and he is good to me," she said getting up and pouring him a glass of water.

As she was handing him the glass he asked, "I'm glad to hear that, but does he love you?"

"If you mean does he love me like you love me, no. But I think he loves me, just differently." Rick closed his eyes and lay there quietly. "With you I miss you every second that I am not with you and begin missing you before you actually leave. With Barone," she said hesitantly, "I want to miss him because I know if I do then that means that in some way I love him or at least care for him, but I don't. I want to miss him but I don't. Is that wrong? Your love for me placed you here now. How, why, and who had a hand in this occurrence can only be explained as divine providence. I will say this, though, I am sure He had everything to do with you being here now…and all this."

"All I know is that the chances of all of this occurring, like it did, are beyond the mind to imagine. What has happened here recently is impossible to decipher. I promised you I would find you, providence heard it, and now I am here; broken, but here. So, now what?" Rick said with a sigh. "You have children?"

"No," she said thoughtfully. "The doctors think that maybe I can't have children."

Rick, looking right into her dark eyes, said sincerely, "Lucia, I'm really sorry. You will keep trying, right?"

"I don't know. Barone and I are not close in that way. I'm not sure if I want a family with him. It's probably just as well, really."

"That's nonsense and you know it. You need a family. You were born to have kids, a lot of them. Maybe it is him who has the problem. Did you or the doctors ever think of that?"

"It is not something we talk about here. It is my job to bear the children. If it does not happen, it is my fault, period. I don't ask the questions. I just do what I need to do, nothing more. Nothing else is expected."

"That's not the Lucia I know or the one full of life that smiled and played in America. That's not the Lucia that I heard about; that, with dark eyes of determination, kicked the ass of that Duke tennis star."

"I told you that things are different here. You will see that firsthand while you are here. I've changed. I feel different."

"You feel different because you are not happy. We can get the happiness back again."

"How? How, Rick? I'm married now. Things are not as simple as they were. Italians are still dying and every night I tremble in fear wondering if Barone will…" Then she stopped suddenly catching herself in mid sentence.

"Will what, Lucia? He doesn't hit you, does he?" Rick said with dire concern in his voice.

"No. He has never hit me. It isn't like that. He is involved in something that I can't talk about. Not yet anyway, OK? Just be patient, Rick. Please."

"Sure, Lucia, patience is my middle name," Rick said with concern and not wanting to complicate her life any more than he already had.

Esta came into the room after a polite knock and asked Lucia if she was staying for dinner or the night.

"That is very nice to ask, Aunt Esta. I think I will. Barone is gone for the weekend and the time will allow me time to catch up on things with Rick."

"Paolo will be glad to hear it," said Esta.

After Esta left, Rick took Lucia's hand. Standing close to the bed he noticed the dog tags she was holding.

"I see you found my dog tags," Rick said.

When she opened her hand to let Rick look at them, Bodie was right on top.

"I thought my mind was going to explode when I saw them. For the first time in my life my mind went completely blank," Lucia said placing her free hand over her mouth.

Looking at Bodie Rick said, "I never took them off. Bodie led you to me that summer at Kelly's and has led me here to you now. You believe in fate, Lucia? You believe in prayer? I believe in both. How couldn't I? Everything I ever did since you left me in August directed me in little steps to this time and space. *Ti amo Lucia*."

"Shush now," Lucia said putting her finger over Rick's lips. "You have to behave yourself. We are not at Bodie."

Rick took Lucia's hand, opened her palm and kissed it, and placed it on his cheek. "You are as soft now as you were then. I missed you and will wait for you again. I will always wait for you."

"You need to be good until…" Pulling her hand away slowly then reaching back and touching his cheek, Lucia said, "I missed you too, Rick, and never stopped loving you."

After landing back at Celone, Sean's crew could see that he was visibly shaken by the loss of Rick. His last memory of Rick was of him losing altitude by the Alps, one engine out with the other trailing a little smoke, but working. Sean knew that if Rick could keep up he would. Sean did not like the idea that his best friend was going down over mountains with clouds forecasted ahead. It was the longest hour and a half flight he ever had.

Sean got a ride to the operations shack to see if they heard anything, which of course they hadn't. Then he waited outside by the control tower to wait for any stragglers. Everybody came back but four. It was the costliest mission to date except for the Ploesti raids in May.

After it was assured that Rick was not coming back, Sean just went to his bunk and lay there for hours knowing he had to write to Kelly and Rick's parents about Rick. He did not know what to say or how to say it. No one ever did. There was no easy or painless way to explain the loss of a loved one. Next to him was Rick's empty bunk which he just stared at. The core of his body felt as empty as Rick's bunk looked.

"I know you are not gone, Rick. I just know it," he said to himself. Then he thought of something. He just had to ask his squadron commanding officer and the group commanding officer for permission.

The next day, although the group was flying to Vienna, Sean and his crew were relieved of flight status so they could tend to *Kelly's Lucky Prayer's* maintenance needs. Major Patton also had off and was in the operations shack when Sean went in to run his idea past him.

"Good morning, sir," Sean said.

"Good morning, Lieutenant. Glad you're here. You did a good job bringing your cripple in yesterday. Maintenance tells me that you will need two engine changes though."

"Yes, sir."

"I'm putting you and your crew down as standby replacement aircrew until your plane is up."

"Yes, sir, I would expect you would."

"I know you are concerned about Lieutenant Hamilton. We all are. I have thirty-nine other guys I have to wonder about too. I hope they all turn up somehow."

"Yes, sir. It is along that line that I have an idea that I need to run past you."

"Idea? What kind of idea?"

"Sir, I did some planning and estimates and it would not be a hindrance to our mission but in fact will improve it because, if my hunch is right, we may recover a crew."

144

"Lieutenant, what in blazes are you talking about?"

"Sir, after a mission and on the return back to Celone I would like to break formation and divert west to look for *The Lucky Irishman*."

"What makes you think you can find *The Irishman*, Sean? She was last seen over the Alps and going down."

"Yes, sir, but slowly, under control and with a slight westerly drift. I think she made it over the Alps. I would like to take a look to see if I could find her on the way back from a mission."

"Your request is very unusual and you know it," Major Patton said with authority. "I'm touched by the loyalty and depth of friendship you have for Rick. Really, I am. But if we went looking for every lost aircrew we wouldn't have any bombers to fly the next day. You know we are barely able to meet the schedule as it is. Losses are mounting. We can't afford to do that."

"Sir, with all due respect, I don't see how we can't try. Morale is down. If we can locate *The Lucky Irishman* and bring her crew back that just might be the morale booster we need. Like I said I have a hunch…just a hunch, but I would appreciate a try at it."

Hesitantly Major Patton said, "Show me on the map your plan."

Sean took a pencil and drew out what he thought was the likely flight path of *The Lucky Irishman*, plus or minus twenty degrees either side of course.

"OK, if you were to break formation here," Major Patton said pointing to the map just south of the Alps, "and BINGO back to base here that will put you back at Celone about thirty to forty-five minutes behind your ETA but probably about the time the last plane in the group is about to land."

After a brief period of silence Major Patton said, "I will go along with this and propose it to Colonel Kurtz but I want you to have fighter escort. Since this is your mission you arrange the fighter support. If you have any mechanicals, mission is scrubbed. This will happen only when I say, probably on a mission in Italy or one close by for fuel concerns and loss of aircraft on the mission. So get it planned and briefed. Your crew has to be 100 percent on board with this 'volunteer' mission or it is cancelled. Understood?"

"Absolutely, thank you, sir."

"You just find Hamilton."

Sean went right to work on his plan. Since his plane was under repair and he cut a deal with the scheduling officer to keep him off the schedule for a couple of days he traveled north about thirty-five miles the next day to San Severo, where he knew that the 31st Fighter Group was based. They were flying the brand-new P-51D single-engine fighter, powered by the Packard-built Rolls-Royce "Merlin" engine. It was the fastest and most maneuverable propeller-driven airplane in the sky. It provided cover for the heavy bombers all the way to the targets and back. She was absolutely beautiful. The 31st FG was familiar with the squadrons of the 463[rd,] having flown fighter cover for them many times before. Seeing a P-51 flying cover overhead put a smile on the faces of the bomber crews faster than seeing home base. There was a certain comfort that seeing the shiny new Mustang provided, more so that any other fighter in theatre.

After driving his Jeep for almost two hours he arrived in San Severo. Sean went into the mess tent to grab a bite to eat when he saw Captain Pat Dixon, the former class president of Manteo High, Class of '36, putting his mess tray away.

"Pat? Pat Dixon from Manteo High?" asked Sean vaguely recognizing him.

"Holy crap! Sean Ryan. You have to be kidding me? What the hell are you doing here?"

"Same as you, liberating Europe."

"Are you joining the 31st?"

"No. I am with the 463rd out of Celone."

"Damn, a B-17 pilot. You have a job that I wouldn't want. You have guts, that's for sure. We flew fighter cover for you guys on the seventh. Guts, pure guts, I don't know how you do it. Honestly, everybody here respects the hell out of you bomber guys."

"Look, Pat, can we go for a walk? I have to talk to you."

"Sure," as they both walked out into the yard toward the flight line. "What's on your mind?"

"Rick Hamilton is here with me."

"What? How the hell is he? That's great! We will have to have a beer or…"

"He's missing," Sean said, stopping Pat in mid-sentence.

With a stoic look Pat said, "What happened?"

Sean explained how Rick disappeared on the seventh in detail and the agreement that the 772nd squadron commanding officer and he made to find Rick. The conversation continued into 31st base ops where Sean drew the same diagram he drew for Major Patton and overlaid his search plan for Rick.

"OK, so you want me to be the fighter cover for you?" Without hesitating he said, "Damn right I will. Hell, I will get a couple of squadron buddies and we will fly with you wherever you want to go. Just let me know so I can plan our tactics. We will pick you guys up just south of the Alps around here depending where you are coming from and escort you. I will clear it with

Colonel Warford. He owes me a favor. Not that this is a big deal because we control this area. We haven't seen a 109, 190 or 110 since the seventh in this area," Pat said pointing to the map south of the Alps.

"Once our operation is underway, switch call signs to 'Redskins' after our high school mascot. You will be Redskin One, I will be Two and I will tell you later about the others. I think I can get three Mustangs to protect your ass."

"Thanks, Pat. Be ready to go. I will give you as much notice as possible."

"Don't worry, Sean. We will find him."

"We have to," Sean said as the two young officers shook hands. Sean drove away feeling better than he had in several days thinking confidently that he would find Rick.

Once Sean got back to Celone he briefed Major Patton of the plan and escort that would be provided by the 31st FG. He also told him that he would write Rick's parents, which Major Patton was grateful of because he knew that it was his responsibility as the commanding officer. It was only because Sean requested to write the letter and his close relationship to Rick and his family that Major Patton agreed.

"Please pass along my deepest respects," Major Patton requested.

He was surprised that Sean got fighter support so quick and glad that he did not have to get involved in the planning. Group operational tempo was hot and he had many issues to deal with.

Sean went back to his bunk and began writing a letter to Kelly and the Hamiltons. At least he had some news of hope to add to the letter. He did not want to write a letter saying, "I regret to inform you…" He mentioned that Rick was MIA (missing in action) and was last seen personally, by him, going down but under control in northern Italy. Sean told them of the search that was being organized, planned and briefed by him and Pat Dixon, who he knew everybody at home was familiar with. "Don't worry," he wrote, "I will find him. He is probably at some 'locanda' (tavern) having a glass of vino laughing, knowing that I am going nuts with worry!" He signed it "Love Sean" and mailed it via V-mail so it could, hopefully, get there quicker than normal mail.

Sean's airplane was ready for a mission by the nineteenth and he was again airborne flying with his crew over Munich with excellent results and no damage to his plane. Sean and his entire crew flew until the twenty-second, when they had to repair some battle damage from the Brux, Czechoslovakia, mission. They missed the Ploesti mission on the twenty-second of July, which he was internally grateful since those missions were costly. The group came back without any losses and little damage, completely surprising the mission planners.

On the afternoon of the twenty-third, Major Patton came over to Sean and told him that his opportunity to search for Rick had just arrived. "Tomorrow we go to Turin, Italy, early morning raid on a tank-repair facility. After forming up on our return flight and after our check in, I will give you and the flight the call 'Mars.' That will be the order for you to break off with your escort. Check in at Celone with your mission call sign."

"Got it. I will notify Captain Dixon of the 309th right now," Sean said.

The mission to Turin was a milk run. The Wild Ducks of the 309th Fighter Squadron (FS) which were a squadron of the 31st FG joined up with the 463rd, on schedule and as briefed with thirty-five Mustangs at Angels Twenty (20,000 feet). After a formation turn southeast and a join up and check in, the call "Mars" was heard over the radio. *Kelly's Lucky Prayer* did a descending right turn on the course planned by Sean, immediately being joined by Pat and two other Mustangs, one off each wing and one about 500 feet higher and back about half a mile.

"Redskin Leader to flight, thanks for the cover," Sean broadcasted.

"Roger that, Lead. Concentrate on the mission. We have your back. When you get in low, Redskin Three will fly ahead to scout for un-friendlies," said Pat in Redskin Two.

Sean got to 1,000 feet AGL (above ground level) and proceeded on course to San Gimignano as fate would have it. Thinking that he might not have another shot at this, he called out to the flight.

"Redskin One to Redskin Two."

"Go ahead, One," Pat called.

"Let's fan out here. Have Three and Four take up positions a couple of miles off either side of course at Angels two. Cover more area. You stay with me."

"Roger. Redskin Three, go left; Four, go right."

After ten minutes of flying and near Florence, Redskin Three broke the silence. "Redskin Three to Redskin Flight, German convoy at my ten o'clock, about five miles."

"Redskin Two to Three, attack as briefed."

Redskin Three made one low-level pass with all six .50-cal guns firing setting three of the six trucks on fire then resumed course on the search pattern.

"Lawman to pilot," called the left waist gunner, Staff Sergeant Trent Marshall. "I have something that looks like a tail nine o'clock three miles."

Sean broadcasted the sighting to Pat, "Redskin One to Two, nine o'clock, three miles."

"Redskin Two, Rog, I see it. I'm going in."

Sean's heart began to race as his face was getting flushed with hope. "Redskin Two to Redskin One. I have a bomber with 463rd markings over here."

"Redskin One coming over," Sean called, banking nearly 60,000 pounds of steel and fuel into a forty-five-degree-angle-of-bank turn adding power and pulling back on the control column to keep his altitude and a little left rudder to keep the airplane in balanced flight.

About the time they got over the wrecked B-17, Sean's crew started breaking over the intercom with elation that they found *The Lucky Irishman.*

"Pilot to crew. Pipe down. You see any signs of where the crew might be?" as Sean began a turn to make another pass.

"Redskin Two to Redskin One. I see crosses on her left side."

"Redskin Four. Confirm, I count…I think ten."

Sean leveled his wings and approached the wreck site at 500 feet and 170 knots. "Pilot to crew, get all the information you can on this pass. We can't loiter out here too long," Sean said with a lump in his throat. The pass was clean and straight. Everybody strained their eyes to get any sign at all that someone survived, but the count of ten crosses was a testament of the crew's fate and Sean knew it.

"Bubble to pilot," came the call from the ball turret gunner. "Yes, sir, I count ten crosses," he said sadly. A hush came over the crew.

"Redskin flight, join up on me. We will make one more pass, west to east to get our bearings," called Sean.

Redskin Flight did a right echelon forming up diagonally off Sean's right wing. A beautiful formation in honor of the crew of *The Lucky Irishman* they flew in at her at 500 feet and 160 knots; three silver Mustangs with red peppermint diagonal lines across a sleek tail and with the green *Kelly's Lucky Prayer* in front. A sad flyby was being prepared as a final salute.

Meanwhile, Rick was recovering at the Marzolis', moving around in the yard getting some air and sun but still had the rib brace on. Lucia was with him that afternoon checking up on him when all the commotion over the crash site was heard. Rick immediately recognized the sounds as B-17s and P-51s and even saw a Mustang as it passed quickly by at 500 feet. Esta came outside when she heard the planes. Gino and his crew were in the vineyard watching the air show also. Excitement and pride filled every part of Rick's being.

Lucia said as she was standing next to Rick, "These are your friends?"

"Yes. The silver plane is a fighter that usually provides my group protection on our missions. They are based not far from where I am based in Celone. They are far from where they should be. This area is not on their ingress or egress routes. They must have stumbled on my airplane and are checking it out," Rick said with professional curiosity.

"Celone? Celone is your base?" she said inquisitively. "I have family in Celone."

As Lucia was asking those questions Rick was just in a daze, totally oblivious to her inquisition, watching the planes flying in the sky as sharks in an open sea. The four-plane formation flew directly overhead Rick and Lucia with a rumble that shook the ground. Rick recognized the nose art of the B-17 and jumped forgetting his injuries. Reacting to the sudden burst of pain, he held his side as he said with animated gestures of delight and surprise, "That's Sean! That's Sean!"

"Our Sean? Kelly's Sean?" Lucia asked now understanding what all the excitement was all about.

"Yeah, he must have organized a search. I don't know how the hell he arranged that but it is only a matter of time now when they come to get me. Now this is all making sense. The Americans and the Brits must be close by."

At 500 feet during the final pass, Bubble called Sean, "Bubble to pilot, don't look now but I saw a man with a woman down below waving. I think he could have been American by the trousers he was wearing."

"Redskin One to Redskin Two, go back to the farmhouse and check out who was out front."

"Roger. You suspect something?" Pat said as he made a climbing left turn maneuvering to fly directly back

"I just have a feeling," Sean said slowly with anticipation.

"Redskin Three and Four, accompany One to base. I will catch up," called Pat.

On a re-pass, Pat flew in a circle around the farmhouse at 500 feet. Rick, on the ground with Lucia, just waved since there was not much else they could do. Pat had a funny feeling so he circled down to 300 feet, slowed the Mustang and in a steep bank recognized Rick.

"Redskin Two to Redskin One. Tally Ho on Rick."

"Confirm Rick?" asked Sean.

"Confirm," called Pat.

Pat did one more pass and waved his wings letting Rick know that he had identified him. Rick returned the salute by waving back and hugging Lucia.

Climbing to 15,000 feet Redskin Two joined the flight.

"Redskin One to flight. Super nice job, Two, super nice. I cannot possibly thank you guys for what you did today. It would be impossible."

"Redskin Two to Lead. You just let me know when you go get him because I'm going with you."

"Deal. Three and Four, drinks are on me and Rick as soon as I get him. Thanks, guys."

Redskin Flight called Celone tower and requested a low pass and it was granted since all bombers had landed and there were no casualties. The Mustangs remained in their echelon and got real tight on *Kelly's Lucky Prayer*. They flew with their engines tuned to perfection matching their RPM with each other, fueled with 110-octane aviation gas and testosterone. With silver metal skin shining like mirrored birds, the P-51s flew so close to the beautifully sleek and designed B-17 it seemed as if they were married, a groom to his bride. At 500 feet and 180 knots they flew right over the flight line. Everybody knew the significance of the flyby. They were excited about the beauty of the formation and what it stood for. An aesthetic sight rarely seen and seldom felt, it defined American pride, righteousness, and determination to do the right thing, of love for a comrade in arms, a brother, a friend.

Upon landing at Celone, Sean briefed Major Patton the details of the flight and the facts as he knew them. "You realize that he is still in German-occupied territory and we can't go get him right now, but I will say this, the Allies are moving up and should be in Florence next month. Once we move up to, through, and past his location then we could possibly organize a trip to get our AWOL lieutenant," Major Patton said, happy about the news.

"Yes, sir. Thanks, Major," Sean said in deep appreciation and respect.

Returning to his bunk he was able to write an addendum to the V-mail he sent a couple of weeks earlier, the best chore he ever had. Sean knew that Rick just had to stay out of trouble and out of the hands of the Germans until August or until he could get to him. That might be the hardest thing he could do. For Sean, it would be the waiting that would be stressful. It would be flying every mission not knowing what Rick was doing or if he was in trouble. It would be wishing the Allies would hurry in their push through to Florence and hoping that he could assist, every day, in their advancement. He had a new resolve, to fly every mission for Rick and his family, to get his buddy home.

10

Lucia went back home to Sienna with her friends, who had family also in San Gimignano, the day after Rick was discovered. There was unusual activity in the towns along the road to Sienna as well as on the road. Civilians were running about and the Allies were in convoys moving north when she approached closer to home. Lucia spent a great deal of time along the roadside. She did not want to get in anybody's way and to get any unwanted attention.

When she got home Barone was there waiting for her out front of their *camera*, or house, with one of his foremen. "Hi, Lucia. I was getting worried about you," Barone said standing with a note pad in his hand.

"The town is going crazy. The roads are getting crowded. What is happening?" Lucia asked.

"The Allies are pulling out and heading north towards Florence and Pisa. The Germans are apparently getting ready for a stand along the Foglia River. Everybody is anxious about the change again. Things will settle down soon." Changing the course of his conversation he inquired, "You have been spending a lot of time with your aunt and uncle lately. Is everything OK?"

"Everybody is nervous about the advancing Allies and what the Germans might do when they leave. The few Germans that are still there belong to the Reichsfuhrer SS Division and that makes everybody tense. Besides, I'm close to them as you know."

"Reichsfuhrer SS?" Barone said dismayed. "I thought they have moved on. You sure?"

152

"That is what Papa said."

"How are Mama and Papa?" Barone asked, knowing that she had not seen much of them in the past several weeks.

"Papa is worried, too. Papa does what he can to comfort her. I go by and visit but I don't spend too much time there. I enjoy the country."

"I am sure your papa is enjoying retirement. The money we make from the business is not much now but once the Germans are gone we can get back to normal. Your mama and papa will be set. I promise that."

"You are a good man. Thank you for all you do for Papa and Mama."

Barone went into the bedroom and opened a backpack. "I have to go north in a couple of days for a week or so. I took care of all of the business necessities so you don't have to worry about it. Make sure they repair the stands up north...oh, and I have a shipment of bottles arriving next week. Have the crews stack them in the cellar. I will be taking Ignazio and Santo with me to Lucca."

"Why? What's going on in Lucca?" Lucia asked.

"The partisan movement up there is gaining strength and they need help. What you just told me about the Reichsfuhrer SS explains everything. I did not know they were still in Tuscany," he said amazed. "This is an opportunity to give the Germans the farewell they deserve. Ennio Tassinari told others to tell me that the partisans there need some organization and some experienced leadership in attacking the Germans. I have to go," Barone explained.

"I get so worried when you go away like you do. Not knowing..."

"I have not forgotten about the murder of my countryman and cousin in Rome on Via Rasella last march. Murdered for just having an address on the street," he said throwing a shirt into the bag and stuffing it with his hand. "I'll never forget that day."

He took a break in trying to explain his reasoning for wanting to wreak havoc on the German withdrawal. He thought about March 23, when 335 Roman citizens were gathered together and shot in the back of the head at a network of caves near the Via Ardeatina after a German SS Polizei regiment was ambushed along the Via Rasella, the street that his cousin lived on. Barone's partisan group played a part in that ambush and he felt responsible for the deaths of his Roman friends and family. His disdain and hate for the Germans ran deep and made him a determined adversary. He intended to follow them on their withdrawal to the Italian Alps, harassing them every step of the way.

"It is best that you do not know too much," he said. "It is safer for you and the resistance. I am just glad that Uncle Gino pulled out when he did. He was superb in getting intelligence for the Allies prior to Anzio in January and February, but he took too many risks. Italy owes him their new freedom. If ever there was a man who deserved the peace that San Gimignano can give, it is him," Barone said being extremely proud of him. "I don't like having to worry about him, Esta, and Paolo. If anything happened to me, it is comforting to know that he is there to help you." Holding Lucia by her shoulders, he said, "I'll be back. The war, for us, is just about over."

Barone kissed her cheek and went outside. Lucia looked down thinking about what she told Rick about missing Barone. She searched her heart, near and far, praying for a feeling that would indicate that she wished he would stay home because she wanted to have a nice romantic dinner and a walk with him through the hills of their property, but she just thought of Rick and the love she felt when she looked at him. Feeling guilty of this innocent emotion she again tried to feel a life with Barone, some warmth or security, but logically knowing that the two of them were distinctly different. They had dissimilar interests and lifetime goals. They had different kinds of friends and liked to do different activities. The chemistry or mental link that had to exist for any relationship to succeed and endure did not exist. It was the one thing that was almost always absent in a pre-arranged marriage, her parents having been a remarkable exception. She knew that she would never feel for Barone what she felt for Rick, not that she had not searched her heart and soul, because she had on many nights and strolls. But she couldn't make something real if there was no substance, no heart, no love to begin with. It was the life she had, that she was born into. It was numbing, it was reality, it pulled at the light of her mortal essence and rested sharply at the door of her immortal soul. Lucia had thought all this through many times before. She looked deep within herself one more time for a glimmer, a parcel of darting love for Barone and felt…nothing. Placing her face into her hands, she cried.

Gino Marzoli was working his vineyard with his workers as Rick was recovering from his injuries and helping Esta with some domestic chores that didn't involve serious lifting or bending.

The aviation activities from the previous couple of days got the attention of the German army in the surrounding area. Late in the morning Paolo came running to where Gino was working.

"Papa, there is a German patrol about a mile down the road coming here," Paolo said out of breath.

"It was only a matter of time. I'm surprised it took this long," Gino said to Gennaro standing on the other side of the vine. "Paulo, run quickly to Mama and tell her to hide Rick. She knows where to put him and tell her what you told me. You all know what to do. Run along," he said, turning him around facing the most direct trail off the road to the house and tapping his butt.

"Gennaro, Filippo, follow my lead. Act normal and keep working. Do not stir suspicion. Treat them as guests," Gino said with serious urgency and confidence forged from years of dealing with political and uniformed combatants.

About ten minutes later on a slow leisurely pace, the German patrol arrived. They walked along the sides of the dirt road about fifteen feet apart. When Gino saw them he stood up and walked over to the *oberleutnant* (first lieutenant) who was leading the patrol. The lieutenant called the patrol to stop.

"Good day, *Oberleutnant*," Gino said to the German officer in Italian.

"There were reports of American aircraft flying low over this area several days ago. Do you know why they took particular interest in your farm?" Lieutenant Doll asked.

"Yes, I do. Let me show you something." Gino put his pruning tools down and told Filippo to stay and continue working, asking Gennaro to come with him. Gino lead the German patrol, who had their weapons at the ready, on a short walk over a hill to where *The Lucky Irishman* was resting. As soon as the tail section was seen, the German lieutenant told his squad to spread out and search the area. Lieutenant Doll also told Gino and Gennaro to stay there as he and his radioman walked to the wreck leaving a German guard to watch Gino and Gennaro.

The German squad walked gingerly through the wreckage searching for any signs of survivors or anything that might be of interest to the German high command.

The German corporal came to the lieutenant and reported not seeing any signs of survivors but that there were ten crosses in a row by the tail section. The lieutenant, noticing the crosses as he approached the wreck site, said, "Set up a perimeter around this site and start a search of the wreck for intel."

The lieutenant, looking at his German sentry guarding Gino and Gennaro, called for him to bring the two men to him.

"How long has this plane been here?" the lieutenant asked.

"The best I can figure it, it has been here since the eighth. I came across it when I was walking to my vineyard one morning."

"Why didn't you report this to the German commander?"

"I think I am dong that now."

The lieutenant, getting a bit annoyed at his smart but accurate response, knew that the Germans didn't normally patrol the fields around San Gimignano, asked, "Were there any survivors?"

"A pilot was alive, but barely. He died shortly after we removed him from the plane. He is buried over there with the rest of his crew."

"If I was to dig up those graves I would find ten bodies?"

Gino, alarmed at the thought of digging up graves said, "Of course. I attached an identification tag to each cross and placed the other one on the body anticipating that question when someone came looking for them," Gino said clearly and looking the lieutenant right in the eye.

"Lieutenant, we searched the plane and found these maps, notes, and radio cards," the German corporal said.

The lieutenant looked at the things the corporal found and placed them in his map case. He looked over at the American cemetery and with a nod ordered, "Corporal, confirm that there is a body in each grave."

"Sir?" the corporal asked with surprise. "Those graves are over three weeks old. Do you really think…?"

"Do it, Corporal!"

The lieutenant, looked at the Italian farmer and asked Gino, "Why would you take the time and care to bury these Americans and place a cross over them?"

"They are human beings and are deserving of a decent Christian burial. Hell, Lieutenant, I would even bury you."

Being amused at his statement and respecting his courage to say that, said, "Well said. Let's see what we find in the graves. There better be ten."

It was well known that the normal compliment of a B-17G was ten aircrew and ten, therefore, was what he expected.

After a brief dissection of each grave the corporal reported back to the lieutenant that he confirmed that there were ten corpses and confirmed it with their identification. It was just as Gino described.

The lieutenant turning to Gino asked, "Where do you live?"

Gino, getting a bit concerned as to where this question was leading, knew that he could only answer truthfully and hoped that Esta had the time to prepare Rick and the house for the infiltration of their home and property.

"I live with my wife and son down that road about a mile and a half," Gino said pointing.

"Corporal, form the squad," the lieutenant said.

At the same time a crackle came over the radio with the radioman answering.

"Lieutenant, we are being recalled back to base," the radioman reported.

The lieutenant looked at Gino and looked over the wreck and the hills said, "In five years this place will never show the scars that the last five years have grown. Land heals and forgets. I wish man could be so great."

With silent pause and a reflection of history, listening briefly to the birds and the sounds of the wind, the lieutenant said, "OK, form up. Let's get out of here." The lieutenant and his patrol left single file back down the trail that brought them there.

After he knew that the Germans were well clear and were no longer a threat, Gino went back to his home and called together his family. He embraced each one. He looked at Paolo, kissing him on the top of his head, and said, "You are the bravest little man I know and better than most."

Gino looked up and saw Rick standing by the corner of the brick house with Gino's Mannlicker-Carcano, Model 91 rifle and his rib brace off.

"I would say you are all healed up, Lieutenant," said Gino.

Rick looked down at his rifle and said, "If I had to move quickly to protect Esta and Paolo, well, the brace would just slow me down."

Gino smiled and looked back to his family, realizing again, as he had done so many times over the past several years, just how fragile life was and how in an instant all life could change. He felt proud of his family, of the courage they displayed every day by living. He felt blessed by having Rick standing guard over his family and by having the friends he had in Filippo and Gennaro who had been with him through the best and worst of times.

"I don't think the Germans will be back. They are pulling out to the north towards Florence," Gino said to Rick and the others.

"How do you know that?" asked Rick.

"I heard 'Florence' mentioned on the radio the Germans were carrying. The Allies will be here any day, which means you will be going home soon. I am going to San Gimignano to see what is happening there. I will be back in a couple of hours. Filippo and Gennaro, head back to the fields and gather our tools. Tonight we will have a dinner and wine like no other. Tonight we celebrate life and friends!" Gino said raising his arms over his head.

Rick leaned the rifle against the wall of the house and said to Filippo and Gennaro, "I am going with you." He looked over at Esta and squeezed her arm with his hand as he walked by and smiled.

On August 4, the British Eighth Army marched into and liberated Florence. With the Germans being well north of San Gimignano the people of Tuscany were free for the first time since Mussolini regime took power and the Germans invaded in '43. In traditional Italian style a festival was planned for Saturday, August 5, by the people of San Gimignano.

It was Rick's first venture from the Marzolis' home. While they rode the cart to town, he was emotionally taken by the gentle rolling hills and peace that exuded from her simple slopes. In the distance he could see the city on a hill. It was a city unaffected by war or time. Frozen in space, born from the mind of Shakespeare's dreams of Verona and Mantua, San Gimignano was her own. She represented the fortress of the Italian people to endure and to overcome oppression. She represented the promise that there would be a tomorrow, of a corporal knowledge that a fellowship existed between the people of San Gimignano and the land that supported their life. The townspeople knew that for every second of toil and sweat they placed into the land they would be rewarded a hundredfold with juicy fruit, cool water, olives, wheat, and blessings from all over their little country. They knew with the land that no one stood alone. Everybody existed for the other and everybody knew it. Rick counted at least twelve maybe fifteen spires of various heights that made beautiful bell tones that called the citizens of Tuscany together, to share in their celebration of freedom and life. Everybody answered the call and everybody brought something to share.

The night prior to the celebration, Lucia arrived with some of her friends to San Gimignano. Sienna had been celebrating every night for the past week. She knew that the festival at home in San Gimignano would be just as good because the people there had such a strong sense as to who they were. They were a community. Not many places could honestly claim that. The festival at San Gimignano, if for no other reason, would be better because her family and Rick would be there.

Saturday afternoon started off with all of the local farmers bringing their wares in from the fields and giving free samples of various types of wine, cheeses, foods, and spices and an assortment of handmade articles of clothing such as dresses and shirts, as well as baskets and crafts made from wheat stalks and wooden toys for the children. The atmosphere was alive with summer and spring and all the sunshine in between. Song and music filled every void which was very infrequent.

Rick met Lucia's parents. Her mother had a physical elegance very similar to Lucia but with aged maturity dressing her superb feminine attributes. Her language and fashionable gestures and manners came from centuries of enlightenment and excellence in family cohesion and understanding of education in the arts and language and their intimate interplay with each other. Her father was a man of position and earned respect and carried himself like a seasoned gentleman. If you were to separate the two of them, you would naturally place them together as they complemented each other in ways that only the two of them could. Lucia was their obvious spawn. She received the strongest characteristics from both of them. Everybody in town knew them and respected them.

"Papa, I want you to meet Lieutenant Rick Hamilton. He is the young man that I told you about when I was in America," Lucia said, introducing Rick to her father.

"Lieutenant, I heard about you. You were very nice to my daughter, a great comfort at times. I welcome you to my country and my home. There is much that I owe you."

"Please, sir, the honor is all mine. Lucia is..." Rick said catching himself, knowing that he couldn't say too much and certainly nothing about the feelings he has for Lucia, "wonderful, just wonderful. And I love your country. I would like to come back to visit after this war is over. It should not be long now," Rick said with confidence.

Looking over to Mrs. Bellamonte, Rick politely nodded and kissed her hand when she gave it to him. In Italian, having practiced it often since he was in the country (he was getting quite good), Rick said, "*La mia signora giusta, posso dire da tutto che sia allineare questo giorno che siete l'anima più bella che abbia benedetto mai questi colline fiorite da cui, Lucia è il fiore più grazioso sviluppato nella valle di amore e di vita,*" which means, "My fair lady, I can say by all that is true this day that you are the loveliest soul that has ever blessed these flowered hills from which, Lucia is the prettiest flower grown in the valley of love and life."

Lucia's mother was touched by his capture of the Italian language and his poetic kindness. Lucia's father put his arm around Lucia's mother and kissed her head.

Lucia's mother said in response to those kind words, "*Non ho sentito le parole come quello parlato me da quando ero un bambino. Siete un caro ragazzo ed avete un cuore caldo. Lucia è molto fortunato averlo come amico. Sarete sempre nei cuori del mama e del papa del Lucia,*" she said placing her hand over her heart.

"*Permetta prego che noi siamo la vostra famiglia mentre siete qui in Italia. Conservazione del dio di maggio voi sicuri.*" Translated she said, "I have not heard words like that spoken to me since I was a child. You are a dear boy and have a warm heart. Lucia is very lucky to have you as a friend. You will always be in the hearts of Lucia's mama and papa. Please allow us to be your family while you are here in Italy. May God keep you safe."

Mr. Bellamonte, holding his wife, said to Rick in English, "Your Italian is very good, Rick; my compliments to your teacher."

"Thank you, sir. I have learned the basics from college but have learned the style from the people here in Italy. I love it here."

The morning activities continued through into the afternoon. Rick and Lucia went touring with Lucia acting as the tour guide. The first stop was Torre Grossa which was the tallest tower in the city at 177 feet tall or seventeen stories. The stairs to the top were in bad shape so Lucia and Rick had to take their time.

Lucia, leading the way, looked back at Rick and said, "Doesn't this remind you of something?"

"Funny, I was just going to ask you the same question."

"At the top you have to climb a ladder to view the city but it is worth the trip," Lucia said.

"I'm looking forward to it."

At the top they came across a large bell they had to navigate around but the view was spectacular. They could see 360 degrees in every direction. Every villa and village for miles could be seen upon tiny Tuscan hills filled with orchards of olive trees and grapes.

Their next stop on their tour was the Rocca. The Rocca was a ruined fortress on the highest part of the hill that San Gimignano was built on. It was surrounded by the buildings, parks, and groves of different varieties, shapes, and colors that 800 years of civilization had cultivated. While there, Rick and Lucia sat sipping wine and eating cheese from one of the festival street vendors. The most popular wine along the street leading up to the Rocca was the Vernaccia di San Gimignano.

Rick was really enjoying the afternoon and the wine. "This is really good. It's different. I have never had anything like it," Rick said.

"This was the first wine my father started to produce here that was different from the traditional Chianti. Vernaccia is produced like a red wine but it is made from white grapes. That is why it has a golden color. It has a fruity and floral bouquet that has a great aftertaste. It is becoming very popular."

"I don't know for sure but there could be a market for this new taste in America after the war. It is something I hope your father will consider."

"Barone and I run the business now and it is in the plan. You are the first American to try it. I'm glad you like it. Your opinion means so much to me. It always has."

"I could help when the time comes to try your marketing strategy. I hope you will allow me to..." he hesitated, not wanting to pressure her into anything she would not feel comfortable with, but wanted to test the waters, "...be involved in your American venture or plan. I mean even if it is purely professional."

"Do you actually think that you and I could ever be strictly professional?" asked Lucia with a little smirk.

"I don't know," Rick said taking a sip of his wine. "But I think of the alternative, of not seeing you. I would like to try."

"We'll see. It is a long way off. A lot could happen in the meantime."

The tour continued to the many arches that were around the small town and to the Duomo, which was a church adorned with ancient frescoes on the inside walls. From the outside it was simple. It was a very unimpressive-looking building except for its large Romanesque appearance.

"My family has been going to Mass here for over a hundred years. Benozzo Gozzoli was one of the fresco painters who did one of these paintings. He was related to the Bellamontes. I don't know which one for sure he did but I like coming here, for the quiet sometimes."

"It's beautiful, Lucia. Just amazing," Rick said staring at the ceiling and the details on the walls and the floor. "The talent and workmanship, skill and patience to do all this, to do everything in this town is...is...amazing."

On their walk back to the center of town Rick said, "Lucia, thanks for showing me around. This was an amazing day and being with you just made it something I will never forget."

"Well, this day is not over. The night is almost here and that is where the fun really begins, with dancing and lights and the laughter that quickly follows."

When they approached the Piazza Della Cisterna the moon was rising overhead. It could be seen in between the ancient brick bell towers of the city dressed by potted plants in windows below. Rick and Lucia took their seats reserved for the Bellamontes near the front. The moon was larger than usual and lit the passing cotton candy clouds giving them a ghostly light blue hue. The inspired shadows they cast on the buildings were like a moving silver curtain revealing a stage at the opening of a show. The moon's subtle dawning acted as a washed-out spotlight on the stage before the seated crowd of a hundred or more. There were even more positioned along the sides talking and enjoying each other. Each one had a glass of wine. Most were eating something such as bread, olives, or cheese or a combination of the three.

The night's highlight was a small concert in the middle of town at the Piazza Della Cisterna where local string players playing violins, cellos, violas, a mandolin, and a beautiful harp were gathered to complement the tambourines, flutes, clarinets, an oboe, tuba, a couple of trumpets, and an upright piano. The musicians from San Gimignano and the surrounding towns formed the ensemble that was gathered to accompany singers from all over Tuscany. The stage was lit like the streets, with an assortment of low-intensity colors, bright enough to light only the smiles, the faces, and the hearts of the people watching and living the moment. At one point in the performance the master of ceremonies asked Lucia to sing a song from Verdi's *Requiem* which they had performed with her before she left for the States. Lucia did not want to perform because it had been years since she sang the song, at least in public, but after some coaxing with a loud and excited applause, she went to the stage. The stage was nothing more than a large front porch in front of a public building located prominently in the Piazza.

Lucia began to stand up from the table, with Rick adjusting her chair away as the perfect gentleman that he had become when he was with her. Lucia approached the stage glamorously wearing a white and light pink dress that touched her shoulders facilely like the light from above and addressed her legs like the water of a tranquil ocean inspiring an unblemished shore. "Stars, behold thy beauty as you walk the earth with thy grace. Love has no better covenant than that that lives and breathes within her heart and mirrored in the actions of her unclouded soul," Rick thought.

"The lights could go out and she could still be seen," he whispered to Esta. Esta reached over and squeezed his hand.

Lucia began singing after a brief musical introduction from the medium-sized orchestra. Nothing sounded more perfect or beautiful. She hit every note sharp and clear in an effortless vibrato. Her expressions and gestures were heartfelt as if she lived every word and note in the song.

Standing in the shadows at a corner of a street as it enters the square were four figures in American uniforms standing side by side watching the performance. Sean, Pat, Bunky and Jack, all officers from the 463rd, were on their way to the crash site when they heard the music. Sean was beyond amazement when he recognized Lucia. "You have to be kidding me," he said to Pat in a breathless tone of total disbelief.

"Kidding what? What do you see?" asked Pat.

"That woman singing is Lucia. The girl I was telling you about that visited us in Manteo and stayed with Kelly over the summers."

"That's Lucia? You have to be kidding me," reiterating Sean's phrase a moment before with the same disbelief. "She's stunning."

"Wow, five years has done her good. Real good," Sean said.

"Hey, isn't that Rick sitting over there?" said Bunky to Sean.

"Sure as shoot'n is," said Sean.

"Let's go get 'em," said the eager Jack Nelson, known as "Admiral" to his friends, as he began to move towards him.

"Hold on," said Sean putting his hand out stopping his approach. "Let's wait until the song is over, then we'll go over. I will get the first word in. Stay cool."

When the song ended, Lucia took her applause and walked back to her seat. When she arrived at the table Rick stood again and helped her with her chair. Sean and the guys walked over, unseen, and approached the unsuspecting pair.

Getting close to Rick's ear that was the closest to Lucia, Sean whispered, "Do you know what happens to airmen who don't return back to base?" Rick slowly turned, recognizing the voice, and stood in awe, marveling at the spectacular sight of friends not seen in a month and wondering at a time if he ever would again, knocked his chair over in a rush to give Sean a brotherly embrace.

"I never thought I would be so happy to see such an ugly person," said Sean. "Look who else I found," Sean said turning Rick to Pat.

"Pat Dixon? What the hell are you doing here?" Rick asked.

"Finding you," he said laughing, vigorously shaking his hand and slapping him on the shoulder.

"Bunky and Admiral too? How did you guys get here, find me here?"

"We found you on that flyover, or did you forget? Once the Brits pushed through Florence we knew it would be safe to come up here to look for you. Fifteenth Headquarters will be moving to Cortona about fifteen miles from here soon," Sean said.

"We got a jeep from the motor pool and starting driving up here this morning. Roads are terrible," said Pat.

"Try riding in the back!" said Bunky, rubbing is butt.

Sean moved Rick aside as he stole a close-up look of Lucia. Lucia, noticing Sean's smile, began smiling herself and slowly stood facing him.

"Lucia," Sean said in a playful voice. "Wow, give me a hug like you missed me!"

"I did miss you," she said hugging him. "You look great. How is Kelly?

"Didn't Rick tell you? We got married a year ago last July."

"Of course he told me. I also got the wedding invitation, a little late though. Next time I need a little more notice than a couple of weeks!" she said, kissing him on the cheek. "Congratulations. That is from me to you and this," she said, kissing his other cheek, "is for Kelly."

"Hi, I'm Pat," said Pat introducing himself.

Clearing his voice first Bunky said, "I'm Tom. My friends call me Bunky."

"I'm Jack. My friends call me Admiral," said Jack, impatiently eager to meet the prettiest woman he had ever seen.

Taking all this in, Lucia said, "I am Lucia and I am very glad to meet each of you. I never knew America had so many good-looking gentlemen," she said encouraging their playfulness. "Welcome to Tuscany. Please, I want to introduce you to my family."

The introductions took a while as most people in attendance were related or familiar with Lucia and her family in one way or another. The festive party of liberation turned into a party of reunion and didn't end until early the next morning. The wine was sweet and plentiful and the food was rich and tasty. The entire town turned out to meet the American airmen. The first Americans to walk their streets as liberators were treated with the utmost courtesy, gratitude, and admiration.

The next day Rick got up earlier than he normally would have but the thought of leaving Lucia and his new friends was resting heavy on his heart and made his night restless. He took an early walk through the vineyard and sat on a green hill that overlooked the Marzoli house and vineyard. In the far distance he could see San Gimignano in the misty lap of repose that nature so kindly relinquished to her beloved people. Rick thought of the events that brought him there and those that brought him to that moment since. He felt very lucky and was not certain that he deserved to be so fortunate. He thought of his crew and the lovely graves that Gino and his men took such loving care of.

Through the still air he saw Lucia walking up the hill to be with him wearing a long gown of cotton, plain and simple, with her hair uncombed and curly from the humidity.

Approaching him she said, *"Buona mattina."*

"Good morning, Lucia," he replied. "How did you sleep?"

"Not well, I thought about you and how empty my bed felt. It has always felt cold since I was with you at Bodie that night. I fear that I will never feel that way again, so I was restless, especially since you were just in the next room," she said smiling. "You will be leaving today, won't you?"

"I will. It's my duty. I knew that this would not last long. Nothing good ever does, it seems like," Rick said, looking at her then back to the hills. "It is beautiful up here. You are a very lucky lady. You have a great family and future here. This land, this country is yours and you are hers. You belong here," he said with certainty in his voice. After a brief pause he said, nodding, "You were right. You said that I would have to see and experience Tuscany to understand. Well, I have and I do. When I began this crusade, this search for you over a year ago…no, really it was ever since I made love to you at Bodie, I was hoping that when I found you I could take you back with me, never to be separated again. After all this, what has happened to me here over the past month, I know now that I can't, that I wouldn't."

"Rick…" Lucia began saying.

"Lucia," Rick said, interrupting, "I love you and have since the first time I saw you," he said taking her hand and she pressing her palm into his. "Shakespeare said, 'Hear my soul speak. Of the very instant that I saw you did my heart fly at your service. Who ever loved that loved not at first sight? When I saw you I fell in love, and you smiled because you knew.'"

Lucia smiled at Rick at his warm and sweet words and remembered that she did smile the first time Rick tried to speak to her.

"Rick, this place is my home but my love is with you. Shakespeare is right about love at first sight. I felt it too. I have never felt anything like I feel when I am with you. I don't know what will happen a year from now, tomorrow or even after we walk down from this hill, but I do know that I will love you like no other for as long as I shall live."

"I don't want to go on like I have for the past five years. I need to be able to communicate with you somehow."

"I don't know how that is possible, Rick. I know you have some ideas about helping me promoting my business in America, but I have to stay faithful to my husband and I will. If he ever knew of my feelings for you," she said pausing, "it just wouldn't work."

"I know. Really, I do. I will not complicate your life. I just want you to know that if you ever need anything, you come to me. You know how to contact me."

"I will always know how to contact you."

For an hour the two of them sat and talked about their lives, her family, Barone's activity in the partisans, Rick's flight training and how he decided to fly and how he got so good at speaking Italian. What time does not allow, a marriage of the heart makes up for. Rick understood Lucia and would never compromise her security, health, and well-being. Although he knew that this would probably be the last time he would spend any real time with her, he was comfortable with the knowledge that she was OK and taken care of. The smell of Tuscany and the love that came from the smiles and the warmth that spilled from the sunny sky, the fields, and the hellos at every turn was more than any one person could ever ask for. Love was there, Lucia was there and it was there that she belonged.

They walked to the house together and had breakfast. Bunky and Jack were a bit hung over but Sean was fine. As they loaded up the jeep with supplies and a couple of provisions from the Marzolis, including a case of their wine given as a present by the family, Rick said to Sean, "I want to go to my plane and crew one more time before I go."

"Sure, I would like to go with you if it is OK," Sean said being extremely considerate of Rick's feelings and perhaps wanting to be alone.

"I would like that."

Sean looked back at the others and said, "We'll be right back."

"Sure, Sean. You and Rick go. Take your time. We'll finish up here," said Pat.

Rick, Sean, and Lucia boarded the cart and went to *The Lucky Irishman*. Sean walked over to the nose of the bomber and patted the clover on the nose while Rick went straight for the graves with Lucia. Nobody said a word. Nobody had to. It was a farewell from a captain to his crew. A closure to a chapter covered in courage, fear, bravery, valor, and of duty. Rick stood silently with his head bowed, eyes closed, saying a prayer to the Almighty, the keeper of their souls, asking that He would grant their souls the peace their bodies and hearts fought so hard for in life.

Lucia put her arm around Rick and rested her head on his shoulder. She looked up to his face and saw a tear fall from his eyes. She kissed each one then kissed his forehead. Sean walked over and stood on the other side of Rick with deep respect and taciturn sorrow. They stood awhile then walked with Rick to the nose of the bomber. He stopped, and upon the nose of *The Lucky Irishman* he wrote from memory a sonnet he recited as part of a Players production in the fall of 1940 at the Greek theatre when he attended Richmond College:

SONNET 30

When to the sessions of sweet silent thought
I summon up remembrance of things past,
I sigh the lack of many a thing I sought,
And with old woes new wail my dear time's waste:
Then can I drown and eye, unused to flow,
For precious friends hid in death's dateless night,
And weep afresh love's long since canceled woe,
And moan the expense of many a vanished sight:
Then can I grieve at grievances foregone,
And heavily from woe to woe tell o'er
The sad account of fore-bemoaned moan,
Which I new pay as if not paid before.
But if the while I think on thee, dear friend,
All losses are restored and sorrows end.

Wm. Shakespeare
I will remember you always, my friend. Until we meet again....
R. Hamilton

Rick turned to Sean saying, "Sean, could you leave me and Lucia alone for a moment."

"Sure, bud, I will be in the cart."

Rick turned to Lucia and held her by the hands. "I won't be able to say good-bye to you at the house the way I would like so I want to say good-bye to you here. Lucia, you are the best thing that has ever happened to me. I love you. If ever an opportunity…"

Lucia putting her forefinger over his lips said, "Say nothing more. I feel as you do. I am sure I will see you again, someday. You come back and visit if you get a chance. You have friends here."

"I have more than friends here. I guess that is the way we should approach this. I will come back to visit." He looked deep into her eyes that were beginning to fill and said, "I am going to miss you so much."

She quickly kissed him to stop the cry from happening but mostly because she wanted to kiss him in the way she had been dying to since she saw him a month ago. The kiss was moist and full of undeniable feeling and love for the other. Lucia walked with Rick back to the cart and stood by its side. Rick, taking her hand, said, "Let me give you a hand in."

"No. You two go ahead. I want to walk back."

"Oh no, you don't. You are coming with us. I can't leave you here."

"Oh yes, you are," she said sternly but as a passionate plea.

Rick, knowing when there is no sense arguing, kissed her cheek again and said, "I will see ya. Write or something, OK?"

"Something," she said sadly smiling. "Good-bye, Sean. Give Kelly a kiss for me."

"I will, Lucia. Good luck and be careful. Celone is not that far."

With a wave Sean and Rick began the trip back to the house. Lucia stood there watching as Rick rode away looking back once more before he went over the hill, obviously distressed with the scene. Lucia covered her mouth and cried.

Upon arrival at Celone, Rick was met by handshakes, pats on the back, and greetings of all kinds. Once Colonel Kurtz heard about Rick's flight and landing he put him in for the Distinguished Flying Cross. Rick would rather go to his bunk and rest but the boys of the 463rd were just too excited about his return. The morning after his return he had to check into the base hospital to get a flight physical from the flight surgeon to evaluate his flight status. The doctor grounded him for at least two to three weeks until his cracked ribs healed. He was glad to hear they were not broken but the pain he experienced the first week certainly convinced him otherwise.

Sean went back to flying on the ninth of August on a mission to Hungary. Rick worried every time Sean went on a mission. Rick knew that Sean had twenty-five missions under his belt and was quickly reaching the thirty-five required missions and a ticket back to the States. He had his fingers crossed every time the group took off for a mission and was always out by base ops when the group returned with binoculars counting planes along with everybody else.

On August 15, the group conducted a night bombing mission on a bridge in Valence, France. The group did not do many nighttime missions and that made the squadron pilots a tad nervous. The lead aircraft had a "Mickey Ball" in place of the ball turret, which was a radar dome to find targets at night and when the target was overcast. On missions like that every bomber would "toggle" their bombs on the lead aircraft. Toggling was strict procedure when Mickey was used. The group had an excellent strike but lost four planes and their crews. It was still dark early in the morning the next day when the planes returned. Familiar flairs were shot from the planes prior to landing notifying ground personnel of aircraft damage and injuries. They lit the sky with an awful story of bravery and sacrifice with red, green, and yellow cascading colors. Fortunately Sean returned but he shot a red and a green flair indicating that they had casualties and a damaged plane. Upon landing, it was seen that Sean had lost his bombardier and had a wounded waist gunner. His plane ran into some serious flak trouble when they entered the box. He had an engine shot out and lost part of his left wing and elevator. *Kelly's Lucky Prayer* got real lucky and Sean knew it. He was getting more and more nervous with each flight as the thirty-fifth mission got closer and closer. Rick always knew Sean as a man of calm and fearlessness but he could tell that Kelly was on his mind. Rick also knew of the added dangers and problems that were self-induced if a pilot was not fully engaged mentally in his flying duties and this troubled Rick greatly. Sean had to fight off the Germans and now his own thoughts of home.

Rick took some time to visit the Amicis. He missed Cara, the darling little girl with the prettiest eyes, and brought her a soda from the mess hall. He also brought the usual pantry items that would not spoil along with some laundry soap he found near the washers. They were all elated to see him again. Mr. Amici was out in town doing odd jobs for pay. They heard that Rick was shot down and worried that he was hurt or killed. They were relieved and thankful to hear from Sean, who paid them a courtesy visit telling them that Rick was alive and on a farm near San Gimignano.

"*Potevate visitare il San Gimignano e la gente là?*" asked Mrs. Amici, meaning, "Were you able to visit San Gimagano and the people there?"

Rick responded, "*Sì, dopo Firenze è stato liberato. Ognuno ha avuto una festa che ha durato tutta la notte,*" which meant, "Yes, after Florence was liberated. Everybody had a fiesta that lasted all night."

Mrs. Amici said, "*Abbiamo famiglia in San Gimagano.*"

Cara being held close by her grandmother looked up and said, "Mama?"

Mrs. Amici, quickly redirecting the conversation, said, "Shhh Cara." Then talking to Rick said, "*Sta ottenendo ritardato e devo ottenere il pranzo aspetto per il Grandpapa,*" translated meaning, "It is getting late and I have to get dinner ready for Grandpapa."

Rick, being a bit puzzled at the last several exchanges of conversation, stood and excused himself with a promise he would return again later.

Walking back to his barracks he was scratching his head running that dialog through his head over and over again. "There was just not enough information passed to get a hook on anything that meant anything," he thought. "Odd. I wonder who they know, probably partisans. That would explain why they wouldn't want to say too much."

"Mama?" he said questioning Cara's word. "Mama. Now that is a word," he said to himself with undeniable certainty. "It is the one word of all that was said all day that might have the most important meaning. Undoubtedly her mama is alive," he thought. "Mama."

Rick came across an Italian newspaper from Rome lying about in the mess hall on the morning of the eighteenth. It was almost a week old but it was still news to the Americans who didn't have a paper of their own. Their world consisted of briefings and music on the radio. Some guys tried to start a paper of their own but it never really amounted to anything but group news, such as who had a baby and scores from the ball games in the States.

Rick was reading about the massacres and atrocities the Germans were committing as they were withdrawing from towns and territories. One town stuck in his mind like glue, Lucca. The article read that on August 12, between Lucca and Currara, just north of Pisa the small village Sant' Anna di Stazzema was the target of a mass slaughter. The Germans were being ambushed at every turn and corner and skirmishes went on continuously for miles along the route of retreat. When the 16th Panzergrenadier Reichfuhrer-SS Division reached the outskirts of Sant' Anna they rounded up over 560 men, women, and children and shot them in cold blood, without reason, but suspected them of being, assisting or hiding partisans. The houses were then burned to the ground along with the local church. A pyre was constructed using the pews as fuel. Bodies were thrown on top, doused with petrol, and set on fire.

"This was less than thirty miles from San Gimignano," Rick thought, "A good way from Sienna but too close to the Marzolis and Lucia's parents." He also recalled that Lucia said something about her husband being in the Lucca area.

He saw Sean walk into the mess hall and quickly hid the paper, not that Sean could read Italian but there was no point taking the chance. Under normal conditions Rick would not hesitate to discuss his concern with him but since his mind was already occupied with Kelly, which had its own risks, there was no point in complicating matters with this. "Besides," he thought, "it is probably nothing, nothing at all." In either case Rick wished he could talk to Lucia to see how she was doing but that would have to come another day.

On August 22, Rick was given back his flight status. The next day he was given a refresher flight. It was odd beyond belief to fly with a different crew. It was ghostly in more than one way. Eerie and sad, he felt out of place, like being at a reunion and not recognizing anybody. The instructor pilot giving Rick his first flight in seven weeks was junior to him, but that did not bother Rick. He was anxious to meet his new co-pilot, however. The crew came from crews that were shattered from combat or were replacements, fresh from the States. Prior to takeoff he introduced himself to each member and tried to get familiar with their names, nicknames, if they had one, and position on the crew. The officers were experienced except for the bombardier, which was not that big of a deal by this time in the war as most of the time they toggled their bombs anyway. This would give Rick's bombardier, Lieutenant Todd Tygesen, time to get the experience he would need to be cool and calm on missions.

It was not long when Rick was back in combat flying off the wing of the lead in the second flight to Brno, Czechoslovakia. It was a Twenty-seven plane daylight raid on an airfield. The resistance was light with only about five minutes of flak and no damage to his plane. Bombing results were excellent which made his twentieth mission a milk run.

His missions continued deep into Europe mostly. They hit a railway bridge in Aviso, Italy, with good result on August 26 and submarine pens in Genoa, Italy on September 4. He was glad that there were but a few missions in Italy as it indicated that the Germans were either gone or that the Italian targets were considered unimportant.

He continued to keep up with local and national events ever since he read about the Sant' Anna massacres. He read that the murders continued in Bardine San Terenzo and Mezzana on August 20. There, hundreds of civilians—women, children, and men of every age—were indiscriminately murdered. Rick just closed the paper wishing this war would hurry up and end.

Operational tempo was consistent. They flew for the first time on a mission to Athens, Greece, on September 15. He told Todd to make sure his bombs hit the intended target as he loved Greek and Roman history and did not want to be responsible for any damage to any historical site where history was as old as civilization. Every mission that had a target in a historically significant area was briefed that way by the operations officer. Every mission considered the historical significance of the area. Red "No Hit" areas were placed on target maps. This mission was on an airfield so it was well clear of the Acropolis.

The mission had excellent results and the group did not have any losses. After the mission Rick brought his crew to the front of his plane and told them that he wanted to name her *The Lucky Irishman, II.* They all liked the idea and accepted the name enthusiastically. Most of his crew did not know the crew of the first *Lucky Irishman* but knew of their reputation. They all hoped that they could live up to that standard. Rick told them that his crew wasn't anything special except that they were very professional, personally close as a family, and worked like a team. "Don't try to live up to their reputation but establish your own. Communication," he said, "is the key. Back each other up. Keep your weapons and equipment clean and operational. Hang out and eat with each other as a crew. Get to know everybody's hometown, girlfriends, parents, and favorite foods; everything you can. Knowledge is power and power will end this war."

"The Lucky Irishman, II" was painted on the nose a week later. It was usually considered bad luck to rename a plane, but since the nose of the bomber was completely reworked, flown to Celone from another group without a name on her, Rick decided that it was OK. He even had the Catholic chaplain, Captain Gene Gomulka, come over and bless her, just in case. Gene said some prayers and sprinkled *The Lucky Irishman, II* with holy water he got from a holy fountain near the Vatican in Rome. He gave Rick and his crew a playful baptism with the water that was left over in the pail by throwing it on them.

Sean's count continued; twenty-nine, thirty, thirty-one. On his thirty-second mission and on Rick's twenty-seventh, they flew again to Blechhammer, Germany, on October 17, where there was a stubborn oil refinery that just refused to stay dead. The missions to Blechhammer were always dreaded because the Germans protected it well with flak. With the P-51s escorting the bombers all the way to the target and back the 463rd was well protected from German fighters. On this mission, however, the 463rd saw her first Me-262 as it screamed by at a closure rate of 800 mph. It was the fastest airplane in the sky, being powered by the first jet engines. No bomber was shot down by the two Me-262s because the Mustangs of the 31st FG engaged them and chased them off. It made the crews thankful that this war was just about over and that their "Little Friends" were above acting as guardian angels. The flight continued to the target. When the group entered the box it was intense as anticipated. The Germans knew they were coming as the 463rd have been there before. Sean and Rick both took hits that damaged their planes almost right away. One plane from 772 was hit, taking off one of its wings. The plane was seen twisting through the sky with eight chutes opening. Sean and Rick were able to drop their bomb loads but were unable to keep up with the flight on their return to Celone. Pat was with his squadron mates of the 309th FS providing cover all the way back. Rick had a wounded crewman and Sean did also but nothing was considered life threatening. "Thank God for the small blessings," Rick thought.

Upon arriving at Celone he noticed that there were two B-17s resting on their bellies off the runway, as several others were still circling the airfield. Pat and the other Mustangs broke off and went back to their base in San Severo. Rick and Sean shot the required red and green flares and had the ambulances waiting when they arrived. Rick went to Sean after his crew was taken care of and saw him standing with blood along his right shoulder.

Rick asked Sean, "You OK?"

"Yeah. Bunky got hit pretty good. A piece of 88 came right through our cockpit and hit Bunk right in the shoulder. Andy came up and bandaged him up," he said, noticeably disturbed. Shaking his head Sean said, "I don't know, Rick, three more missions. You have five more than I do. You think we will get out of this?" he asked Rick, knowing his answer.

"We have to. We have come so far already and have so much to live for."

"We don't have any more or any less than any of these guys here. We all deserve to go home," Sean said slapping his cover on his right thigh in frustration as he began to walk to the jeep that was waiting to take him to the debriefing tent. Rick stood there and watched his friend drive off with his crew feeling his pain and anxiety, just wondering if anybody really appreciated the sacrifices that he, Sean, and every American made every day of their lives there. He then walked to the truck where his crew was waiting and began the quick trip to the debriefing area.

Since Rick and Sean's planes were so badly damaged, their respective crews flew as replacement aircrew if they were not involved with the repair of their own plane.

Rick, with special permission, was able to fly with Sean on his last several missions. His last one was on board *Kelly's Lucky Prayer* on a special low-altitude mission ranging from 300 to 500 feet AGL. It involved three planes from the 773rd BS to hit the Florisdorf Oil Refinery in Vienna, Austria. It was considered to be a special operations raid with the 31st FG providing close escort support. The briefing confirmed the intensity and importance of the mission. It was felt that a large bomber formation would bring too much attention and that the cost in American crews would not be worth it. It was felt, however, that three B-17s with their entire 6,000-pound complement of 500-pound bombs placed in key, strategic areas of the plant could do the damage requested by Fifteenth HQ. Missions of this kind were usually reserved for B-25 Mitchell bomber but HQ wanted as few planes as possible with the greatest impact. As the 463rd was not committed and the B-24 groups were, the choice became obvious.

The mission was briefed, launched and flown with the 309th FS picking up the bombers over Pescara before going "Feet Wet" over the Adriatic Sea at 15,000 feet. When the flight approached the Croatian mountain range, the bombers dropped to within 300 feet of the surface and flew towards Vienna through Hungary at a top speed of 270 mph. Engines ran so hot they had the engine cowl flaps open. Everything was running well within the operational parameters of Pratt and Whitney and Boeing.

The skies were scattered to partly cloudy, allowing the bombers to maintain some semblance of a formation all the way to Vienna with radio silence. Five minutes prior to reaching Vienna, the Mustangs broke off to the bombers' perimeter looking for targets of opportunity. The B-17s, with *Kelly's Lucky Prayer* in the lead, climbed to 800 feet, got tight and opened their bomb-bay doors. Suddenly triple-A opened up all around with 20mm, 37mm and 40mm rounds with tracers guiding German eyes upward looking for Yankee blood.

Sean, being very focused on the mission, said, "Pilot to bombadier, you got her," giving him control of the plane.

"Got her, Skip," came the quick reply from the nose.

Less than fifteen seconds later the anxiously waited call, "Bombs away," was heard over the intercom. Every bomber in the formation dropped their explosive 6,000-pound cargo when Sean dropped his.

"OK, Skip, let's get out of here!" cried the bombardier.

Sean took the bomber on a right turn out away from the built-up areas. The other bombers turned with Sean and joined up staying at a 1,000 feet. The Mustangs were seen behind strafing some of the triple-A sites and some oil storage tanks not hit by the bombs. After leaving their calling card, the Mustangs joined up on the flight looking for bandits that were sure to be waiting for them now.

Sean, knowing that they were not out of trouble yet, called the flight to check in.

"Two good. Everybody OK."

"Three hit but OK right now."

Sean, glad to hear that no one was badly hurt, began to climb to an altitude that they could fight at.

Over Hungary Pat called, "Bandits, six o'clock. Bullet (which was the call sign of one of the Mustang pilots), stay with Able Flight. Duck Flight, let's get 'em."

The Mustangs climbed at full military power and engaged the flight of five FW-190s, killing one on the first pass. Each Mustang had his turn getting personal with the 190s. One German got on the tail of "Duck Two" and put a couple of holes in his tail but was quickly shaken by the superior maneuverability of the P-51. The Folke Wolfes did not have much stomach to fight so fled after several minutes. Duck Flight quickly rejoined Able Flight.

"Duck One, Able One," called Rick to Pat.

"Go, Able One."

"Sean's been hit. A round came in from above and hit him in the back of the shoulder. We are going to have to push it," explained Rick. Everybody knew that this was Sean's last flight before heading home, but now everybody was wondering just *how* he was going home. Rick did not sound well and that alarmed the flight.

It was one of the longest flights of Rick's life. Sean was bleeding badly and there was not much anybody could do about it.

"Come on, Sean, stay in there," Rick said trying to encourage his best friend in the whole world.

"I'm OK. Just fly the plane," Sean said painfully and not fooling Rick at all.

Rick remembered the last flight of *The Lucky Irishman* and Tab bleeding to death. "I lost one pilot. I will not lose another," he silently thought. He reached around his neck and removed his dog tags with his scapular medal, St Joseph Cupertino and St. Christopher medal and Bodie attached and hung them from the number-four-engine feathering switch.

Sean looked at them and asked him what he was doing.

"They saved my life before. They will save yours and get you back to Kelly. Just don't you worry about it now so be still, damn it," said Rick trying to tweak more power from the already stressed engines.

Approaching the Celone airfield Rick shot the red flare and was the first to land with Pat flying off his wing as he touched the runway. Across the radio as Rick was taxing in Pat called, "Able One, God speed, my friend. Call me as soon as you know something."

"Able One to Duck One. You will be the first I call. Duck flight..." Rick began saying but being forced to pause because emotion was swelling up in his throat. After gaining some composure he continued, by simply saying, "Thank you."

Sean was removed from the cockpit, laid on a stretcher, and rushed to the hospital. Rick looked about the flight line and saw the celebration that the group was preparing for Sean and his crew on his return. "Congratulations

Lieutenant Ryan and 'Kelly's Lucky Prayer'" was scrolled across a banner and attached to the control tower. Long tables with tubs of ice were positioned as refreshments by the base of the tower with only a couple of airmen and mess men standing by. What was to be a jubilant occasion turned out stifled by worry and concern. Sean's crew and the other crewmen of the flight somberly walked by the table and grabbed a bottle of pop and a sandwich. They stood about talking about the flight reassuring each other that Sean would be fine, which allowed for the occasional smile to be seen and laugh to be heard. Rick was having a pop with them when members of his crew came over to give him the support they knew he would need. The HQ staff was also there and got an informal debrief around the table from Rick. The captains from Able Two and Three gave the formal one, not wanting to bother Rick. The mission was a complete success. Sean's crew was going home thanks to his leadership. They all wished he was walking away from his plane rather than being carried from her. Rick just headed towards the barracks after he finished his pop and sandwich to change and shower before he went to the hospital where he knew he would end up staying the night.

The next day the surgeon came out to Rick, who was sleeping in a chair, to tell him about Sean's condition.

"Lieutenant Ryan will be OK. A spent .50-cal round from one of the Mustangs grazed the upper part of his latissimus dorsi just under his right armpit. It was just a freak random shot. Fact is the .50-cal bullet fell to the floor when we removed his jacket. He will be on his way home tomorrow on the C-47 with his crew. He can recover just as well stateside as he could here. Better I would say."

Rick took his first full breath in nearly eighteen hours.

"Damn, Doc," he said slumping back into his chair. "Thank God Almighty. Thank you, God. When can I see him?"

"You can go in now but he is heavily sedated. Don't wake him if he is sleeping."

Rick went into his room and Sean was sleeping peacefully. He went to a table next to the bed and began to write a note to him in the event he did not wake so he could say good-bye to him.

6 Nov 44
Dear Sean,

You are the best friend any guy could ever have. I stayed here with you all night while you were in the hospital just hoping in the event you woke that I could tell you, in person, just how much you mean to me. You hurry up and heal and make love to my darling Kelly and have many kids. Tell my mom and dad, Kelly and her mom that I miss them and that I am OK. I will see you soon in Manteo.

Your co-pilot and friend,
Rick

Sean woke for a brief moment as he was being lifted into the C-47 the next day and saw Rick standing in the crowd cheering and wishing him a safe trip home. Sean had the letter in his hand and waved it to him mouthing the words "I will see you at home."

Rick stood there smiling and nodded in the affirmative, giving him a casual salute.

For Sean the war was over; as for Rick, he had eight more missions to go. Time in Celone was going to seem like an eternity without Sean around.

11

With winter settling in over Europe, the weather was getting worse and overcast the targets most of the time. The Mickey plane led most of the flights using a "spot jammer" as well as "chaff," which were thousands of pieces of tin foil deployed over triple-A emplacements to distract enemy triple-A radar that was accurately targeting the American and British formations. The use of the Mickey was effective but the American fliers could not confirm their results the same day because they could not get a visual confirmation of the damage. It was frustrating everybody who risked life and limb to hit the target. It was normal to want to know how they did right away.

Rick was getting close to the end of his countdown. He had two more and he was going home. Being so close to Lucia he wanted to see her, but the new group commanding officer, Colonel G. W. McGregor, did not want his crews gallivanting about Italy in their off time. Rick completely understood. They were highly trained pilots and could not be risked so foolishly.

Rick was again faced with not being able to write Lucia. It ate at his heart to know that she was not far away but could not get to her or even talk to her. Not knowing her physical and emotional condition, not to mention her safety, was affecting his concentration. He came to the stark realization that he just might have to wait for the end of the war to go back to see her and the Marzolis. On the bright side of that thought, he knew that Germany was just about through resisting. He came to that conclusion because the missions were concentrating on oil refineries in Austria and Germany. Missions like that, in the past, were often covered with German fighters who were noticeably absent from the skies now.

Hitting the marshalling yards like they had was taking a terrible logistic toll on the once powerful German war machine. They could no longer send supplies to repair the war damage or to the troops who needed them on the front lines which were becoming more indiscernible everywhere. Without supply, defeat is inevitable. It was being drastically seen in Europe and being played out every day in the air, on the ground, in the cities, and towns by armed combatants. It was seen in the destituteness of the civilians who had to live in the scars and rubble of the homes they once lived.

Rick did take the time to see Cara from time to time, but the family was gone more often than not. The reason for their absence was never clear, but Rick suspected that the Amicis had to travel to where the business opportunities were. As long as Cara was taken care of he felt OK but he missed her terribly.

On Christmas Eve, Rick got a V-mail from Sean and Kelly wishing him a Merry Christmas and telling him that all was well back home. Sean was released from the 17th General Hospital in Italy two weeks after he arrived there then flown to Charlotte via England for rehabilitation and leave. His note was short but it said the important things. "Not long now," Rick thought.

Rick went back to Cara's house Christmas day with some presents for her and the family, but again there was no one home. Looking in the window he saw dust on the furniture and the empty cabinets.

"Where did they go?" Rick asked himself. He went to a neighbor's home and inquired as to their whereabouts, but they were not sure. They expected that they would be back one day because they were certain that if they were not coming back that the Amicis would have told someone. Rick did not share in their belief. He felt something strange was going on. He gave the presents he had for the Amicis to their neighbors and walked back to the base via the place he saw Cara the first time. "I will come back, Cara," he said looking at the spot where she played and at her house that was not far away.

Prior to Rick's last mission he was filled with different emotions, excitement, eagerness, fear, but mostly reflection of everything he did to get himself to that mission. He thought of Cara, and the Amicis, the Marzolis and, of course, the diamond in his sky, Lucia, and all she meant to him and to his personal world. He could not overlook thinking about the aircrews that would remain behind to finish that war and how some would not make it home at all. "Their chances are better than mine nine months ago," he thought, "and mine were better than those who started our offensive on the Axis in '42."

Rick's last mission was to be an attack on the marshalling yards in Vienna on January 15, 1945. It was a twenty-six-plane mission with the 31st FG flying escort again. The mission had its flak but no enemy fighters. Rick saw a new crew aboard *Day Dreamer* go in after she dropped her bombs. She went into the final approach to the target with number three engine trailing smoke, then started taking a gradual right descending turn from which she did not recover. Ten chutes were seen opening, which everybody was glad to see, but all were puzzled as to why she crashed to begin with.

Upon reaching Celone, Rick requested permission to make a low pass on the airfield, which was graciously granted. At 500 feet and 200 mph *The Lucky Irishman, II* did her final pass with Rick at the controls. All of the aircrews from the mission landed first so everybody could be on the flight line to watch Rick and his crew grease on his final landing, taxi, and park. The crew of *The Lucky Irishman, II* traditionally kissed the ground with Rick being the first. His flight crew carried Rick on their shoulders to the tables of soda and beer that waited for Rick and his crew.

There were not any missions planned for the group the next day so a festive atmosphere filled the camp. It was what Sean would have had if he was not hurt and Rick felt his absence. It was a day he looked forward to since he flew his first mission but was also saddened by the thought that he was leaving his first crew behind and the woman he hoped to find a way to bring home to Manteo.

After most of the beer was gone the group commander came up to Rick and asked him a question, "Lieutenant—Oh, I'm sorry, Captain. I was asked to give you these," holding out a pair of used captain's bars, "...by Mr. Weldon, who just happens to be my brother-in-law. He knew that you would be promoted soon and knew that I was taking over the 463rd."

"Crud, Colonel, you have to be kidding me? I owe my life to Mr. Weldon. It was because of a little trick he taught me in flight school that I was able to bring my plane in...in July."

"I heard about that. Everybody in the Fifteenth heard about it and that is why they rushed in this decoration," opening the case with the Distinguished Flying Cross in it.

The executive officer standing close by ordered the group to attention. Colonel McGregor pinned the captain's bars onto his collar, shook his hand, and patted him firmly on the shoulder.

The executive officer then read the Distinguished Flying Cross citation:

For heroism and extraordinary achievement in aerial flight as Pilot of a B-17G, The Lucky Irishman, attached to the 463rd Bomb Group, 772nd Bomb Squadron (Heavy), in action against enemy German forces in the vicinity of Blechhammer, Germany, on July 7, 1944. Leading a flight of three B-17s of a multi-flight formation of over 215 planes in a strike against oil and shipping sights, 1st Lieutenant Richard Hamilton pressed an attack in the face of intense antiaircraft fire and enemy fighters. Although his plane was hit and set afire and with one engine out he continued toward the target area and succeeded in dropping his bombs on the target. Returning to base he was attacked by two Me-109s, knocking out a second engine, killing his entire crew and leaking fuel from all of his tanks, he successfully "Dead Stick" landed his plane into a foggy field ten miles east of San Gimignano, Italy. His courage, skill, and devotion to duty were in keeping with the highest traditions of the United States Army Air Force.

For the President,
Henry L. Stimson, Sect'y of War

After the reading and the usual congratulations that followed a promotion and decoration, Colonel McGregor took Rick to the side walking to *The Lucky Irishman, II* and said, "Rick, I need you to do me a favor."

"Yes, sir."

"I need you to fly your plane back to the States and turn it in to the Boeing plant at Wichita."

"Yes, sir, but Boeing Wichita just builds the 29."

"I know, but they want to do some structure analysis on the repairs we did here at Celone. On paper they like what we did here to repair your plane. She has been here from the start and deserves a flight back. What do you say, Captain?"

"Absolutely, sir."

"OK. You will be leaving early tomorrow..."

"Excuse me, sir," Rick said interrupting. "Tomorrow? I was hoping to go to San Gimignano to see some friends before I leave."

"Sorry, son, we are expecting a front through here tomorrow night and will probably be socked in for a week. That is why we are not flying tomorrow."

"Oh, I see," Rick said disappointed.

"Besides, your friends will be here when the war is over and you can come back to do humanitarian flights. I am sure we will be looking for volunteers to do that."

"You are right, sir. I'll do that."

"Good. Go get some real chow, shower, and pack. Your crew is a deserving crew and has already been notified. As you can see," pointing to the airplane, "they're already getting her ready."

The morning of the sixteenth could not come fast enough. Rick could hardly wait to get airborne again. It would be the first time he had flown for the pure enjoyment of it. No mission to kill anybody, no bombs, just passengers and .50 cal's for self-defense. It was a beautiful Tuesday morning. Other than his crew being on the mat and maintenance personnel working, the rest of the group was still resting in their bunks. A sleepy fog covered the ground as Rick threw his duffle bag aboard. He briefed the crew and passengers and introduced himself to Captain Ted Bonner, a veteran from the Eighth Air Force returning home after two tours of duty. His second tour was to train replacement pilots with the 463rd.

"Hi, Ted," Rick began to laugh.

"Watch it, wise guy," said Ted.

"I can't help it. I love your nickname, 'Boner.' I am going to have to call you Ted. I won't be able to fly straight otherwise. You are going to have to tell me how you got it," Rick said, beginning to break into a roar.

"Never mind," said Ted.

The flight back was the reverse of the flight over and took four days. Weather was good and, aside from getting lost for a little while flying over the Azores and contemplating ditching, the flight was uneventful.

Their flight plan took them to MacDill Army Air Field in Florida for a one-night stay prior to heading to Wichita, Kansas.

Rick convinced his remaining crew, consisting of a mechanic, the navigator and Ted, to fly to North Carolina first, parking the plane at Warren field in Washington and staying with him at Manteo for the night.

Rick contacted Kelly for the first time since he began his trip back to tell her to be looking for him. Sean got on the phone and was absolutely euphoric.

"How you feeling, Sean?" asked Rick.

"Not as good as you will be after I see you."

"Yeah, what do you have planned?"

"Nothing," Sean said thinking of their flights together and the times they had in Italy which seemed long ago. "I missed your ugly mug. Kelly missed you."

"OK, I will be there tomorrow morning. Be at the house about ten o'clock."

"What, ten o'clock tomorrow? Where the hell are you?"

"MacDill."

"MacDill? You must be flying in then."

"Oh yeah, I'm flying in," Rick said in a tone to indicate that a big surprise was coming.

"You have to be...no way!"

"Just be looking overhead at ten hundred and have Kelly and everybody out front of her house."

"You got it! Rick, God, it is going to be great to see you again. Kelly and I do have a surprise for you too. Hurry up and get here."

"See ya tomorrow. Pick me up afterwards at Warren Field in Washington.

The morning of January 22 was cool and bright. Rick expected a smooth flight of about three hours. His route of flight took him northward along the Florida, Georgia, and South Carolina coast, then to Wilmington and a northeast turn to the Outer Banks. Rick dropped down to 500 feet after he passed Wilmington to give everybody on board *The Lucky Irishman, II* a bird's-eye view of the beaches and to give, what few beachgoers were there, a passing view of the greatest bomber ever built.

Rick flew by the Cape Lookout Lighthouse with its distinctive black diamonds along its side. They flew by the tiny white seventy-six-foot Ocracoke Lighthouse, the oldest in North Carolina having been built in 1823, then the Cape Hatteras Lighthouse with its black barber pole stripes. Rick's eye strained as he looked forward to see the light of his childhood, the assemblage of towering stone, brick, and masonry from the North Carolina earth and shore painted with three black and three white horizontal stripes. In the distance he saw her and began to slow the B-17 down. Addressing the Carolina shore he majestically turned the green plane with a newly painted yellow rudder identifying the plane as being from 772nd BS. He dipped her left wing like the pelicans below as he approached the first love of his life with respect and excitement. Rick noticed that there were several people on the beach with children playing and cars passing on the street running parallel to the shore on the other side of the sand dunes. "What a peaceful sight," he thought. "She was protected from the horror of war by a vast open ocean and by men and machines born and built for victory." Rick continued his left turn so he could get a kiss from Bodie from above and file it in his brain for a time in his life when this view would no longer be possible. He leveled his wings and flew over his house in Manteo and his high school then turned south again to fly over Kelly and Sean where he knew that his family and the Stewarts would be waiting. Approaching from the north he saw the little street filled with balloons blowing in the wind and with American flags flying from every house and corner. Kids and families were waving. In the front yard was Kelly with Sean dancing and jumping as high as excited children at Christmas. Rick's mom and dad were waving. He saw his dad's arm around his mom's shoulder and her head resting proudly in the saddle of his arm as she wiped a tear from her eyes. Mrs. Stewart stood waving small flags with the neighbors. The men were waving their hats. Rick took another low pass directly overhead waving his wings in greeting and thanks and did a climbing left turn to head for Warren Field.

Sean said to Kelly, "I love you, Kelly. Wasn't that a great flyby?!"

"Beautiful, Sean, just beautiful. That was the first B-17 I ever saw flying. I am so proud of you and Rick. You two really accomplished something. You shared your talents and were willing to give your life to free a world. In doing so, you and Rick secured our freedom for our family," and pointing to the people on the lawn, "and theirs for the rest of our lives." He kissed Sean and he kissed her sweetly back.

Looking over at Mrs. Stewart with Kelly under his arm Sean said, "Mrs. Stewart, I'm sorry," Sean said correcting himself, "Mom, I am going to go get Rick and his crew. I'll be back in several hours." He kissed Kelly again and said, "Today will be a day Rick will never forget. I told him I would get him back. I'm so excited I could burst. See ya in a little." Looking over at the Hamiltons Sean said, "I will be right back. I'm going to get your boy."

Rick and Sean met at the field with much anticipated excitement. It had been months since Rick saw a groggy Sean being carried into the C-47. Between that moment and now Rick had seen more death, missed a Thanksgiving, Christmas, New Years, got promoted and received a medal. He was not selfish or resentful of missing those special events with people he loved in any way, but was measuring the time since he saw Sean last. He had his health and all of his limbs and a chance to go back to Italy to see Lucia again. In that respect he had all that he needed and more than some to look forward to.

Sean's last conscious and visual memory of Rick was when he was being removed from his bomber and Rick was standing outside the hatch as he emerged from the plane. Sean did not really remember much of anything else.

The crew threw their gear in the back of a truck that followed Sean. The mechanic hitched a ride there while the rest drove with Sean in the '42 Ford sedan that the Stewarts were able to purchase with the money they earned from the successful construction business.

Upon arrival at the Stewarts' house, Kelly ran out to the car and jumped all over Rick. Sean got out of his side of the car, pulled the back of his seat forward so the guys in the back could get out. The guys stood there with Sean just looking at the hugs Kelly was dishing out and the exciting display of affection between two friends.

Ted said to Sean straightening out his uniform and rubbing his palm across his hair to get it neat, "Can I expect the same hello from her when she is done with Rick?"

Sean said elbowing his side, "Not on your best day, pal."

Ted, looking at Rick and Kelly still in the front seat, said calmly and in a matter-of-fact way to Sean, "So, how long will this be going on," smiling and loving every minute of it.

"When she is done," Sean said as a matter of course. "Come on inside, guys. There are people inside that are dying to see some real war heroes. The whole town prepared a lunch fit for kings."

After the mauling, Kelly and Rick went to the front porch where his mom and dad were waiting.

"Hi, Mom," Rick said giving her a hug and a kiss on the cheek.

"My boy," she said tears falling freely from her eyes and a hug so tight as to put him back into her body where he grew over twenty-three years ago.

Rick, separating as his mom wiped the tears from her eyes, shook his dad's hand and said, "Hi, Dad."

"You look good, Rick. You really do," pulling him close by his hand and giving him a fatherly embrace, father to warrior son who quickly became a man. The embrace in strength and love described pride perfectly which amplified the respect and admiration from a father to his superhuman boy who helped save a world.

Rick looked over at Mrs. Stewart and walked over to her in a sassy swagger saying, "I have been waiting a long time for this. Mrs. Stewart, you are as pretty as ever," Rick said, giving her a hug.

"Rick, you are all grown up. You are so handsome," Mrs. Stewart said just looking at him.

"Isn't he, Mom? He is drop-dead gorgeous!" Kelly said giving him another hug.

The house was a buzz of activity. Laughter, music being played from the radio, featuring Jimmy Dorsey's "Carolina in the Morning," food and drink were everywhere. The party spilled out onto the porch and into the front yard where tables were set up with cakes and pies. People milled about with smiles talking about the flyover and the young flyers from the war who had become Manteo's most special guests. There were boys playing, pretending they were flying and young girls chasing them. It was a reunion that Rick's wildest imagination could not create.

Kelly looked at Sean and pointed to his watch. "Right," he said.

"Rick, my friend, I hate to tell you this but you need to go to Bodie right away. Rust has taken its toll on the lantern room and I need you to go out there now before it gets dark to tell me what you need to repair it."

"Now?" Rick said in disbelief.

"Yep, right now. I'm leaving tomorrow to get the supplies I need for the business and want to pick up the stuff you need at the same time.

"OK, I'm taking the Ford."

As Rick was walking to the car Sean said, "Hey, you will need these," throwing him the lighthouse keys.

Rick took the keys and walked to the car. As he pulled away he saw Kelly and Sean with their arms around each other smiling back at him.

After Rick pulled way Kelly looked up at Sean and said, "You are the dearest man I know. You are Rick's angel and I love you for loving him the way you do. I don't know how you do it." She kissed him and went back inside with Sean.

As Rick was approaching Bodie he was remembering the hundred drives he had made down that road before. The years had reshaped the dunes but they were still there, and on the horizon stood Bodie. With the motion of his car and his imagination Rick could see her swaying with excitement to see Rick again. The passing clouds made that imaginable thought real and genuine.

Pulling up to the caretaker's house he saw the peeling paint and tall grass. He remembered Lucia and their last night together in the room upstairs. He looked at the rocking chairs remembering the Gaskills and the nightly rocks and casual talks that he had with them.

Looking left at Bodie she looked as magnificent as ever. He walked to her and unlocked the door after brushing away the spider webs that had accumulated over time. He noticed the dusty floor and the staleness of the air inside. He walked up the stairs and emerged from the top onto the gallery and marveled at the sight. He looked over the lantern room, the panes of glass that housed the lens, and the vast ocean, thinking about the war that was just 3,000 miles away. Rick thought of Lucia and her living a life of pale uncertainty. "Lucia," he reflected, "Where are you? I miss you and love you."

Thinking of a line in one of his drama books and thinking of the relevance it had to his life now he recited looking out over the ocean, "So long as I can breathe or I can see, so long lives your love which gives life to me."

As his eyes moved slightly a couple of degrees below the horizon, he noticed a figure sitting on the beach facing away towards the ocean with a child playing on the beach frequently running back to her mother. Rick studied the shape of the woman and his heart stopped as it looked astonishingly familiar. Not paying too much mind to the shape at first, he just marveled at the loveliness of the situation. When the figure turned slightly it caught his attention again. Realizing the impossibility of his thoughts he said, "No, it couldn't be. It looks like it could be but there is absolutely no way that…" He stopped and again strained the focus of his eyes and brought every sense he had to bear on the distant semblance of human treasure he has ever known.

Looking at this tormenting illusion he knew he had to get closer to be sure. He turned and entered Bodie walking down the steps that picked up at a point where it became a run. He bolted from the lighthouse and ran the quarter mile to where this familiar shape was sitting. Rising over the dune he stood and stared at the woman with her hair blowing in the breeze. He walked down the other side of the sand dune to where she was sitting, getting warmer and warmer with each step as the shape became more and more familiar. The little girl playing and kicking the sand turned and saw Rick slowly walking towards them.

"Rick!" the little girl screamed in a cry of excitement and surprise. She began to run to him.

"Cara?" he said softly to himself in the incredulity that even angels with perfect, unblemished souls could not dream this blessing to become a reality.

Rick went to his knees, his eyes filling with tears, while he was still on the dune to catch Cara's tiny approach. She fit perfectly between his knees and against his chest and bent his head around hers. He hugged her gingerly at first, not to tempt God with a dare. He feared that if he breathed too hard she would disappear in the wind from whence she came. Feeling her warm and racing heart he knew she was real, that this was no dream.

With a slow and graceful turn with her hair blowing across her face, Lucia smiled and stood facing him observing Rick with Cara.

Rick stood still taking the miracle of life's unbelievable scene into his mind through his eyes, his mirrored soul of hope and love. He began his walk to Lucia with Cara holding his finger the same way she always had.

Cara ran back to Lucia excitedly holding her leg through the lightly blowing material that formed her dress. Rick walked to Lucia and when he came within reach of her she held out her hand inviting his. He took her hand with both of his and placed it over his mouth and kissed her palm, inhaling as he did so. Placing her hand upon his cheek he reached for her and kissed her perfectly. Perfection has no equal as this moment would testify. Cara embraced Rick's leg with her right arm and Lucia's with her left. A common bond was formed that linked forever with today. Lucia was Rick's forever and Cara was Rick's child. Created from the love and the light of Bodie on that rainy summer night born under a Tuscan sun and lived through a war with Lucia's aunt and uncle until such time when Lucia could be the mother she wanted and prayed she would be.

Rick, still flushed with surprise and lightheaded, asked the obvious question the best he knew how, "What...how...Cara...here...?"

"Take it easy, my gentle heart," she began to explain, placing her open hand on his chest. Sitting on the beach facing the ocean Lucia began telling the story, beginning with Cara. "I was pregnant with Cara my last year at Meredith and graduated not showing any signs of my condition. Kelly knew, of course, but was a dear friend not telling anybody, not even Sean. I arrived in Naples and my aunt and uncle brought me back to Celone, where I had Cara on April 2. I stayed with her for about four months when I had to go to Sienna. No one knew I was back in Italy before I arrived there. They all just figured that I was still in college. I would visit Cara at least twice a month for several days or weeks at a time. She was never in need or want of anything. I was always in close contact with my aunt and uncle there and could arrive in Celone within a day when needed. On one of my visits to Celone, after March, I saw the airplanes on the base. I had no idea that you were there or even in the military. My uncle told me of a young flier that took an interest in Cara and who provided food and items for them. I was deeply touched at the gesture. I never asked who it was as it would not have made any difference since I would not have known the American. I just hoped that one day I could show my appreciation in person."

"This is unbelievable," Rick said.

"Then you arrived at Uncle Gino's. You mentioned Celone a couple of times and I wondered about it but didn't give it too much thought. Barone was killed in the Sant' Anna massacre in August. He was very aggressive, too aggressive, and I feared he would get killed and he did. It was probably the subconscious reason I could not get too close to him, physically and emotionally. He was not a man you could persuade so I did not try after a while. He always made sure I was taken care of but was never focused on me or our marriage. Our marriage was a matter of ceremony and tradition, nothing more. He was set to remove the Fascists and the Germans from Italy and never turned down a request to help the partisans."

"He was a very brave man, a patriot for Italian liberty. You should be proud of him," Rick said with deep respect.

"I am, don't get me wrong, but I also knew that I would be a widow before this was all over, so I emotionally distanced myself when I could so I would not be devastated when the inevitable happened. When it did happen, I grieved of course. How could I not? For three years I lived with Barone and served him as a wife should. I never denied him anything and he never denied me anything.

"I contacted Kelly and told her of Barone's death. She told me in October of Sean's injury and in December asked me to come back to North Carolina, saying that you would be home soon. And the rest, well, you know."

"This story is unbelievable, Lucia," Rick said. "I have so many questions. How long can you stay?"

"I have taken care of the business in Sienna and in San Gimignano. It is self-sustaining right now, so to answer your question, for as long as you will have me."

With Bodie Lighthouse looming in the background and with the sun beginning her sleep under the curved blanket of earth, Rick began a matrimonial promise to Lucia.

"I will have you forever and will live where you live," Rick said, beginning to stand and helping Lucia to her feet. Lifting Cara and holding her between the two of them, Rick placed his dog tags with Bodie clearly seen over Cara's neck. Lucia then took off her necklace, kissing Bodie and placing it over Cara also. Rick, touched by the sight of Cara wearing both halves of Bodie making one lighthouse for the first time, said, "I swear by the sun and the moon that graces the night sky and the stars that are your bridal attendants that I will love you and marry you this day. That I will be your husband and Cara's father. I have searched for you all my life. Our souls dodged from one corner of this earth to the other until by fate and war we were brought together. Now let the peace that was bravely won and borne of man be blessed by God. This promise that I make to you now is forever; that I will love you and will always be where you are."

Bodie smiled that night, knowing that Rick and Lucia would live forever under her protection. She brought them together twice. Always knowing where each one was separately, and always knowing where they would finally rest and love. Bodie, and the spirit that lives within her, always knew the love that existed between Rick and Lucia before they even met.

Rick and Lucia looked at each other holding the other's hand, fingertip to fingertip, as Cara whispered an embrace, "Where you are."

Printed in the United States
69367LVS00006B/157-216

9 781424 155972